A Brush with Fate

CAMRYN VAN LINGEN

For those who have ever felt unworthy. May you one day see yourself as the priceless masterpiece God created you to be, with not a single brushstroke wasted to form the unique painting of your life.

Scintillia
Capital City of
Mentera
N
W
E
S
The Chrysalis
The Docks
Eden's Cottage
Wildflower Field

The Palace
Marketplace

Eden

The first time I painted a portrait, I saw my mother's death.

Even now, ten years later, the memory rises unbidden as I lift my brush to paint myself again. Not for the first time. Not even the tenth.

But no matter how many times I capture my reflection, that moment still lurks beneath each stroke—my mother's face, tight with worry as I explained my vision through terrified sobs; her gentle voice, promising she wouldn't let it happen; and the hollow ache of betrayal when she couldn't keep it.

The shame burns worst of all. Because even with my supposed divine gift, I couldn't prevent her death.

My hand falters, paint dripping onto the pristine paper. I smear it before it stains too deeply, ruining the portrait I've barely begun. The brush strokes come on instinct now, a familiar rhythm as I shuttle my gaze between the mirror and the page.

I start with the jawline, a soft curve inherited from her, and trace upward toward my cheek. In my mind's eye, a vivid image flashes: her cheek pressed to the grass, skin bone-white against the fierce green of spring. I blink it away, forcing my hand to move on.

My nose is next, the slight upturn replicated with soft shadows underneath. Then my lips—shades of pink forming the contours, the corners set in the same unreadable line hers once held. A lie in paint, this composed girl I'm rendering. She doesn't look haunted.

But I am.

Green meets my brush next, the hue of my eyes, made brighter today by the emerald gown I wear. It used to shine, once. Now it's dulled from too many occasions and too few replacements. I match the faded color, careful not to romanticize it on the page.

The water in my jar turns a weary gray as I rinse out the green, then reach for brown to shape my hair. With a few precise brushstrokes, I imitate the intricate braid at my temples, then paint the soft waves that tumble down my back.

Another image claws its way forward—my mother's hair whipping wildly in the wind. The strands catch sunlight moments before her body meets the ground, her hair pooling like a halo around her lifeless body.

My brush slips from my hand and clatters against the desk. I suck in a breath, gripping the edge of the desk to ground myself.

Get a hold of yourself, Eden.

I meet my own eyes in the mirror. The girl staring back wears my mother's face. Same lips. Same brow. Same panic swimming beneath the surface. On the day I discovered my fated skill, she wore that same look. Hard to hide when your daughter just predicted your death.

I glance at the silver hourglass etched into the skin of my left wrist. Its sands swirl and spin, never still when my skill is active. The soft pulse at the base of my skull returns, a quiet thrum building beneath the surface.

I turn back to the painting. My hand moves faster now, adding final touches before the vision comes—before the future demands my attention.

My pulse quickens.

And then it happens.

The sensation blooms across my skin, and I go still, surrendering to the tide.

My breath catches as the world slips away, the painted lines of my portrait dissolving into darkness.

The future unfurls.

And I'm pulled into its depths.

I see myself in the throne room, curtsying before the royal family. My dress swishes elegantly as I lower myself. But just as I'm about to rise, I lose my balance, stumbling forward in a graceless display. The crown prince watches, the glint of amusement in his eyes as he fights to suppress a laugh.

The vision shatters, and I'm left staring at the roughly finished portrait. It's enough to give me a glimpse of what's to come. I release a small breath, mentally noting to practice my curtsy again before I leave. The last thing I want is to make a fool of myself in front of the royal court. No need to make my vision a reality.

As I pack up my paints, there's a knock at the door.

"Eden?" my dad's voice calls from the other side.

"Yeah, Dad, I'm still here."

He pushes the door open, a warm grin lighting up his weathered face. "Well, don't you look like a princess!"

I smile, unable to resist the urge to drop into a dramatic curtsy before him. "How do you do, good sir? I'm Lady Eden."

He chuckles, pulling me into a tight embrace. "You're sure to dazzle the crowns right off their heads! I'm proud of you, Eden."

I hug him back, breathing in the familiar scent of cedar and sawdust that always clings to his clothes. "Thanks, Dad."

He pulls away, smoothing a hand over my hair. I reach up to check my braid, making sure it's still in place.

"You look perfect," he says, his voice gentle.

Then his gaze shifts past me, settling on the still-wet portrait. His expression falters, and he lets out a small sigh. "Eden, you know I wish you wouldn't do that."

I snatch the portrait off the desk, crumpling it up and tossing it into the bin nearby. "It's just… reassurance," I mumble, avoiding his eyes.

"You don't need it." His tone is firm. "Why can't you trust in yourself? You spend so much time looking into the future, trying to control every little detail. Life isn't meant to be lived like that."

"It's not about control!" I reply, a touch defensive. "It helps me prepare. What's so wrong with wanting to know what's ahead?"

He shakes his head, crossing his arms as he leans against the doorframe. "Because you're so focused on the future that you forget to live in the present, Eden. You're always chasing after something that hasn't happened yet—something that might not even happen the way you see it."

My jaw tightens. "I need it, Dad. I can't just go into things blind, hoping for the best. I've seen what happens when people don't use their skills. They falter, they fail, they get left behind—"

"Like me?"

His words quench the embers of my growing anger. "I didn't mean it like that."

"I know. But what happens when you rely on your skill too much? When you only feel confident by seeing the future? What does that say about you, Eden?"

I falter, taken aback by the raw honesty in his words. My dad has always been wary of my fated skill. But it's a part of me. How could he ask me to ignore it?

"I'm not asking you to stop completely," he says, softer now, as if reading my thoughts. "I just don't want you to forget who you are without it. You're more than just your skill. You've got talent, heart, and a brilliant mind. Don't let your visions define everything."

My fingers curl into the fabric of my dress. "I just want to be ready."

He steps forward, gently tipping my chin up so I'm forced to meet his eyes. "You are ready. Even without your foresight. You'll face whatever comes your way with grace, because that's who you are. Not because of some vision."

For a moment, we stand there in silence. His words hang in the air between us, and despite the knot of anxiety in my chest, I know he's right. But I also know I can't turn my back on the thing that's always given me an edge—the thing that sets me apart.

"I know you want to help, Dad," I reply, "but I need this. Just for now. My skill gives me confidence."

He lets out a slow breath. "I just don't want you to lose yourself in it."

With that, he presses a kiss to my forehead, offering one last smile before turning toward the door. "I'll be downstairs if you need me. But remember, Eden—whatever happens, you're already enough."

The door clicks shut behind him, leaving me alone with my thoughts. I stare at the crumpled portrait in the bin, chewing the inside of my cheek.

Enough? I wish I could believe that.

I return to packing, mentally rehearsing my plan, only to be interrupted by another knock on the door. Before I can even respond, my siblings burst into the room.

"We're here to help you practice speaking to royalty!" Soren announces, a paper crown perched atop his chestnut hair.

I stifle a laugh, grateful for the distraction. "A prince in the making, I see. I'm honored."

Aria sighs dramatically but grins, standing inside the doorway with her arms crossed. "Soren insisted on the crown." She arches an eyebrow. "But we're serious about this. You're not just speaking to anyone, Eden."

"It's stunning. Soren looks just like a prince."

With all three of us crowded in the room, there's not much space to move around. Aria and I share the space, our beds dominating the small area. Soren sits on Aria's bed with folded hands, assuming a regal posture, and giving me his best royal glare.

Aria steps closer, adjusting a stray lock of my hair as she speaks. "Remember, they expect confidence. Clear, steady words. Your voice is just as important as your talent."

I grab the edges of my skirt and give them both a curtsy—graceful, elegant, and wobble-free. "Your Majesty." I bow my head. "It's an honor to meet you."

Soren smirks, mimicking a formal tone. "Speak up, Lady Eden! I can barely hear you!"

Shaking my head, I give my best impression of poise, clasping my hands. "My sincerest apologies, Your Grace. Is this to your satisfaction?"

"Better." Aria takes my hand, her warm smile calming my nerves. "Exactly like that. You'll be unforgettable."

"I hope so." I take one last look around the room.

Satisfied, I bend down to give Soren a brief hug before moving over to Aria. She wraps her arms around me in a tight embrace. After a long moment, she pulls away to straighten the neckline of my gown, casting a critical eye over every detail.

A gifted dressmaker, I trust her to catch any flaw in my appearance. I never go anywhere without her fashion expertise.

"I wish I had finished the gown in time." Aria casts a wistful glance at the half-finished gown pinned to the dress form near her bed. "If there were any day for you to wear a new dress, it would be today when you're meeting the royal family."

"Perfection takes time. And a gown that beautiful deserves to be worn to a ball or a fancy dinner, not a painting session where it could get ruined."

"You're probably right." She turns back to me with a sigh. "I still feel bad. If it hadn't taken so long to save up for all the fabric, it would be done by now."

I smooth my skirt. "Aria, it's okay. This dress will get me through. And if I do well, we should have plenty of extra coin to purchase fabric for several more of your projects."

She gives a slight nod. "If all goes well, maybe you can still wear that gown for the royal family."

"That's the goal," I say. "You're in charge while I'm gone. Don't let that crown go to Soren's head."

Soren pats his paper crown with dignity. "Oh, it's already too late for that."

We dissolve into a fit of giggles, our laughter filling the room. But it isn't enough to banish the growing pit of anxiety in my stomach.

If I don't paint well, I'll lose my only chance to work for the royal family. Worse than that, if I fail to keep my fated skill a secret—if I slip, even for a moment—I won't just lose my freedom, I'll lose myself.

They'll never let me go, and I will be forced to paint not as the court artist, but as another weapon in their arsenal.

After years spent hiding my gift, I'm willingly walking into the one place equipped to expose it.

Cassian

The curtains are opened against my will, the morning light blinding me. I roll onto my stomach and bury my head under the pillow with a groan.

"You must get up, Your Highness," my attendant pleads. "Your royal portrait is being painted today."

"I'd rather stay in bed." I sprawl across the satin sheets, still shielding the light with my pillow. It does little to block the brightness, though it successfully muffles my attendant's persistent fussing. I relax into the feather mattress. Just as I'm on the brink of drifting back to sleep, the chill morning air hits my bare skin. My eyes snap open.

I prop myself up on one elbow, scowling over my shoulder. "What are you doing?"

My attendant stands triumphantly with the sheet clutched in one hand. "The king will be displeased if you are late."

"The king is never pleased," I mutter under my breath, reluctantly sitting up to stretch. "Fine. I'm up."

"You've already missed breakfast, Your Highness. And part of your lesson. You must dress quickly."

Unbothered by my attendant's rushed demeanor, I take my time getting out of bed. The second I'm standing, more servants rush in to help me dress. One of them hands me a pair of pants while another pulls a cotton shirt over my head. As they produce more layers of clothing, I break through the circle of servants.

"I'll just wear this, thank you," I say, unwilling to indulge the ridiculous ensemble. "No doublet."

"But Your Highness—"

"No. I'm done being dressed." I grip my attendant's shoulder, preparing the right words to ensnare his emotions. "Let go of your cares, for once. I'm old enough to dress myself, don't you think?"

I grin reassuringly. My attendant returns it with a smile that is his downfall. It's proof he's swayed by my words, allowing my fated skill to do its work. He nods numbly as it takes hold.

Satisfied with his silenced protests, I step into the bathroom and run a comb through my unruly black hair. But my bedhead refuses to be tamed. The servants swarm in to assist me, and I dismiss them with a wave of my hand.

They heed my command, scurrying off to make my bed. I exit my chambers without another glance. My guard, Silas, moves from his post by my door to follow close behind as I veer left toward the kitchens, my stomach growling.

I ignore Silas's quiet sigh of disapproval.

The moment I enter, the kitchen staff lower their heads. "Your Royal Highness," they murmur in unison.

"Carry on," I say, weaving through the busy space in search of something to eat.

I spot a basket of fresh-baked croissants and snag a couple. Without turning around, I throw one to Silas, who catches it easily. A few wide-eyed servants hover nearby, but I don't acknowledge them as I grab an apple from a bowl on my way out.

As we head to my lesson, I casually toss the apple in the air. A maid I pass stares for a moment too long and I wink at her. She blushes and practically trips over her own feet trying to flee down the hall. I chuckle to myself, biting into the apple.

"Your charm has no boundaries, I see," Silas observes, earning a smirk from me.

By the time I reach the study, the apple is half-finished. My tutor awaits inside, standing by the desk, adjusting his spectacles. He's new, and I can't be bothered to remember his name.

"Your Royal Highness." He bows his head. "We must begin immediately. You have missed half of the lesson."

I pull out a chair and prop my boots up on the table. My teeth crunch into the apple, and I raise a brow at him. "What is your name again?"

"Lorenzo, Your Highness."

"Ah, yes. The human abacus. Blessed with the skill of arithmetic, aren't you?"

He clears his throat, pulling parchment and ink out of his bag. "A divine gift from Delayon, Your Highness."

"Wonderful," I say dryly, tossing the apple core onto the desk. "Our Creator may have blessed you, but have you perfected your skill enough to teach me? The last tutor fled the palace declaring I'm unteachable. Let's see if you fare any better."

Lorenzo swallows nervously but stands his ground, sliding some parchment my way. "Then we have much work to do."

I lean back, balancing the chair on two legs. "Tell me, Lorenzo, why should a king have to know mathematics, anyway?"

"Well, Your Highness, a well-educated king is a successful king." He meets my gaze with surprising steadiness.

"Clever answer, Lorenzo." I set the chair back on all fours. "You might last longer than the others, after all."

I leave Lorenzo in the study, no more eager to learn arithmetic than when the lesson began. Silas falls into step behind me as we make our way to the throne room.

It's time to meet with Eden Asher, the common-born artist we've hired to paint my portrait. It's one of the more tedious royal obligations. I'll never understand why royalty must be immortalized in paint.

We move through the grand halls, morning light casting long shadows on the polished marble floors. The blue and silver banners of our house decorate our path, a reminder of lineage and legacy. Of everything I can't escape.

"Your Royal Highness, the king expects you in the throne room," a herald announces as we approach.

I nod, jaw tight. The grand doors swing open with ceremonial slowness, revealing the throne room in all its gilded splendor. At the far end, my father sits on the raised throne, his commanding presence tainted by a sour expression. My mother sits beside him, her gaze disapproving. Lyra, my sister, stands next to mother with raised brows.

I avoid looking at them as I stride towards my place beside my father's throne. Before I've even turned around, the disapproval begins.

"I expect you to change before your royal portrait," Father says, his tone razor-sharp. "Your appearance is a disgrace."

This is the reaction my attendant was hoping to avoid. I shift my weight, resisting the urge to roll my eyes. "Yes, Father."

Out of the corner of my eye, Lyra mimics Father's stern expression while wagging a finger at me—her attempt to lighten the mood. Suppressing a laugh, I train my gaze on the door, hoping that's the end of my father's lecture. The silence doesn't last long before my mother joins the conversation.

"I assumed you'd greet your prized painter with a bit more dignity, Cassian." She accepts a cup of tea from a servant. "You went to great lengths to convince your father she was worth considering."

"And I fear it was a mistake to leave the task in your hands," the king adds without looking at me. "I allowed you the opportunity to prove your discernment. Let's hope you haven't squandered it with this simple village girl."

I keep my voice calm. Detached. "She won the Midsummer competition last season—took first place."

The king scoffs. "A festival art show. Hardly court-worthy."

The queen lifts her teacup without looking up. "Didn't she paint that gloomy self-portrait? The one in the rain with her reflection in a puddle?"

I'm not surprised Mother remembers. With her Aetherean blood, she'd sooner forget her crown than miss a promising painter from Mentera. "That's the one."

"She's not a Morphi," Father snaps.

I spin the ring on my index finger. "Then let her fail. It will reflect me, not you. And you'll finally have proof that talent without divine blessing is nothing."

The king narrows his eyes.

"But if she succeeds, it could be an olive branch to the commoners and those with lower ranks."

A proud smile breaks through my mother's poised demeanor. She hides it with her teacup, taking a sip before speaking. "Sometimes talent blooms in the soil no one bothers to tend. Let's see what she paints before we decide, Leopold."

Guilt distorts my grateful smile into a grimace. Though this commoner is talented, part of me hopes she *will* fail. That her portrait won't be good enough. That a flawed painting might stall the betrothal process long enough for me to find a way out.

But as the moment draws nearer, dread pools in my stomach. What if she doesn't fail? Today is more than a portrait. It's a reminder that the crown draws closer every day. And with it, the end to what little freedom I have.

Eden

My heels click on the stone bridge as I approach the palace gates. Sculpted ivy adorns the silver metal, elegant and threatening all at once. The walls are imposing, guards stationed on every tower, and two standing at the gates. I wipe my sweaty palms on my smock, swallow my nerves, and steady my voice.

"Eden Asher," I project, announcing my presence. "I'm here to paint the crown prince's portrait."

I'm thankful I didn't stumble over my words, but I'm nervous all the same. One guard scrutinizes me, unblinking. I try not to fidget. He studies me like a micro-expression reader, searching my face for a lie. My pulse jumps at the thought, and I take deep breaths, trying to maintain my composure. Though I'll be lying all day about my fated skill, I'm not lying now. I earned this invitation.

I smile at the guard.

He frowns. The seconds stretch by, and I try not to let my panic grow. They haven't rescinded the offer, have they? I've worked too hard to get here for them to take it away at the last second. Finally, the guard waves his hand, and the gates open with a groan.

I stifle a relieved sigh as two more guards greet me just inside. One takes the lead while the other follows behind, keeping close as they guide me into the palace. It's massive and more luxurious than I could've ever imagined.

Golden light spills through the towering windows, glinting off the crystal chandeliers that hang every few feet. The ceiling arches high overhead. Mentera's royal colors sweep across the walls—silver and blue like sea and starlight—welcoming me into a world I've only dreamt of. Even the pillars are works of art, each embellished with intricate sculptures.

The guard behind me coughs conspicuously, prompting me to stop gawking at the palace. It's hard not to, having grown up as a commoner. I glance down at myself. Dressed in my finest attire, I still feel out of place.

Maybe I should've waited to tie on my smock, I think, noticing even the servants wear pristine uniforms. I grip my supplies tighter, calming my nerves by running through everything I know about greeting royalty.

My rehearsal is cut short when the guard stops at a giant set of double doors. They open to reveal a breathtaking throne room. The floor is marbled with blue and silver, the swirls sparkling in the sunlight. A skylight makes the space seem larger, permeating the room with an ethereal shine.

At the front, a staircase leads to an elevated platform where two people sit on silver thrones, flanked on either side by someone standing.

The guards escort me to the base of the stairs, where I take a deep breath to steady myself. The royal family looks down at me with a mix of curiosity and scrutiny.

On the left throne sits King Leopold, a stern man with a commanding presence. His silver crown glints in the light, matching the streaks of gray in his dark hair. Beside him, Queen Clarissa radiates elegance, her poised demeanor softened by the warmth in her eyes. She regards me with a kind smile, a welcome contrast to the king's intensity.

Standing to her right is Princess Lyra. Her cerulean and silver gown is stunning, and I can't help but think of my sister. She would love it.

Then there's Prince Cassian, the subject of my commission. His features are sharp, almost severe, with eyes the color of storm-swept skies. He stands to the left of the king, dressed in a loose cotton shirt and scuffed brown boots. Not the most princely attire. Paired with his ink-black hair, tousled and falling over his forehead, he looks more like a brooding traveler than a prince. For a moment, I'm uncertain if it's truly him. But the way he watches me—measured, calculating, as if sizing me up—leaves no doubt.

"Your Majesties." I curtsy deeply, keeping my voice from wavering despite my racing heart. The nerves subside when I make it through the curtsy without falling like my vision. "It is an honor to be here. I am Eden Asher, the painter commissioned for His Royal Highness's portrait."

King Leopold nods curtly. "Welcome, Miss Asher. We have heard of your talent, despite your… unorthodox background. We expect nothing less than excellence."

"Indeed," Queen Clarissa interjects, her voice softer. "Your portrait from the Midsummer festival was quite impressive. We look forward to seeing how you capture our son's likeness."

Prince Cassian shifts his stance. "Let's hope you don't squander this opportunity, Miss Asher," he says, a hint of a smirk playing on his lips.

I meet his gaze, refusing to be intimidated. "I shall endeavor to do my best, Your Royal Highness," I reply, my voice unwavering.

King Leopold rises from his throne, signaling the end of the audience. "We will provide a space to work and any materials you require. My son's time is valuable, so I trust you will work efficiently."

I nod. "Of course, Your Majesty."

The guard steps forward to lead me to the designated studio, but before I turn to follow, I take one last look at the prince. His smirk has faded, replaced by an inscrutable expression. What lies behind those piercing blue eyes?

As I'm led through the opulent halls to my workspace, my mind races. This is my chance to prove myself, to rise above my station. I will paint the prince, and perhaps in doing so, I'll uncover the layers of the man who stands so nonchalantly beside the silver throne.

The studio is spacious, filled with natural light, and equipped with all the supplies I could ever need. I feel foolish for even bringing any, setting my measly supply next to the other materials.

Running my fingers over the smooth wood of the easel, I marvel at the quality of everything. This is a place where I could lose myself in a painting.

A knock at the door startles me from my thoughts. It opens to reveal Prince Cassian, now dressed in more regal attire. He steps into the room with an air of casual authority, closing the door behind him.

"The sooner we begin, the sooner this will be over," he says, his tone lighter than before.

I nod. "Very well, Your Highness. Please, take a seat." I gesture to the chair the servants prepared, angled to catch the best light.

As Cassian sits, I study his features, committing them to memory. Despite his earlier bravado, he appears restless, his eyes darting around the room as if seeking an escape.

"Do you find sitting for a portrait tedious, Your Highness?" I ask, breaking the silence.

He shrugs, a hint of a smile returning. "I find many things tedious, Miss Asher. Small talk, one of them."

I bite back my retort, annoyed by his aloofness. He raises a brow at my silence, eyeing me with a tilt of his head.

"But I'm curious to see how you plan to keep me entertained," Cassian adds, taunting me with his words.

I smear yellow ochre across the canvas with force. "I assure you, Your Highness, I am full of surprises."

"Is one of them being terrible at painting? Because that color is hideous." He lazily props his chin in his hand.

"If you're going to comment on every step of my process, this will be a long session," I blurt, my mouth moving without thinking. I awkwardly clear my throat, trying to regain my composure. "Please refrain from moving too much, Your Highness."

He chuckles, his lips curving into a half-smile before he straightens into a more regal pose.

I glance up to study his features once more. Up close, he is far more normal than I expected—just a young man cloaked in princely attire. Dark circles rim the underside of his eyes, like sleep has eluded him for more than a few nights. His fingers toy with one of his rings, pulling it on and off with repetitive ease. Most would mistake the gesture for boredom. But I recognize the nervous energy, the same kind that causes me to spin my own ring at times. What is he so worried about?

"Is something the matter, Miss Asher?" he asks, his voice smooth with a hint of levity.

I shake my head, a slight blush creeping up my cheeks. "No, Your Highness. Just making sure I capture every detail accurately."

Cassian's lips curve at the corners, making him seem both regal and approachable. "Well, let's hope you do. I wouldn't want my likeness misrepresented."

I try to relax as I begin the underpainting, blocking in his strong jaw and the proud set of his shoulders.

I can do this.

I've painted many portraits before. The prince's will be no different. As long as I match every color perfectly, and don't let my visions break through my focus, I'll be fine.

Except Prince Cassian is far more perceptive than I imagined. Which means this commission might be the biggest masterpiece of my life—or my last.

Cassian

 itting here is torture.

I've always hated having my portrait done. The artist's scrutinizing gaze makes me uncomfortable, and sitting still isn't my strong suit. My foot taps against the studio floor. Eden's eyes stray from the canvas, all but burning a hole through my boot.

I stop.

I can't wrap my brain around her. She's outspoken, far more than most women I meet. They spend their time trying to get on my good side and batting their eyelashes. It's insufferable. Eden does none of that.

I watch her work, her green eyes flitting between me and the canvas. Her gaze is focused and resolute. I wish I could see the painting as she works—something to keep my mind occupied.

Our last court artist was quite gifted. When he wasn't drunk, that is. After too many of the portraits reflected his drunken focus, he was dismissed. Father couldn't be bothered to replace him, so the role went unfilled for a while. Until the search for my bride grew more serious. Then, he handed the task to me. So I made an unconventional choice: a commoner.

Talented, yes—but not a Morphi.

All I need is for her to buy me time. Distracting her seems like a good place to start.

"You've made quite a name for yourself in the village, Miss Asher," I say, hoping she can't talk and paint very well.

"Is that so? I hadn't realized," she mumbles, her eyes never leaving the canvas.

My lips quirk into a small smile before I school them back into place. She continues working, refusing to engage.

"How else do you suppose we found you?" I ask.

"I thought you found small talk tedious," Eden retorts, squinting at the painting.

I notice her deflection, annoyed she's using my own words against me. "Aren't you curious how we stumbled upon your midsummer portrait?"

"I assume through the usual means—like sending your servants to snoop around where they don't belong."

The words hang in the air, sharp and unrefined. I raise an eyebrow, caught off guard by her bluntness. "You don't mince words, Miss Asher," I say, my tone now edged with interest.

She finally looks up, her expression a mix of defiance and frustration. "I've never found it particularly useful, Your Highness. In my experience, people rarely listen when you're polite."

"Is that so?" I resist the urge to lean back, studying her. "And what has made you so… disenchanted with the world?"

Eden's jaw tightens. "Not the world, Your Highness. Just those who think themselves above it."

Her meaning is clear, and I feel a twinge of irritation. "You seem to have a rather low opinion of royalty."

She shrugs, her brush never pausing. "I've seen enough to form an opinion, yes."

I'm silent for a moment, unsure whether to be offended or impressed by her candor. "And what, pray tell, have you seen?"

Eden hesitates, her eyes flicking to mine before returning to her work. "I've seen the way people suffer while the nobility feast. I've seen lives ruined by decisions made in gilded halls far removed from reality."

Her words cut deeper than I care to admit. "You assume a great deal about people you do not know," I say, my voice colder.

She finally sets down her brush, meeting my gaze head-on. "Maybe. But I've lived it. I've seen my family struggle while your kind looks down from their towers."

For a moment, we just stare at each other, the air thick with tension. She's more than just an artist; she's a voice of the people, raw and unfiltered. I can't decide whether to respect her or put her in her place.

"Perhaps," I say slowly, "you'll find not all of us are as detached as you think."

She snorts softly, picking up her brush again. "We'll see, Your Highness. We'll see."

Eden returns her full attention to the portrait. I remain silent, watching her paint for what feels like an eternity. With nothing better to do, I rehash our conversation, finding it ironic that I attempted to refute my detached demeanor. I'm the last person who can say that.

Eden appears unbothered by my words, once again lost in the painting. My fingers twitch, wishing for my own escape. The longer I sit here, the less time I'll have to myself.

"You can relax your face." Her voice sounds loud in the stillness of the room.

I blink, surprised by her instruction.

"I finished your face, so you can relax it now," she reiterates, glancing at me momentarily.

I stretch, trying to ease the tension in my neck. It's hard to tell how much time has passed. As each section of my body is completed and I'm allowed to relax, my anticipation grows. The prideful part of me wants the portrait to be good, proving my father wrong. But the larger part of me hopes it's the worst portrait of myself ever painted, that I look nothing like marriage material.

By the time Eden has finished half the portrait, it's taking all my concentration to stay still. When the door behind her swings open a crack, and my sister's head peeks through, my body sags with relief.

A leaf is stuck in Lyra's long, dark hair. She gives me a mischievous grin. I shake my head at her, internally envious of her escapades.

Eden must notice where my gaze has shifted because she turns to look behind her. "Greetings, Your Royal Highness." She curtsies hastily, her long brown hair narrowly avoiding the palette of paint.

Your Royal Highness? She didn't use the full title when addressing me, I think, my brow scrunching together.

"Good day, Miss Asher." My sister steps into the room, rushing towards the painting. "You're quite talented!"

A slight blush colors Eden's cheeks. "You flatter me, Your Highness."

"Nonsense! You've managed to make Cassian look like the future king, for once. If only you could make him look this regal in real life, too."

"Lyra." I glare at her, a silent warning not to continue.

"What, brother? All I'm saying is you'd make quite the crown prince if you finally accepted the responsibility." Lyra shrugs.

I glance over at Eden, aware of the smile she's trying to hide. Our conversation must amuse her.

"I'm sure you have better things to do than flatter a common painter." I fix my gaze on Lyra, but can't help noticing Eden's rigid posture.

"Ignore my brother's callous words, Miss Asher," Lyra says, jutting her chin out defiantly. "He's always like this."

Lyra leans in close, whispering something in Eden's ear. Her eyes widen at my sister's words, and she curtsies low.

"I hope to see more of your work."

"I live to serve, Your Royal Highness," Eden replies, dipping her head in farewell as Lyra leaves the room.

Turning back toward the canvas, Eden stares down at my feet. Her brow furrows.

"Is something the matter, Miss Asher?"

"It's nothing, Your Highness."

"Your Royal Highness," I correct, clenching my jaw.

"My apologies, Your Royal Highness." Her tone is full of disdain. She purses her lips.

"Is there something else?" I ask.

"Please refrain from moving your… lower half… until I'm finished."

"Certainly, Miss Asher." I keep my tone light. "As long as it doesn't take all day."

She gives a slight curtsy before resuming the portrait. Though my head is free to move as I please, I find my gaze focused on her. Eden's shoes are worn, the green of her dress having seen better days. In spite of that, she holds her head high, embellishing her appearance with silver jewelry. Her wrist turns, the bracelets shifting to reveal a familiar hourglass shape—her fatemark. The light hits it as she adjusts the palette in her hand.

Instinctively, I glance down at my own.

The silver sands of time are still. They only move when I'm actively using my fated skill. And even then, it's hard to see. I remember the day my fatemark first appeared—how astonishing it felt to discover my gift, a mark which proves my worth.

After perfecting my skill at a remarkably young age, the sands of my fatemark have had many years to dwindle. But only half the sand has fallen, and my father couldn't be more disappointed. He thinks I should've already ascended into a Morphi, like him, something all who bear a fatemark strive for.

I can't wait for my hourglass to drain. When the sands are gone, replaced by the Morphi's distinct black butterfly mark, I may gain some of my freedom back. Ascending means receiving divine clarity, a mind elevated to that of our Creator. But that will just be an extra benefit of my true reward—freedom from my father's overbearing presence.

I look back at Eden's wrist, trying to see how far her sands have fallen. But no matter how long I stare, her fatemark remains a mystery. I scrutinize her further, realizing the care in which she chose to present herself.

She's trying too hard to appear noble.

I watch as she blows a stray strand of hair out of her face. It doesn't budge, and she swipes it away with her hand. White paint smears across her forehead.

Do I say something?

I open my mouth, then close it.

Eden steps back from the canvas, assessing her work. She's still for several seconds, her eyes glossing over. I tilt my head. Is her fated skill at work?

Eden blinks back to focus, glancing over at me. I avert my gaze, annoyed she caught me staring.

Overwhelmed by a sudden urge to flee this wretched room, I stand. "I trust you are talented enough to finish the rest without my presence?"

She presses her lips together before bowing her head. "As you wish, Your Royal Highness."

I pull down the cuff of my sleeve before crossing the room to the door. My boots sound loud against the wood floor. Clenching the door handle, I debate whether to give her the satisfaction of looking at the painting. Curiosity wins me over and I turn to look.

It's remarkable. Lyra is right—she really has made me look like the perfect prince.

I'm doomed.

My gaze flickers to the smear of white across Eden's forehead.

I step closer.

"Be sure to clean up before you leave, Miss Asher."

She steps back, biting the inside of her cheek.

I point to my forehead, and she reaches up to her own. When her fingers come away flecked with white, she hurriedly scrubs the rest away.

As I turn to leave, she clears her throat.

"Assuming you're having this portrait sailed to another kingdom…" She hesitates. "I would wait until next week."

I glare over my shoulder. "And why, Miss Asher, would I do that?"

"I hear storms are brewing. You wouldn't want to sit for another tedious portrait, would you, Your Royal Highness?"

I straighten, my hand tightening around the handle. "Are you an expert on the weather, too?"

"Forgive my insolence." Eden curtsies, staring at the ground. "Your Royal Highness doesn't want advice from a *common painter*."

My muscles tense. "You're right. I don't."

I nearly rip the door off its hinges in my eagerness to leave. If I never see her again, it will be too soon.

Eden

Cassian's portrait wasn't difficult to finish, though our parting conversation kept looping through my mind. The prince is every bit as infuriating as I assumed he'd be, despite his arguments.

Although a part of me wanted to leave the studio a mess just to spite him, I resisted the urge. If I have any hope of being invited back, I can't leave a poor impression on the king and queen. And so I left the room spotless.

The palace gates close behind me as I emerge onto the stone bridge. I clutch my art supplies closer and begin the descent. Scintillia is beautiful from up here, but I'm careful not to get too close to the edge.

Light dances across the flowing water, reflecting off the houses lining the coast. Boats pass underneath, most carrying goods to and from the marketplace. As the capital city of Mentera, it's always busy.

To my right, the glittering dome of the Chrysalis rises above the city, catching the light of day like a beacon. Perched on the tallest cliff, it's hard to miss, especially with the steady stream of people climbing its endless steps like ants to an anthill. The poor tourists have no clue they won't get to see the farion, the Mimicry's Ascended One. Said to hold the greatest wisdom on how to "ferry on to higher things," as the saying goes, they don't know he spends most of his time behind palace walls.

Still, the Chrysalis is beautiful. From the palace's vantage point, even the city itself is enchanting.

I admire how the houses bleed into one another like smears of color on an artist's palette. It's lively and inviting, each house a reflection of the people who call it home.

Squinting, I scan the horizon, searching for mine in the distance. It would be nearly impossible to pick out if not for the distinct blue of our roof—a shade my mother chose. At last, I spot a speck of cerulean like the endless blue of Scintillia's waters. It's a bit of a walk to get there, especially in heels, but I don't mind. I've always enjoyed venturing through town.

As I walk, I attempt to interpret my earlier vision. I regret mentioning any part of it to Cassian and hope he thought nothing of it. If not for the strange, insistent tug to tell him, I wouldn't have said a word. But something told me it mattered. That it would play into fulfilling the rest of my vision.

The royal ship sinking at sea was only the beginning.

What unsettles me most is the image that followed—Cassian standing outside my home. The idea still rattles me, though I try to take it as a good sign. Maybe it means he'll hire me again. Perhaps even name me court artist.

It helps that the last part of my vision ties it all together—Cassian's portrait being repainted. Only time will tell if the crown prince heeds my advice. If I learned anything about him today, it's that he'll ignore a common painter's advice just to prove her wrong. And when he does, he'll need me.

A brush of fur against my leg startles me.

I stumble back and almost trip, my heel catching on a cobblestone. Clutching my chest, I glare at the innocent-eyed tabby cat staring back at me. Any sharp words I had ready, dissolve instantly as it meows softly.

"Who could stay mad at you?" I croon, crouching down to scratch the tabby behind his ears.

He purrs in reply, arching into my touch before slipping away.

I continue in that direction, the hum of conversation and laughter growing louder. As I enter the heart of the marketplace, the clatter of footsteps surrounds me. I'm jostled by the crowd, righting myself before falling face first into the cobblestone. The same cobble streets where they found my mother's body.

A shudder ripples through me, and I clench my fists.

I've long since overcome the fear of meeting the same fate, and yet the image comes unbidden every time. A part of me still blames myself for her death. I'm not sure I'll ever be able to let go of the guilt.

The scent of fresh-baked bread floats by on the breeze, grounding me in the present. I've always had a weakness for it. Squeezing my way through the crowd, I head toward the origin of the delicious smell. The detour will be worth the reward.

Up ahead, I spot the bakery—a quaint teal building with a delectable spread of pastries and bread on display. Flowering vines snake up the side, their red and orange petals a beautiful compliment to the teal exterior. This time of year, their blossoms are so bright they look like flames.

A bell chimes when I open the door, mingling with the crackle of fire. The sounds and sweet scent of delicious food bring a smile to my face.

Mateo stands behind the counter, concentrated on kneading dough. His muscles flex, flour-covered hands moving in a rhythmic trance. It's clear he's using his skill, enchanting a specific memory or feeling into the dough.

"Eden!" he exclaims without even turning around.

"How'd you know it was me?"

He turns, a wry grin on his face. "You always smell like oil paint."

I sniff my sleeve. "Do I really?"

Mateo shrugs. "Or maybe I just know you've got a nose like a hound. The scent of fresh-baked bread always brings you in."

"You must be the one with the nose like a dog—saying you can smell the paint on me," I grumble, sticking my tongue out at him.

He chuckles, disappearing into the back for a moment.

"Your flowers out front are beautiful, by the way," I call. "I wonder what brilliant person decided to decorate with them?"

"You've already heard me say it many times. Do you really need me to say it again?" His voice is muffled by whatever he's doing in the back.

"Just one more time will suffice. Hearing I'm right never gets old," I tease, leaning against the front counter.

Mateo and I have known each other since we were kids. Our parents are close friends, so it was inevitable we would be stuck with each other. We're basically siblings.

"Hey now, is that any way to treat the owner? I assume you'd like your usual discount." He emerges through the doorway, his amber eyes sparkling.

"The usual would be perfect," I reply, dropping a sack of coins on the front counter. "No discount necessary."

Mateo gapes at me, his gaze flicking from me to the money. "Where did that come from?"

"I did it!" I say giddily, pointing at the oven in warning.

He glances back, realizing the fire is growing out of hand. With precise movements, he extracts the loaf of bread from the oven before it burns and ruins his enchantment. "You were invited into the palace?"

The bread's scent drifts over to me as it rests on the counter nearby. I inhale the smell greedily. "Mm-hm. I painted a portrait of the crown prince."

"Eden, that's amazing! I certainly don't mind taking advantage of the small fortune that your commission must've been."

I laugh softly, watching as Mateo skillfully packs my usual purchase—a loaf of crisp ciabatta and buttery brioche, one good for focus, and the other for connection and warmth.

My eyes wander over to his famous diamond-dusted donuts. Thick granules of sugar coat the white frosting, making it shimmer like diamonds. My mouth waters just thinking about it. One bite and you feel determined to conquer the world, the resilient-inducing enchantment the source of its name.

He must notice me eyeing them because he grabs several out of the display case and places them neatly in a box.

"Diamond Donuts on the house."

"You don't have to do that, Mattie! I can pay," I argue, digging through the bag of coins.

He stills my hand with his own, shaking his head softly. "My gift to you and your family. I haven't stopped by in a while. Say hi for me."

"I will. But you should stop by and say hi yourself, sometime. Soren would love to see you."

"Definitely," Mateo says, ringing me up. "The bakery keeps me pretty busy these days, but I'll find the time."

The bell chimes, interrupting our conversation. Two young women walk in, eyeing Mateo before staring intently at the pastries.

"Uh oh, more of your devotees have arrived."

Mateo smirks. "You should get going. Your dad will be eager to hear your news."

He makes a show of reigniting the oven, the flames flaring to life behind him as he turns back to me. I stand on my tiptoes, mussing his sandy-brown hair as I set another coin on the counter. "See you later!"

He shakes his head at me as I leave, but I know he's grateful. Through the front window, I catch him fixing his hair before addressing the women. His signature smile appears, and I turn away, knowing his routine by heart. Mateo knows he's attractive and has never been afraid to use it to his advantage.

I start down the road, humming as I go. My good mood makes the rest of the walk fly by. Before I know it, I'm headed through the field of wildflowers on the edge of town. White petals reflect the sun, covering the hills in a summer snow. Intermingled are patches of blue and purple that mirror the beauty of Scintillia's sea.

I pick them as I go, making a small bouquet for the house. As I snap the stem of an Azulia, its cobalt petals stretched wide to catch the sun, something iridescent shimmers nearby. I crouch lower, pushing aside other flowers to find the source.

There, nestled in the field like a hidden treasure, is the crystalline Edenia flower. Its translucent, prismatic petals look like crystal or glass, framing a glowing silver center. Its beauty is a testament to the artistry of Delayon, our Creator. But appearances can be deceiving. Why does something so beautiful cause so much destruction?

Digging through the grass to find the base of the flower, I pull on the stem, the roots coming up easy. Edenia flowers are an invasive species—a weed from the fallen kingdom of Divinia. It's well known in Scintillia to uproot them when found, for they leech off surrounding nutrients, killing anything nearby. It's a pity, for they are one of the most beautiful flowers.

But they still add a magical touch to any bouquet. I tuck the Edenia amongst the other flowers I gathered, admiring it as I wade through the field back to the path. My skirts catch on the flowers several times and I'm careful to untangle myself lest I snag the fabric.

By the time I'm home, my hands are full, and my feet are sore. I tap my foot against the door. There's a commotion inside as my siblings fight over who answers. It's my sister, Aria, who wins, but Soren isn't far behind. He sticks his head between Aria and the door, excited by a visitor.

"It's just Eden." Aria's initial excitement is gone.

"Hi, Sis!" Soren grins. "Is that bread from Mateo's bakery?"

"Where else would it be from?" I readjust my grip on everything. "Now can I come inside before you have to eat bread off the ground?"

My siblings move aside, and I follow them in, kicking the door closed behind me. Afternoon light bathes the house in warmth, making the space feel large and inviting despite the clutter. Evidence of my family's escapades lies around—books from Soren's reading, scraps of fabric from Aria's dressmaking, and a trail of sawdust out the backdoor. Dad is always woodworking out back.

I shove aside Aria's dress designs and set the baked goods on the dining table. The coin purse is next, landing on the wood with a satisfying thunk. As I walk the last few steps into the kitchen, Soren's footsteps patter across the wood floor behind me. The clanking of coins soon follows.

"It's heavier than I expected! How many coins are in here?"

I grin over my shoulder. "Enough to last us a while."

Placing the wildflowers on the counter, I hike my skirt up and squat in front of the cabinets. I rummage around under the sink until I find the vase I'm looking for. It's a beautiful sky blue, the intricate carvings on its surface making it look like crystal.

It was my mother's favorite.

The sink groans as water from the spout spills into the vase. I meticulously arrange the flowers within, satisfied that the vase's enchantment will make them look fresh forever.

My stomach growls.

I picture the glittering, sugary delights on the table behind me, my mouth watering at the thought. Spinning on my heel, I freeze.

The box of donuts is already open. Soren and Aria chew contentedly, their lips dusted with sugar.

"Dessert before supper?" I cross my arms.

Soren gulps, glancing between me and Aria. They're both silent as they wait for the scolding.

I stalk toward the table, stopping just short of the box. My eyes narrow as I inspect the remaining two donuts. Then, I pluck one out, wink, and take a big bite.

Their mouths fall open.

I burst out laughing, trying not to choke. "Who said I'm against it? I just wanted to make sure you saved some for me."

Aria rolls her eyes. Soren giggles, resuming his sugary feast.

"Did I hear dessert?" Dad enters through the back door covered in sawdust.

I lift my donut in reply.

"You spoil us, Eden."

"It's easy to do when the royal family paid me triple my usual fee."

Soren grabs the bag of coins and gives it a satisfying shake. A symphony of clinking metal fills the room, cut off in an abrupt metallic thump as Soren drops it on the table.

Dad raises his eyebrows. "They recognize your well-renowned talent." He joins us at the table and grabs a donut for himself.

"Soon to be world-renowned," I say. "My painting is sailing overseas to another kingdom to secure the prince a bride."

"Finally," Soren says, mouth full. "Then maybe Aria will stop swooning over him."

"Being married won't make him any less handsome. There's no harm in staring from afar, is there?" Aria leans into the table. "What was it like getting to stare at him for hours, Eden? I bet it was magnificent."

Dad huffs but holds his tongue. He finishes his donut and relaxes in the chair. Soren reaches for the loaves of bread. I swat his hand away with a warning glare.

"I suppose he's objectively handsome," I say. "If you can get past the smirk that's perpetually on his face. But the prince is not as charming as he appears."

Aria finishes her donut with a wistful look. "That's just how I picture him—attractive but cold-hearted, able to break women's hearts with a single look."

"And that's what you're fantasizing about? Sounds like a poor choice, Aria."

"Your sister is right." Dad gives Aria a pointed look. "You should want a man who will treat you like a princess, regardless of his station. Not one that looks down on you or regards your heart as easily disposable."

"Yeah, I know, Dad. I aspire to find a man who loves me as much as you loved mother."

We're all quiet at the mention of our mother. Although Soren and Aria were very young when she died, they grew up hearing our parents' love story. Maybe that's why Aria is such a romantic.

I could do without another distraction in my life. Love is finicky, something that can be ripped away before you can blink. My focus is, and will always be, my work.

"No issues with your skill?" Dad breaks the silence.

I shake my head. "None. My color matching is convincing, and they have no reason to question it. You know I'm skilled at hiding my visions."

"I know, but it's best to remain vigilant. Underestimation can easily become our downfall." Dad runs his finger over a nick in the table. "I don't want to see you exploited by the royal family. We all know they covet skills like yours for their court."

"I'll be safe, Dad. I promise. If I could live without seeing the prince's smug face again, I would. But the role of court artist is what I've been working for, and I have a feeling it's in my grasp."

Eden

"Let's go, ladies! We're going to be late," Dad calls from outside.

Aria and I check our appearances one last time before rushing out of our bedroom and down the stairs. Soren is already outside, waiting impatiently beside our dad.

"You're going to walk in those shoes?" Soren wrinkles his nose.

I look down at my blue heels, surprised he noticed them beneath my skirts. The rising sun glints off the silver details, making them appear almost magical. These are my best heels, worn only for special occasions—one of them being the monthly Ascension Rite.

"I know how to walk in heels," I retort.

"And so do I," Aria chimes in, linking arms with me as we walk down the path into town.

Soren sighs dramatically. "Why do they expect us to dress up every time, anyway?"

"It's a ceremony, Soren. One led by the royal family. It would be disrespectful not to," Dad explains, falling into step beside him.

I glance over my shoulder, smiling at my brother in his blue and silver tunic. Dad wears a more mature version of Soren's outfit, his tunic in a deeper shade of navy. He's attended many more Ascension Rites than we have, making his tunic a bit faded with age.

"Well, I think the royal colors look great on you," I compliment, beaming at my brother.

"Whatever you say, Eden. I just want this itchy thing off." He pulls on the short collar around his neck.

"Good thing your paper crown was fake. If you were royalty, you'd have to wear a tunic or a doublet every day," I reply.

"No way. If I was a prince, I'd wear whatever I wanted."

"Just like the current prince," I mutter under my breath, thinking back to Cassian's unseemly attire in the throne room.

Aria nudges me. "What are you talking about? He always looks so regal at the Ascension Rites."

"Only because he has to," I explain, trying not to picture him in his doublet from the other day.

I distract myself by looking up at the gleaming glass dome of the Chrysalis. A spire rises from the top, stretching toward the sky as if reaching to the heavens. Beneath the dome is a row of stained-glass windows, each one depicting a scene from the origin story of our fated skills. The rest of the temple is too high for me to see, hidden by the cliff's edge.

We pass by the field of wildflowers, our conversation dying down. The rising sun makes Scintillia shine in the distance. I unloop my arm from Aria's and bend down to pluck a couple of flowers. Snapping the stems close to the petals, I stand and tuck one behind Aria's ear. The other slips nicely into the braid by my temple.

It's become a routine, finishing our appearance with a flower to honor the story we've heard since childhood. They symbolize our soul, their radiant blooms representing our strong connection to the vine of life.

Aria smiles, her steps lighter as we enter the village. The dusty roads are busy, everyone on their way to the Ascension Rite. Many of them are also adorned with flowers.

As we make our way through the sea of blue and silver, we stick close to each other. The air thrums with anticipation and excitement, everyone eager to see who's become a Morphi this month. I try to avoid the uneven spots in the road, but the crowds leave little room. The closer we get to the cliff, the more my unease grows at the sheer height of it.

People line the stairs all the way up, the rising sun turning them into walking shadows. It isn't long before we join their ascent. I hike up my skirts, glancing up at all the steps with a sigh. This is my least favorite part of the walk.

By the time we reach the top, the back of my neck is damp with sweat and I'm nauseous from the height. I grab a fistful of my long brown hair and sweep it over my shoulder, letting the cool morning breeze hit my skin. Aria fans herself beside me with her hand. Soren tugs on his collar once more, and I look around for Dad. A few steps behind us, he ascends the final stairs.

"Aldo!" someone shouts.

A tall, older man pushes through the crowd behind me. I recognize him as one of Dad's few loyal customers.

"Good news! I've got a job for ya," the man says.

"Is that so?" Dad smiles while he converses, motioning us toward the Chrysalis.

With all of Scintillia here, finding seats is a priority, and his conversation won't be quick. We join the line of people filing inside, and I wonder for the hundredth time how we all fit.

The marble statues of past kings look down on us as we slowly approach the large front doors. They stand tall between stone pillars that line the Chrysalis's solid foundation. Everything about the temple is a work of art.

Finally at the entrance, we hold our wrists out for the guards to see. They briefly inspect our fatemarks before allowing us to step inside.

I glance toward the balcony overlooking the space, but the royal family remains out of sight. People pour into the temple around us, crowding the entry. There aren't many empty spaces among the tiered stone seats.

"Our usual spot is taken," Aria groans, pointing towards the front right where we usually sit.

"That's alright, we'll find somewhere else." I scan the crowd for a familiar face.

"But how will Dad find us?" Aria questions, glancing back the way we came.

"How about I wait here for him?" Soren suggests, casually leaning against the stone wall by the doors. "I'll watch where you find a seat and lead him your way when he gets here."

I nod once, hoping Dad won't be much longer.

Aware of the slight ache in my heels, I decide not to dawdle in making a decision. Grabbing Aria's hand, we head left. As we ascend the stone steps, I'm desperate for a seat near the ground; the higher we go, the more my stomach twists.

"Eden!"

I look around, sure someone called my name. Though I'm uncertain where the sound came from, I stop my ascent and scan the crowds.

I lean close to Aria, straining to be heard over the murmur of conversation. "Did you say my name?"

She shakes her head before continuing up the steps. With one last look at the crowd, I finally spot someone standing in the middle of a row, waving his hands high above his head.

"Eden!" he shouts.

It's Mateo.

I grab Aria's hand and pull her into the next row. "Excuse us," I say, trying to keep my dress out of the way as we step through the seated people.

"About time you spotted me," Mateo says when we get close. "I started wondering if you'd gone blind."

"And I thought you were some crazed interpretive dancer." I mimic his flailing arms before smoothing my skirts to sit on the stone bench beside him.

Aria leans forward, looking over me at Mateo. "Thanks for saving us seats!"

"Although I wish they were closer to the ground," I mumble, worried one wrong move will send me tumbling over the rows of people below us.

"It could be worse, Eden. There are plenty of open seats at the top."

Mateo's retort surprises me. I didn't mean for him to hear my complaint. "Sorry." I grin sheepishly. "I'll try not to look down."

His mother and father sit beside him, and they wave politely at us. Seated next to each other, it's easy to see Mateo's resemblance to his parents. They all have the same sandy-brown hair, the sole difference being the gray streaks that now run through his mother and father's. His mother smiles, her dimples the spitting image of Mateo.

"Where's Luca?" I ask, referring to Mateo's older brother.

"Sitting somewhere with his wife," Mateo's mother replies. "Now that he's all grown up, he wants nothing to do with us."

Mateo's father pats her hand reassuringly before turning to Aria and me. "Where are Aldo and Soren?"

I steel myself before looking down toward the entrance but can't see Soren over the wall. "Dad is outside talking with one of his customers. Soren is waiting by the entrance for him."

"I hope Aldo's doing alright," Mateo's mother chimes in.

Smiling politely, I reply with a nod. Though I'm thankful they care enough to ask, I don't need any more of their sympathy. Mateo's family knows how mother's death shattered our family—and how it ruined Dad's work. People stopped buying his pieces after that, whispering he was cursed.

We fall into a comfortable silence, listening to the murmur of conversation all around us. Aria nudges my shoulder, pointing to a familiar head of dark-brown hair as my brother emerges from behind the entrance wall.

Minus the standing, I raise my hands above my head, mimicking Mateo's earlier stance.

"It would work better if you stood, Eden!" He laughs behind me.

His amused expression sends a comical frown across my face before I yell down to my brother. Soren takes much less time to spot me than I thought, and he quickly climbs the steps with Dad in tow. I give Mateo a pointed look. "No standing necessary."

Soren and Dad scoot in beside us, my dress squishing into Aria's. I look up as the sun peaks over the walls of the Chrysalis, its golden light spilling in through the glass dome to bathe everything in a divine glow. It's another marvel of the Chrysalis, one of the many intricate ideas the architects made a reality.

Trumpets sound, signaling the beginning of the ceremony. We all stand, turning toward the upper balcony, where the silver thrones now sparkle in the sun. King Leopold and Queen Clarissa are the first to appear, followed closely by Prince Cassian and Princess Lyra.

Thunderous applause fills the space, echoing off the stone walls. King Leopold raises a hand to silence us.

"We are blessed by your devoted service and attention as we take part in our monthly Ascension Rite." The king's rich voice reverberates around us.

He sweeps his arms over the crowd, and I make the mistake of following his gaze. My knees lock instinctively, legs swaying as I stare down at the rows of people. I force myself to relax, despite the memory of my mother's death flashing through my mind. Aria's hand finds mine with a reassuring squeeze.

"Let's begin with our creed," the king says, his voice recapturing my attention.

I let go of my sister's hand.

"Thank you, Delayon, our Creator," I recite with the crowd, "for the blessing of our skills. Fated to serve." I lift my left arm over my chest, wrist outward to expose my fatemark. "Fated to fight." My right arm crosses my left, fists clenched. "Fated to rise." I raise my elbows, then lower them slowly, letting my hands slide together. My thumbs interlock, forming a butterfly shape in front of my chest.

Everyone does the same, the swish of skin against skin echoing like the whir of flight.

"Please be seated as we begin the ceremony."

The rustle of fabric sounds loud as we all take our seats. Fixing my gaze on the king and queen, I can't help but glance behind them at Cassian. He stands with his hands clasped behind his back, a bored look on his face. *Does he ever look happy?*

A harp begins playing and I quiet my thoughts, eager for the ceremony to begin. The farion enters the balcony with the Royal Codex. He looks like a walking shadow, the black cape draped around his shoulders made darker by the sun's glow behind him.

"The Word of Delayon!" The farion holds the large leather tome up for all to see. "Indestructible, unalterable, life-changing truth. May our ears, eyes, hearts, and minds be open to receiving it."

He places the Royal Codex on a lectern at the edge of the balcony. With ceremonial delicacy, he opens to a specific page— *The Origin of Fated Skills*—a sacred story of the purpose of our gifts.

"Grown from the vine of life, the Gardener's earthly trellis flowered abundantly," he begins. "Like a garden tapestry, each vine entwined with others. Flowers bloomed in radiant colors, a testament to their connection to the Gardener's care. Closest to the vine's heart, the flowers were ethereal. They were the powerful foundation of the trellis, protecting and nourishing continued growth."

I look to my left at Aria, who appears lost in thought. To my right, Soren dramatically mouths the words, each one memorized after years of hearing the same story. I shove his shoulder with a shake of my head. I must be the only one in my family who still enjoys hearing it.

"Yet as they dutifully served, the other flowers grew high above and were bathed in sunlight. These flowers garnered more attention from the Gardener."

I look up at the stained-glass windows, finding the one that shows the radiant flowers at the top of the trellis. I shift my gaze to the one beside it, the trellis now marred by deep red thorns.

"Jealous, one vine developed thorns, attempting to spread them along the whole foundation of the trellis. Several other vines became infected with this envy, working to choke off the top flowers' connection to the vine of life." The farion turns the page. "But the Gardener noticed this and pruned the thorny vines, casting them aside."

I glance at the window with the sword severing the vine before looking at the next one. Roots made of tawny-colored glass connect a shriveled, thorny vine to the ground.

"Cut from the vine of life, the fallen vines shriveled. Though their strength and beauty were no more, their roots took hold nearby. A new vine grew, determined not to flourish, but to fight—to surpass and destroy the life from which it had been cut."

Unable to see the rest of the windows that wrap around the dome behind us, I return my attention to the royal balcony. It's too bad; the last part of the story is my favorite. No wonder I prefer sitting on the right side of the Chrysalis.

"Determined to disrupt the Fallen's influence"—the farion looks up—"the Gardener offered His flowers gifts: small, delicate caterpillars. These creatures held great potential. If nurtured, a wondrous transformation would take place, elevating the soul of the flower into a graceful butterfly."

I pull the flower from behind my ear and pluck the petals one by one. As they fall to the ground, I imagine them shifting into butterflies, ascending into the sky.

"With radiant wings, their new form would carry them closer to the divine, lifting their spirits beyond the earthly trellis to bask in the eternal light."

My thumb rubs over the fatemark on my left wrist, the silver sands showing my progress toward the transformation.

The king steps forward from his throne to join the farion. "And now to honor those who've accomplished their transformation!"

The crowd roars with excitement.

"Finally, we're getting to the good part," Soren yells over the cheering.

I lean forward, eager for a closer look at this month's Morphi. Five people dressed in all silver step onto the balcony. A collective gasp fills the temple, everyone shocked by the high number. Most months it's only two or three, sometimes as little as one. Perfecting your fated skill is difficult, a feat that takes much time and dedication. Very few achieve it quickly.

"We are blessed to honor five new Morphi this month," the king declares, his voice brimming with pride.

I squint, trying to get a closer look at the group. There are two women and three men, all but one appearing older in age. At the far end is a younger man, his sandy-brown hair startlingly familiar.

I reach over to grip Mateo's hand. "Is that your brother?"

He stares back at me, mouth agape. "I think so."

"You didn't know?"

Mateo shakes his head.

I release his hand and watch closely as each person steps forward to receive their recognition from the king. He takes their fist in one hand, raising it high for all to see. Though the distinct butterfly mark is hard to make out from this distance, its black coloration is unmistakable.

"Having fulfilled their duty to Delayon, their minds have ascended beyond this Earth. For with perfection comes divine clarity," the farion says.

An acolyte brings forth a torch. The farion, now holding the Royal Codex, moves to stand to the left of the five Morphi.

"Come forward to cast off your old self," he says, holding the Codex out in front of him.

The first Morphi steps forward as the acolyte lowers the torch onto the Royal Codex. The flames curl around the pages, hungry and bright—but the book does not catch. Not even the corners blacken. The fire dances back, as if repelled.

Even after witnessing the ceremony many times, I gasp, joining the countless others that echo through the Chrysalis.

The farion gestures for the first Morphi to place a hand upon the Codex. "Touch now, the unshaken word. Let its truth mark your soul as your skill has marked your flesh."

They reach through the flames, a faint shimmer rippling across the cover as their palm lays flat against the book.

"Your name is now etched upon the eternal page."

A reverent silence falls over the crowd as the ceremony repeats for the four other Morphi. When they all stand back in line, the Royal Codex glowing blue with heat, the king addresses us.

"To recognize their hard work and transformation, each Morphi will receive wealth, land, and the chance to work for the royal family. Join me in recognizing the remarkable accomplishments of these individuals as they receive the title of Mentera's Morphi."

King Leopold sweeps his hand over the crowd, and we erupt into applause. As the cheers and clapping continue, the farion drapes black capes over each new Morphi. The velvet falls heavily over their shoulders. It's a striking garment, one that exudes both elegance and power. The fabric has a subtle sheen, catching the light in a way that accentuates its rich, inky color.

Along the cape's edges, silver embroidery depicts a flower transforming into a butterfly. It matches perfectly with the silver silk that lines the cape's interior. At the collar, a clasp shaped like a butterfly holds the cape in place.

It's the ultimate symbol of status.

I'll do anything to wear one of my own.

Cassian

As Farion drapes the last cape onto the young man at the end, Father looks at me as if to say, *Why isn't this you?*

I clench my jaw, now keenly aware of the fatemark on my wrist. Another young man already becoming a Morphi puts even more pressure on me than I already had.

The joy of being the crown prince.

The crowd's cheers grow louder as the Morphi raise their fists in the air. Everyone is excited about the large number of people ascending this month. It is rather unusual, but a good sign for our kingdom. The more Morphi we have, the more powerful Mentera will be.

I glance at Lyra on my left.

She still has her fatemark too, though Father puts much less pressure on her. Lyra must sense my gaze because she turns to look at me, giving me a small half-smile.

"Smile," she mouths, her voice drowned out by the crowd.

I muster my best princely smile, rolling my shoulders back and facing the crowd once more. The whole of Scintillia is here. After attending so many Ascension Rites, I thought I'd be used to their stares. But they still make me nervous. It will be even worse when I'm king, all their fates tied to my decisions.

My father raises a hand, quieting the crowd as the ceremony nears its end. His voice cuts through the hush like a blade.

"As we return home today, let us not grow complacent." He pauses, letting the silence linger. "The Fateless still walk among us—those who reject the gifts of Delayon, who cling to the Divinian heresy and hide in shadow."

He steps forward, his gaze sweeping the crowd.

"Though none were brought to justice this day, take heart. I believe—no, I know—that by next month's Ascension Rite, some will be revealed. And when they are, they will face the truth as all traitors must."

The king raises his left arm to expose his Morphi mark. "Fated to serve," he begins, leading the crowd in our creed.

I cross my right arm over my left, joining them. "Fated to fight. Fated to fly."

Swallowing, I wave to the crowd as they cheer, and the ceremony ends. Mother leads the way, and we exit the royal balcony. Farion grabs the Royal Codex on the way out. He clutches it to his chest, always paranoid even though it's a safe journey back to its home in the palace library.

Not far behind him, I enter the stairwell when a hand grabs my shoulder. It squeezes tight, the Moretti family ring shining on one finger. I prepare for the worst as I turn to face Father.

"Soon that will be you up there, Cassian!" he bellows, stepping down to descend alongside me.

The space is narrow, our broad frames mere inches from each other. Though I'm the same height as Father, his presence exudes power and authority. It's something I have yet to master.

I give him a tight-lipped nod, not sure what to say. Now is not the time to get into an argument. I'd like to keep his good mood from the ceremony for as long as possible.

"Remarkable, isn't it?" he asks. "How many ascended this month?"

"Indeed, Father. Mentera grows stronger by the day."

We reach the last step, but Father stops me before I join the others. His firm stare pins me in place, eyes the same cold and calculating shade of blue as mine. It's like a glimpse into the future. Mother always says I look just like him.

"Today you will choose the Morphi who will be honored with serving the royal family."

My mouth goes dry. I school my features into a mask of confidence. "Yes, Father."

I join the others in the receiving area. Lyra and Mother stand along the right wall. Farion is to the left, waiting in the open space to oversee the Morphi. When I head toward him, Lyra raises a brow at me. I flash a smile before taking the king's place next to Farion.

Father takes my place against the wall beside Mother. She glances over at him in surprise, but he pays her no mind. Clasping her hands in front of her blue gown, she gives me a reassuring nod.

I'm always grateful for her support. Especially in the face of a test such as this. Father is always trying to gauge my ability as the future king, springing things on me at the last minute.

Today is no exception.

The newly-ascended Morphi file out of the stairwell, lining up against the stone wall. They eye me expectantly, their anticipation evident. It's well known that the real decisions are made *after* the ceremony. Being offered an esteemed position in the palace is not a guarantee for all Morphi.

"I extend my congratulations to you all," I begin, trying to sound as regal as my father. "You have ascended into Mentera's elite class of Morphi, and you shall be rewarded accordingly."

Pivoting on my heel, I walk to stand in front of the first person in line. My silver cape swishes behind me when I stop. Looking from top to bottom, I assess the woman in line. She bows respectfully.

"Tell me your name and your skill," I direct.

"Emmeline, Your Royal Highness. I am a skilled navigator at sea, blessed with an internal compass of sorts."

"It's nice to meet you, Lady Emmeline."

She lifts her head, and I'm met with her deep brown eyes. I allow myself only a moment to scrutinize her, not wanting to appear indecisive in front of Father.

The subtle streaks of gray in her brown hair hint at her age. Weathered and calloused hands speak of a life of hard work. She looks like she could hold her own, a true naval woman.

Crew members from our current navy flit through my mind as I recall each of their skills. None have one such as hers.

"It is my honor to welcome you into the ranks of the royal navy." I resist the urge to look at Father's reaction to my first decision.

Lady Emmeline's eyebrows raise. She drops to one knee before me. "Thank you, Your Royal Highness. For as long as I shall live, I will faithfully serve Mentera and its royal family."

My throat constricts. There's no taking back the decision now. The next few blur together, the names and faces hard to keep straight as I focus on making the right call. I move quickly through them, keeping my tone steady and focused. I will not disappoint Father.

The second Morphi, a healer who can enhance remedies, is assigned to the infirmary. The third, a glass artisan, goes to the royal workshop. A woman who predicts storms is placed with the scouts.

For a moment, Miss Asher's words of warning flash through my mind. It's a shame this woman wasn't already working for us. I could've looked into the possibility of the ship sinking more thoroughly. Although, if she's right, it could work in my favor, buying me the time I was hoping for.

Clearing my thoughts, I face the last one in line—the young man with sandy-brown hair. His posture is stiff and expectant, eyes shining.

"And your skill?" I ask.

"I craft swords, Your Royal Highness, able to manipulate the metal with my mind."

I nod. "You'll work in the royal forge."

Relief floods his face as he bows. "Thank you. I won't fail you, Your Royal Highness."

Stepping back, I face them all. "Rise. The Ascended One will get you settled into your new roles, ensuring your adequate compensation and lodging."

"Your Royal Highness," they say in unison, heads bowed.

Not wanting to face my father just yet, I leave the receiving area. As soon as I step outside, I drink in the morning air to soothe my pounding heart. I steady my breathing.

Being king doesn't suit me.

I have never wanted to make such important decisions.

The door creaks open behind me, my father's steady gait approaching.

Never a second too long on my own.

Still overwhelmed, I clench my hands together behind my back. Words flow fast and fierce through my mind, a persuasive mantra that activates my fated skill.

I am the master of my emotions, I think. *They do not rule me; I rule them. Feelings are a weakness. I care not what others think. I am in control.*

Numbness falls over me, a cold emptiness settling in my stomach. I turn to face the king.

"Running away from your decisions like the little boy you are. It's clear you have much to learn," he says, nostrils flaring.

"I apologize if I disappointed you, Father," I reply, my tone neutral.

If it weren't for my skill, I don't know how I'd face yet another disappointed lecture from my father.

"If? There should be no question that you did! How could you possibly think inviting all five to serve the royal family was a wise decision?"

"More Morphi means more power," I explain. "You've always said that."

"Not when you hand out the positions as if they are *easy* to earn," he sneers. "Especially when we already have several with skills such as theirs."

A flash of surprise pushes through the emptiness. I tamp it down. "You must be mistaken. Their skills are unique," I say. "I'm sure of it."

"You're sure of it?" He steps closer, his gaze challenging.

I dig through my memories, trying to place who might've been a duplicate. Now that my thoughts aren't a mess, my earlier nerves quenched by my skill, I realize the mistake I made.

"The navigator," I whisper. "And the healer."

"Now you're thinking clearly." Father grabs my left wrist, yanking the sleeve down to expose my fatemark. He squints at the swirling sands. "Ah, finally using your skill, are you? You're blessed not to be controlled by your weak emotions, and yet you do not use it when you should."

I meet his gaze. He's right. I never think to use my skill when I need it the most. I'm pathetic.

"I'm sorry, Father. You're right."

"Of course I am. You lack the determination to do well. When will you finally accept your responsibility as the future king?" He drops my arm. "I hope your future wife has more of a backbone."

The words don't sting, but they will. It's only a matter of time before my focus is drained and I must stop using my skill. There's only so much I can say to myself to keep my feelings at bay.

Father exits the courtyard. The wooden door slams closed behind him, creaking on its hinges. I rub my temples, hoping to ease the strain from my focus. With a sharp inhale, I let go of control. My emotions rush through me like waves crashing over the shoreline.

I move to bite my nails but stop. They're already bitten off. Another disgusting habit of mine, or so my father would say. I bend down, picking up a rock. The rough surface grates against the skin of my palm. Clenching it tighter, I hurl it against the stone wall of the courtyard.

It ricochets, the sound echoing through the space. I jump when the door to the courtyard creaks behind me. It closes softly, Farion standing with the Royal Codex held at his side. He strides over to stand beside me.

"I take it your conversation didn't go well?" His brown eyes meet mine, a knowing glint in them.

I scoff. "Well? It was wonderful. I'll have you know I received high praise from my father, the king."

Farion chuckles, shaking his head. "He'll come around. You know how he gets. And you must admit you do not prioritize your studies like you should."

I kick another rock across the courtyard. "Do I know every single person working for the Moretti family? No. But do I care? Also, no."

"Cassian—"

"No more, Farion. I already know what you're going to say. And you already know that I've never wanted to be king." I walk to the courtyard exit, pausing just before leaving. "If only that was a choice I could make."

Eden

Water sloshes in the basin as I scrub at the dishes. I'm careful with them, not wanting to break the few nice plates we own. As I lift one out to dry, a knock at the door almost startles it out of my hands.

I set it down on the counter beside the sink, breathing through my now racing heart. There is no movement behind me, so I turn to look at my siblings.

Aria is focused on her newest sewing project at the kitchen table. Soren has his nose in a book in the living room.

"I guess I'll get it." I sigh, drying my hands on the apron around my waist.

Crossing to the front door, I run a hand over my braided hair. With a quick glance down to ensure I look somewhat presentable, I muster up a welcoming spirit and open the door.

"Welcome! What brings you to our humble—" The words die in my throat, my outstretched arm frozen in place.

Staring back at me is the smug face of the prince.

He's dressed modestly—the embellishments typical of royal fashion notably absent. His white cotton shirt is left untied, a navy cape draped around his shoulders. A sword is strapped to his belt, his hand resting on the silver hilt. He taps his finger against it, his ring clinking against the metal. He must be the most impatient person I've ever met.

Behind him is a tall, burly man dressed similarly. He clasps his hands behind his back, moving so the sun glints off the sword beneath his cape. It's clear he's Cassian's guard.

I bow my head and curtsy. "Your Royal Highness."

Aria gasps behind me, rushing to the door to get a better look. Her breath hitches at the sight of him, and she joins me in a curtsy.

"To what do we owe the great honor of your visit, Your Royal Highness?" Aria inquires, fluttering her eyelashes.

I mask my disgust, pasting on a smile and smoothing my dress. "Yes, do tell what brings you so far from the palace? It's quite the walk for someone of such importance."

Cassian squints, the corner of his mouth twitching. "I've come to make you an offer. One that's better discussed in person."

I clench the fabric of my skirt, fairly certain what his offer will be. "So important you must tell me yourself?"

Aria steps on my foot, mortified by my undignified behavior. With a deep breath, I channel my inner lady and straighten my spine. Though I know exactly how to act in front of a royal, something about Cassian makes me abandon all manners.

"I'm honored to welcome you inside to discuss further, Your Royal Highness." I bow my head and step to the side, allowing him room to enter.

Several long seconds pass, but I resist the urge to look at him. *Must he make me wait like this?*

"That's a generous invitation, Miss Asher," he says finally. "But that won't be necessary."

Deep breaths, Eden. Deep breaths.

"We understand, Your Royal Highness. You must be incredibly busy." Aria curtsies again.

"Indeed, which is why I won't take much more of your time. Would you allow me a moment alone with your sister?"

Her shoulders slump, but she complies. As if warning me to behave, she gives me a pointed look before disappearing into the house.

It's ironic how our roles have reversed. Usually I'm the one doing the parenting.

Turning to face Cassian head-on, I watch as the guard brushes his cape aside, exposing his sword once again. I swallow nervously, forcing myself to adopt a more lady-like demeanor. I can't keep treating Cassian like any other spoiled noble I'll never see again.

My gaze shifts back to the prince. "Please continue, Your Royal Highness."

Before I can react, Cassian closes the distance between us. His hand darts out and grabs my wrist, the chill of his fingers a shock on my skin. I stiffen, instinctively pulling my arm away, but his grip holds fast.

"What—" I start, but my question is answered as he turns my wrist to inspect my fatemark.

"I must confirm you've perfected your skill." His voice is steady and commanding. He stares at the hourglass etched into my skin, studying the amount of silver sand within. A tense silence stretches between us as he holds my wrist for a moment longer, his expression unreadable.

I'm unsure why he stares for so long, knowing it should only take seconds to notice the sands at the bottom of my hourglass—proof I perfected my skill.

Then, with a flick of his hand, he releases me. I clutch my wrist to my chest, the protective gesture betraying the calm facade I wanted to maintain.

I level him with a glare, not bothering to mask the edge in my voice. "I presume your unwarranted appraisal yielded the answers you sought?"

Cassian smiles but it doesn't reach his eyes. "Congratulations, Miss Asher. I'd like to formally offer you the position of Mentera's court artist."

Though I expected it, my stomach still flutters.

He continues, "If you accept, you will move into the palace and assume your duties at once. The royal court expects nothing less."

My mind races, still trying to grasp the implications of such an offer. Becoming the court artist elevates my social status and wealth. It's exactly what I need to grow closer to being a Morphi. But now that it's finally here, I feel utterly unprepared. Lying to the royal family will become my new normal, every day a balance between using my skill and hiding it.

Cassian's head tilts, his brows raised. "I can't wait for your answer all day, Miss Asher."

I nod hurriedly.

This is what I've been working toward—a way to better provide for my family and be noticed by the king. Why is it suddenly so frightening?

Swallowing my fear, I curtsy low. "I accept. Thank you for the incredible offer, Your Royal Highness."

My heart is pounding as I process what will happen next. There is no turning back now.

When I rise, Cassian is staring at me, his ice-blue eyes scrutinizing. "You're an artisan now, Miss Asher. It's expected you act like one."

He turns away with a swish of his cape, his boots crunching against the gravel. The guard dips his head in a slight nod before following Cassian down the path.

I watch them leave, noticing as Cassian's guard falls in step beside him. It's unusual, considering they're of different ranks. The proud set of Cassian's shoulders relaxes as they walk, a sign of the more friendly relationship between the two.

As the sun continues its descent, they become silhouettes against the backdrop of the village. The palace gleams in the distance, raised above Scintillia on a cliff overlooking the sea. I can't believe that will soon be my home.

I turn and stare at our family cottage. Afternoon sunlight turns the blue roof violet. The flowering vines have taken over since I planted them, but I don't mind. Their blue and white blossoms turn the cottage into a living part of the wildflower field nearby. I trail my fingers along the soft petals.

It will be harder than I thought to say goodbye to this place. With a deep breath, I step inside.

Aria stands from her seat at the dining table. "Tell me everything!"

Soren perks up from his spot on the sofa, setting his book aside.

"You're looking at Mentera's next court artist," I relay, my voice sounding shakier than intended.

The shock on my siblings' faces mirrors how I feel.

"Eden, that's amazing!" Aria takes my hands in hers. "Why aren't you more excited? The prince himself came to offer you the position!"

I smile and nod my head as if trying to convince myself. "I know, I should be. I mean, I am!"

A sigh escapes my lips. I pull Aria into a hug, waving Soren over. He scrambles up and wraps his arms around us.

"I'm just realizing how much I'm going to miss you rascals." I squeeze them tight.

"Don't be silly," Aria reassures. "You'll be glad to have us out of your hair."

I laugh, the sound coming out warbled.

"Don't cry," Soren says. "You can still come visit us. And we can visit you at the palace, right?"

"Absolutely. I'll make sure that's one of my stipulations."

Ruffling Soren's chestnut hair, I bop him softly on the nose. Then I grab Aria's hand, squeezing it gently. They smile up at me, though they'll both soon be taller than me.

"We'll help you pack," Aria offers. "You deserve a life out on your own, Eden—not always having to look after us. We'll be okay."

They follow me up the stairs and into my shared bedroom. With their help, it doesn't take long to pack what I need—clothes, a few sentimental items, jewelry, and my art supplies.

"I hope your bag isn't full yet." Aria spins her dress form to reveal an exquisitely detailed gown.

My lips part with surprise. "When did you finish it?"

"Only yesterday. You simply *must* bring it with you to the palace."

I blink back another wave of tears. "I'd look a mess without you."

"What am I, chopped liver?" Soren asks, lifting a bag he packed.

"Never, Soren. Your clothing taste may be questionable, but I can't deny you are an efficient helper."

He sticks his tongue out.

"I'm going to look through some of Mother's old art stuff in the attic before I go."

"I can do it, Eden." Soren drops the bag.

I wave him off. "I'll be fine. The ladder isn't that tall."

Soren shrugs before packing another bag as I head into the hall. The ladder comes down from the ceiling with a groan. I sneeze from all the dust as I ascend into the small upper room before I can overthink it. It's been a long time since any of us have been up here.

Mother's old paintings and supplies are stacked neatly throughout the space. I admire her work, looking through the canvases at her beautiful landscapes and portraits. In the far back corner, I find a canvas tucked under a blanket. Dust swirls as I slide it off, revealing an unfinished portrait of our family.

My breath catches, the sight of all of us together making my heart constrict.

I crouch down beside it, unbothered by the dust that will dirty my skirts. My fingers trace the loose brushstrokes that capture our round, youthful features now lost to time. I can picture her painting it, beaming as it came to life with each swipe of the brush in her paint-stained hand. Although it's a shame she never got to finish it, I like it better this way. It's as if she replicated the energy in each of us, her brush capturing the memory straight from her mind.

She never liked unfinished paintings. I have the same sort of perfectionism. And yet, I know this painting needs to come with me—a piece of home in an unfamiliar place.

I pick up the canvas, gathering a few other odds and ends before leaving the attic. As the ladder recedes into the ceiling, Soren and Aria enter the hall with my bags in tow.

"Ready?" Soren asks, hoisting one bag over his shoulder.

"As ready as I'll ever be."

"Where have you been?" my mother demands.

She looks regal as ever, her blue gown bright against the courtyard stone. Her eyes narrow as she takes in my appearance. I can already feel the lecture coming.

I'm in trouble.

"Lovely to see you too, Mother," I mutter, trying to sidestep her.

She catches my arm with surprising speed.

"Cassian." Her grip tightens. "Where were you?"

I force a smile, placing my hand over hers. "Just a quick trip to the village."

"Why?"

"To hire our new court artist, of course," I explain with a shrug.

Her brows draw together, suspicious. "Why didn't you send your squire?"

I shrug again. "I prefer doing things myself."

With a gentle tug, I remove myself from her grasp. The servants open the doors as I move past her into the entrance hall.

"Cassian!" Her heels click behind me, a sharp reminder she's not done. "You know you're not supposed to go into the village. You are the crown prince! Something could happen!"

"Scold me later, Mother. I'd like to get out of these clothes before Father finds out."

She lets out an exasperated sigh, but I don't bother sticking around. I take the stairs two at a time. Silas follows easily behind me.

Thankfully, the royal quarters are quiet, most of the servants elsewhere. As I near my room, I glance at the door to my right.

Please don't hear me.

Slowly twisting the silver handle of my door, I breathe a sigh of relief. Almost there.

"Cassian?"

Or not.

I grimace. Lyra's head pokes out from her doorway. A mischievous grin creeps onto her face.

"Why are you dressed like a commoner?"

"None of your business."

She steps out, closing her door with a knowing smirk. "I'm your sister. Everything is my business."

Groaning, I step into my room. Of course, she follows, barging in after me.

"Do you mind?" I snap.

"Not at all. You can change in the bathroom while you explain why you needed such a horrible disguise." Lyra settles onto my bed with an expectant look.

"Are you that starved for entertainment?"

"Yes. This life is duller than most think," she says. "And don't pretend you think otherwise. Or that you have anyone else to talk to but me."

I slam the bathroom door behind me, my frustration building. "I'm not telling you anything. Go ride a horse or something."

Her laughter answers me, but I ignore her. Quickly, I strip off the commoner's garb. It lands in a heap on the floor, the cool air hitting my skin. I exhale. What a day.

I catch my reflection in the washbasin's mirror—black hair plastered to my forehead, a streak of dirt across my cheek. I twist the spout and lean over, splashing cold water on my face, then ducking lower to gulp it down. The chill is just what I need to clear my head.

As I pull on a fresh shirt, Lyra's voice sounds through the door.

"So, what's her name?" she teases, her voice lilting with glee.

I freeze mid-motion. "What?"

"Come on, Cassian, I'm not stupid. You secretly went to the village. You're covered in dirt. And now you're brooding like someone with a secret."

I can practically see the smirk on her face.

Rolling my eyes, I continue dressing. "It's not what you think. I was hiring our new court artist."

Lyra laughs again, the sound grating on my nerves. "I knew you fancied her! She's pretty. Is that why you had to go fetch her personally?"

I yank open the bathroom door, fully dressed but not ready to face her relentless questioning. "Lyra, for the last time, it's nothing like that. She's just a painter. End of story."

She arches a brow, unconvinced. "Oh? Then why are you so flustered?"

"I'm not," I insist, trying to keep my voice calm.

Lyra always manages to get under my skin.

"Whatever you say, big brother." Her voice drips with sarcasm.

She stands from the bed and brushes a hand over her gown. I move past her to grab my coat from the back of the chair. "Don't bring up any of this nonsense when she gets here."

Lyra gasps dramatically. "How dare you assume I'd do such a thing! Although if we become best friends, there's no telling what secrets might come out."

I glare at her. "She's here for one purpose, Lyra—to paint. That's it."

"Oh, come now, Cassian," she says with a grin. "We both know things rarely stay that simple in this palace."

Before I can argue, a knock sounds at my door. I glance at Lyra. She shrugs. Opening the door, Silas stands with a serious expression.

"Your Highness, the king wishes to speak with you in the council chamber. It's urgent."

Great. As if I didn't already have enough to deal with.

I nod, glancing back at Lyra. "Looks like I'm needed elsewhere."

"Of course you are," she says. "Go ahead, dear brother. I'll go prepare for my new best friend's arrival."

With a wink, she sweeps out of my room, her skirts rustling as she goes. I leave shortly after, Silas at my heels.

As we walk through the hallways of the royal quarters, my thoughts drift back to the village. I remember Eden's expression as she hesitantly accepted my offer. There was something about her I couldn't quite place. I thought she'd be elated, but instead, she seemed sad.

I shake the thoughts away as we approach the council chamber. Squaring my shoulders, I brace myself for whatever Father has to say. I give a nod, and the servants open the doors.

The room is empty except for my father. He sits at the head of the table, his silver crown bright atop his dark hair. His attention never wavers from the papers in front of him.

"Your Majesty," I say, stepping into the room. The doors close, leaving us alone.

He's silent, examining a piece of parchment for several long moments. I clasp my hands behind my back. Father hates being interrupted. I know better than to speak out of turn.

At last, he sets the parchment down on the table. His face betrays nothing. He's long since mastered the art of hiding his emotions. Or maybe he doesn't feel anything to begin with.

"Cassian, nice of you to finally join me."

I don't respond. There's always more.

"I heard you hired the new court artist today. Miss Asher, is it?" He leans back in his chair.

I clear my throat. He can't possibly know I hired her in person, can he? "Yes, as we discussed, Your Majesty. Or am I mistaken?"

His head tilts, brows scrunching together. "What is her skill again?"

"True Color, Your Majesty. She can perfectly match any hue," I remind, though I sense he already knew the answer.

"Ah, yes. And that is such a special skill you had to confirm it in person?"

For a split second, my breathing stops. Adrenaline shoots through me, my mind racing through the afternoon's events. I was certain I snuck out unnoticed. Where did I go wrong?

I feign a smile, hoping Father won't notice it's forced. "I've been shirking my duties enough—thought I should take personal responsibility for such an important task, Your Majesty."

He laughs—a cold, biting sound that fills me with dread. "My boy, you should be a better liar than that by now."

My neck is hot. I clench my hands behind my back, trying to maintain my cool. Father always finds a way to belittle me. If I lie too well, he's ashamed of my dishonest character. If I don't lie well enough, he thinks I'm weak and inexperienced. I'll never live up to his expectations.

It's suffocating.

Father doesn't wait for an answer, leaning forward to rest his elbows on the table. He steeples his hands. "No matter. I don't need the truth from your lips when I already know it, anyway. Let's get to the real reason I brought you here."

My mouth tastes sour. I clench my hands tighter, not sure what to expect. I had hoped that was the extent of our conversation.

"Now that the painter is hired, I expect another portrait on the morrow."

"A-Another?" I stammer.

"Yes, of course. Even if the royal ship hadn't sunk, we have many maidens falling over themselves to receive your portrait," Father states. "Though your grandparents in Aetherea still have priority."

"The royal ship sunk?" My mind is muddled, unable to process his words.

Miss Asher's prediction was right. She might prove useful, after all.

Father sighs in frustration. "Keep up, Cassian. You should know all the happenings of this kingdom, especially important news like that."

He rises to a stand, the heavy wooden chair scraping against the floor as he gathers the papers in a pile. Father stalks toward the door. I don't move, staring straight ahead even as he stops beside me.

"I plan to have you betrothed by the end of the month. You'd do well not to get in the way of that." He rests his hand on my shoulder, the gesture more a threat than a comfort.

Pressure builds behind my eyes. A pounding, like that of my own heartbeat, knocks against my brain as if seeking entry.

He's trying to intrude on my thoughts again.

I let my mind go blank. After many years of enduring his skill, I finally realized he could only reach the parts I left exposed. And so I learned to hide in silence, to show him nothing at all.

Father's frown deepens.

He's known for some time that his skill isn't as effective on me as it used to be, and yet he never ceases to try. After several long seconds, he releases my shoulder and the pressure dissipates.

The council chamber doors creak as he leaves. My tense muscles sag with relief, no longer weighed down by his presence. Shame and anger course through me and I will them into nothingness.

But my skill won't activate.

I slam my fist into the wooden table. What good am I if I can't even control my own emotions? My heart pounds, my breathing ragged and uneven. I want to scream into this empty room.

I'm ashamed of how easily my father gets to me—of how much control he wields over me. I'm done being a pawn.

This is my life. Not his.

If I only have a month before I'm engaged, I'll play by my own rules.

I hold my breath, willing my hand not to shake. My face is inches from the canvas, eyes unblinking as a bright white line flows from my brush. Stepping back, I admire how the once dull-gray detailing on Cassian's doublet now shines like true silver.

The thin paintbrush clacks against the table as I set it down, and I collapse onto the chair behind me. Silky green fabric bunches around me. I'm careful not to touch it with my paint-stained hands. If it weren't for the expectations that come with working in the palace, I wouldn't be wearing such an extravagant gown to paint.

Cassian wasn't joking when he said I'd assume my duties as soon as I moved in. Only minutes after I finished my tour, the servants instructed me to meet the crown prince in the studio.

Painting him the second time was easier, having done it once before. But the experience was no less intimidating. Cassian's stare still makes me nervous, even through the portrait, his icy eyes intensely observant. No matter how careful I've been, I worry he'll notice what I'm hiding.

It doesn't help that my own visions continue to shock me. It's hard not to react when I see myself shamelessly flirting with the prince like all the other court ladies. I refuse to become that future version of myself.

The crown prince's charm has no effect on me, anyway.

I wipe my hands on a nearby rag. Though the color is gone, it does little to remove the scent of linseed oil and pigment that clings to my fingers. With a groan, I pack up my supplies, my body stiff from hours of standing with a ridiculously layered skirt around my hips. It's beautiful, but certainly not practical.

I clean up quickly, packing my brushes and palette into the new leather satchel I was given. The studio is too quiet, the weight of the prince's presence still lingering even though he left hours ago. I swing the satchel over my shoulder, dirty smock in hand, and step into the hallway.

A young servant passes, balancing a tray of crystal glasses. I catch her eye.

"Excuse me, do you know where I should leave this to be washed?" I ask, lifting the smock.

She glances at it without breaking stride, nose wrinkling as she disappears down the next hall. I stare after her for a moment, then clutch the smock tighter and keep walking, jaw tight.

"Good to know the palace is just overflowing with kindness," I mutter, low enough that only the stone walls hear me. "Really makes you feel welcome."

The hallway stretches before me, its walls lined with royal portraits—silent witnesses in gilded frames. A fitting path to and from the studio. I slow my pace, letting my gaze drift over each one. This time, I admire them not as a guest on a rushed tour, but as an artist, alone and observant.

The servant's disgusted stare still clings to me like paint that won't wash off. But here, among these masterful brushstrokes, I find something familiar. Comforting. Each portrait is a quiet conversation between artist and subject, frozen in time. Maybe these painted faces will be kinder than the real ones.

After all, paint doesn't judge.

A flash of chestnut-brown hair stands out among the wall of black tresses. I stop in front of Queen Clarissa's portrait. Coupled with her sunflower gold gown, it's clear she's not a direct descendant of the Moretti family.

Her brown-eyed gaze is full of sorrow, an emotion I wouldn't expect from someone in her position. Having grown up hearing about the king and queen's love story, her life sounds like a dream. A loving husband, beautiful children, and a powerful kingdom at her fingertips.

I tear my gaze away from the portrait as the click of heels approaches. At the end of the hall is a young woman, tall and elegant, a silver tiara crowning a head of raven hair.

I instantly recognize her from the other day: Princess Lyra.

She grins radiantly, waving in my direction. I look behind me, certain there's someone else she's looking at.

The hall is empty.

"Oh! I'm—" I fumble for words and manage an awkward curtsy as she stops in front of me. "Greetings, Your Royal Highness."

Lyra tilts her head, smiling as if she finds my nervousness endearing. "Just who I was looking for."

My grip tightens on the satchel's strap, and I stuff the smock further under my arm. "I am?"

Lyra laughs at my stunned expression, a soft musical sound that melts the tension between us. "I was dying to formally meet the new court artist Cassian keeps going on about!"

My heart skips a beat.

She leans in, lowering her voice as if we're sharing a secret. "He says you're *infuriating.*"

I blink. "Oh."

I'm not sure what to do with that. My mind races. *What else has he said?*

Sensing my unease, Lyra places a gentle hand on my arm. "Don't worry, that's a compliment. Cassian doesn't like many people."

"I'm not sure 'like' is the right word," I mutter before I can stop myself.

Lyra's grin widens, her brown eyes twinkling with mischief. "I like you already."

In a rush of lavender skirts, Lyra loops her arm with mine and leads us down the hall. Something about her warmth puts me at ease, and I find myself returning her smile.

"The palace can be a bit much at first." She guides me to the left. "If you ever need anything—or if Cassian gets too unbearable—come find me."

"Thank you," I say, meaning it. The palace halls have felt endless and unfamiliar since I arrived. This is the first time someone here has made me feel... welcome.

We turn right this time, passing by a group of maids. They eye us curiously, but don't say a word.

"You should join us for dinner tonight!" Lyra squeezes my arm excitedly. "It would be lovely to have someone to actually talk to."

Dinner with the royal family? My stomach twists at the thought. "I couldn't intrude, Your Royal Highness."

"Nonsense. It's your first night in the palace. Let us welcome you properly!"

I want to ask if she has permission from the king, but I hold my tongue. The last thing I want is to show up uninvited and leave a bad first impression. But I also don't want to anger the only friendly person in the palace.

Lyra stops in front of a familiar door, unlooping our arms with a small, encouraging nod. "I hope to see you at dinner, Lady Eden. Six o'clock sharp in the Great Hall."

I'm a bit surprised she knew where my chambers were, but I suppose she's lived here her whole life. "Thank you, Your Royal Highness. I will consider it."

"You can call me Lyra, by the way. Welcome to the palace." Her gown whispers against the stone floor as she heads back the way we came.

I stand frozen for a moment, watching her disappear down the corridor. The encounter leaves me strangely buoyant, like I've been pulled from the current just long enough to catch my breath.

With a shake of my head, I gather my bearings and enter my new chambers. Life in the palace is already proving to be more complicated than I imagined.

My appetite is completely gone by the time I make it to the Great Hall. I'm already regretting my decision to come. I glance down once more, running my hands over the light blue ruffles of my skirt.

I changed my gown three times, unsure what to wear for a royal family dinner. Finally, I decided on the gown my sister made. While it's a risk not wearing one from the royal tailor, my sister's dress calmed my nerves the most.

Literally.

When I pulled it from my bag, a note detailed the dress's enchantments. "*Joyful serenity*," my sister called it. To match the carefree nature of the flowers that inspired her design.

I glance down at the gown. The skirts aren't as layered and heavy as typical noble fashion. Its volume comes instead from the beautifully draped ruffles that cascade to the floor like flowing water. The bodice fits perfectly, with lace vines and wildflowers that highlight my curves. A few lace petals shimmer in the light as I move, Edenia flowers hidden in plain sight.

Not only is the gown stunning, it's a piece of home. I still smell the subtle fragrance of cedar, oil paint, and herbs, each breath steeped in memory.

A faint wave of peace washes over me, and I lean into it, counting on the enchantment to get me through the night. With a nod, the attendants open the doors.

The Great Hall is grand, of course—vaulted ceilings, glittering chandeliers, and a long table draped with rich fabrics.

Every inch of the space is opulent, nothing like the quaint simplicity of my family cottage.

The royal family is already seated. King Leopold sits at the head of the table, his sharp gaze cutting across the room as I enter. He doesn't bother masking his scrutiny, his cool eyes trailing from my head to my hem. I resist the urge to tug at my gown.

Beside him is Queen Clarissa, who offers an unexpectedly warm smile. Cassian sits next to her, lazily leaning back in his chair. He swirls the wine in his goblet, uninterested in my arrival. His white shirt is undone at the collar, just enough to suggest a deliberate carelessness that grates on me.

And then there's the princess—Lyra. She's perched in her chair with a wide, bright-eyed grin. She waves eagerly when she sees me, as if we're old friends.

"You're here!" she says with a little clap. "I'm so glad you came."

Her enthusiasm is disarming, and I manage a tentative smile. Suddenly less nervous, I stop at the edge of the table and curtsy politely. "Good evening. Thank you for the invitation."

"Sit, sit," Lyra urges, gesturing to the empty seat across from Cassian. "We were waiting for you."

The king's expression suggests otherwise, but I slip into the chair, nonetheless. I habitually smooth my ruffled blue skirts. My heart thuds against my ribcage, the air in the room far too stifling for comfort.

"Your gown is so unique!" Lyra says, tilting her head as she studies it. "It's lovely—so different from what we wear."

Her voice carries no malice, just unfiltered curiosity, but my stomach knots anyway.

"My sister made it." I give her a tight smile.

"She's quite talented."

I nod, feeling a burst of pride for my sister's work. "It's a thoughtful blend of old and new—a royal take on the wildflowers near my home. Comfortable, too." The words come out before I can stop them, my worries forgotten in the brief moment of friendly chatter.

"Comfortable?" Cassian arches a brow. "That's not a word we hear often at royal dinners."

The queen glances at him, part warning, part weariness. Meanwhile, servants glide into the room with silver platters, setting out roasted meats, steaming vegetables, and fresh bread still warm from the oven. The scent drifts around me, but all I can do is pick at my plate. My sister's enchantment is too weak to overpower my discomfort.

Lyra leans forward, resting her chin in her hand. "I quite like the look of those flowers—so wild and carefree. Nothing like the dainty florals I'm forced to wear."

The king clears his throat.

Cassian gives a soft chuckle. "Wildflowers," he says.

There's something teasing in his tone.

"It suits you," he continues, leaning back in his chair. "Wildflower."

I blink at him, stunned. "What?"

"That's what I'll call you," he declares, his grin widening. "It seems fitting."

I glance around the table, unsure if he's mocking me. Lyra frowns at her brother before offering me a sympathetic smile. The queen is unamused, glancing over at the king's expressionless face. He stabs a piece of meat, uninterested in his son's antics.

My face burns, and I fumble with the folds of my gown, uncertain whether to be flattered or irritated by the sudden nickname. Maybe my sister's gown wasn't the best choice for a royal dinner. Even the enchantment has proved useless.

Cassian notices my discomfort, seeming thoroughly pleased by it.

"Well then, Wildflower." He sets his goblet down with a soft clink. "We'll see if your artistic skills are as charming as your dress."

I fumble for a response, but the words slip away as Cassian stands abruptly.

"Leaving already, Cassian?" the queen asks with a delicate lift of her brow.

He shrugs. "I've had my fill."

With one last glance in my direction—and a wink, of all things—he strolls out of the dining hall.

I stare after him, my heart racing for reasons I'd rather not admit. Lyra sighs dramatically beside me.

"He's insufferable sometimes."

I press my lips together, unwilling to give Cassian the satisfaction of a reaction. The nickname lingers in the air, settling over me like an unexpected gift—or a curse.

Cassian

The portrait hall is eerie this time of night. Shadows settle over the faces of kings and queens that stare down from the walls. Their painted eyes follow me as I head toward the studio. With one last glance, I slip inside the quiet room.

My portrait makes me jump. Eden's painting is so lifelike it's like looking in a mirror.

There's something different about her painting than all the others in the portrait hall. My eyes aren't eerily vacant or serene. They are intense—full of an emotion I don't know how to name. I've never seen myself this way before. The longer I stare, the more I'm seeing myself through her eyes.

I look away, feeling suddenly exposed. Somehow, she's captured more of me than I thought possible. I can't deny her talent. But a part of me still questions who she truly is.

I think back to the way her eyes glazed over at the end of our session, just as they had the last time she painted me. It was like she was seeing something other than the portrait.

Doubts swirl through my mind, prompting me back to the painting to scrutinize the colors. I search for anything to confirm my suspicions. At first glance, there is nothing. And yet it still feels off.

I step closer, eyes catching on the color of my doublet. I hold up my sleeve to the portrait, my gaze flitting back and forth in the dim light, comparing the two.

It's subtle, almost unnoticeable except for the direct comparison, but the colors *are* different. She's lying about her fated skill. Why?

The soft click of the door closing breaks the silence. I whirl around, nearly knocking the portrait off the easel.

It's Farion, his black cape blending into the room's shadows.

"What are you doing here, Your Royal Highness?" His voice is calm as he steps further inside.

I breathe a little easier, glad it's not my father. "Merely admiring the results of today's session."

Farion's gaze flickers to the painting. He nods, slowly. "And does it meet your expectations?"

"It's true to form, I'd say. Looks just like me." I tug on my cuff, trying to seem casual. "Not that I know much about portraits."

Farion's lips quirk. "There's no need to lie to me, Cassian. You may be a touch vain, but not enough to care about the progress of a portrait that's already been painted once."

I clench my jaw. He knows me too well. "You're right."

Farion stands next to me, staring at the portrait as if assessing it himself. Silence hangs between us, my suspicion roiling beneath the surface. I weigh whether to voice my concerns. But I have no proof. Only an uneasy feeling and a barely noticeable color-matching issue. No need to make a fool of myself in front of Farion, too.

"I suppose," I admit finally, "I'm more curious about the artist herself than the creation."

Farion chuckles, a low sound that resonates in the empty room. "You say that as if the entire palace hasn't already noticed."

I pull back, a scoff catching in my throat. "I'm hardly that transparent."

"Oh, Cassian." Farion gives me a bemused smile, the faint glint of light illuminating his teeth. "A pretty young woman arrives at court, and suddenly the Crown Prince of Mentera is interested in art? Do you think people wouldn't take notice?"

I'm about to protest, but his steady gaze cuts me off.

"Careful, young prince," he says softly, almost fatherly. "She may intrigue you, but she is far beneath your station. Allowing your attention to linger on her... it would be a mistake."

I smirk. "Are you saying she's dangerous?"

"Not intentionally," Farion replies, his eyes fixed on the painting. "But she reminds me of someone from long ago." He pauses. "Someone who also hid behind an innocent face but brought more ruin than I care to recall."

I study him, trying to read beneath his usual stoic mask. Who does he see in Eden that gives him such pause?

"Don't let curiosity lead you astray, Cassian," Farion continues. "She may be skilled, but her path is not yours. Remember who you are destined to become."

With a parting glance, he strides toward the door. Before he exits, he looks over his shoulder, his eyes catching mine with a spark of something darker, sharper.

"Whatever her secrets, I suggest you keep her at arm's length."

As he leaves me in the quiet studio, I ponder his words. It's as if he knew exactly what I was thinking. Though I've always valued Farion's advice, I remember the promise I made to myself only days ago.

I'm sick of hearing about destiny—about my future as the king. Discovering Eden's secrets may work in my favor.

Anything to change my fate.

Eden

"Paint me." Cassian shuts my bedroom door behind him.

"Excuse me?" I stammer, surprised by his sudden entrance.

I notice the way his black hair is mussed and falling over his forehead, giving him a boyish charm. His shirt is half buttoned, thrown on as if in a rush.

Cassian clears his throat, sending a fiery blush along my cheeks. I look down, only to realize the thin satin nightgown I'm wearing. Instinctively, I cross my arms over my chest.

"What are you doing here?" I scowl. "Just because you're the prince doesn't mean you can barge in here whenever you want!"

Cassian's lips curl into his signature smirk and he takes a step closer. I back up.

"Actually, it does." He takes another step.

His bold words startle me, and I realize he's right. Though his presence in my room this late at night will spark a wildfire of rumors, the prince may do as he pleases.

"Don't you have any morals?" I take another step back, only to be stopped by the brush of the comforter against my legs.

Cassian closes the distance between us, standing mere inches from me. His gaze is searing, tracing the contours of my body. My heart is thundering in my chest, and I try to calm it back to normal. But my body won't listen.

His proximity is electric.

"My morals are none of your concern, Miss Asher," he says slowly, locking eyes with me.

Something flashes across the ice-blue depths as they flick down to my lips. But when he looks back up, the emotion is gone. His eyes, once the blue of a blazing fire, are now cold and unfeeling.

"Now paint me," he repeats, taking a step back.

I swallow, trying to regain my composure. I don't know why he makes me so nervous.

"Why?"

"It doesn't have to be anything fancy. Just a quick portrait," he says, ignoring my question.

With a huff, I cross to the opposite wall and throw on my robe. I gather supplies from around my room and instruct him to sit in the chair by the window. He sits as I turn on the lamp nearby, staring at me with his usual carefree attitude.

I sit across from him on the bed and draw a rough sketch in my notebook. Opening the palette of watercolors, I dip my brush into the forgotten cup of water on my bedside table. I try to sort through my mess of thoughts as I paint. *Could he know about my fated skill? Is that why he's here?*

The colors bleed across the page, forming the contours of Cassian's face. A familiar pulse begins at the base of my neck, signaling the onset of my power. I continue painting, knowing the release will come when the portrait is complete.

The minutes pass in silence, Cassian staring calmly at me while I work. When I'm satisfied with the results, I try to remain calm as my power pours over me. I've grown skilled at hiding my emotions while the visions flash through my mind.

I see hands. A glittering diamond slides onto a woman's ring finger. She moves to place a ring on the man's hand when the vision shifts. It's nighttime, and I see another pair of familiar hands. The man from before reaches out to grab them, entwining his fingers with hers in the dark of the night.

The moonlight glints off a ring on the woman's index finger. It's shaped like a single arrow, solidifying her identity.

But I already knew it was me.

The portrait of Cassian comes back into focus as the visions dissipate. I painted only enough to get a small glimpse into the future.

"I knew it," Cassian mutters in front of me.

I resist the urge to flinch at his words, not wanting to feed into whatever he thinks he's discovered. Calmly, I raise my gaze to meet his as I turn the sketchbook around. "Is this what you wanted?"

Cassian leans forward in his chair. "What did you see?"

"A disheveled young prince who needs sleep." I set the sketchbook on the bedside table.

He furrows his brow in irritation, a low growl escaping his throat. "You know what I mean."

"I'm afraid I don't, Your Highness."

Suddenly, Cassian is standing over me. His hands rest on either side of me on the bed, pinning me in place. My breathing grows shallow, but I do my best to meet his piercing gaze head-on. I will not let him intimidate me.

"True Color is not your fated skill."

My muscles stiffen. I force myself to relax. He searches my face for any hint of affirmation, and I try to mirror his cold, unphased expression.

"I command you to tell me." Cassian clenches his jaw.

I don't budge.

After several seconds like this, he sighs.

"Eden." The way he whispers my name catches me off-guard, his voice shaky.

His eyes squeeze shut, and he visibly swallows before meeting my gaze again. The blue of his eyes is bright, his usual blank stare cast aside like a mask.

"Please, I need to know what you saw."

I place a hand on his chest and gently push him away, doing my best to ignore my racing heart and the intensity in his gaze. My fingers twist my arrow-shaped ring on instinct.

If I tell him, I risk becoming a pawn in whatever game he's playing. If I don't, Cassian could dismiss me. Or worse. He could have the answer tortured out of me if he really wanted to.

My gaze darts around the room, landing on Cassian, who now leans against the opposite wall. He crosses his arms, fingers digging into his biceps. The silence stretches between us, growing more tense by the second.

"I won't hurt you," he vows quietly.

I chew the inside of my cheek, uncertain whether to trust his words. He stands unnaturally still, watching me think. In the dim light of my room, he's no longer the indifferent, entitled prince—just a young man desperate for answers.

"The exchange of rings." I watch his reaction closely, noting the way his breath hitches and shoulders drop.

He drags a hand over his face, leaving a bitter smile in its wake. "I'm sorry for barging in here at this hour, Miss Asher." He moves toward the door. "I'll be taking my leave now."

"Don't you have questions?" I ask, baffled by his cold response to my admission.

"You've already answered them all."

He leaves without another word, his hardened expression the last thing I see before he shuts the door.

I collapse onto the bed, feeling light-headed. *What just happened?*

I'm immediately furious with myself for giving in to his demands and all but blowing my cover. Who knows what he'll do with that information? If he tells the king, I could lose my position as court artist. I'm not sure what the punishment would be for lying to the king.

But I don't want to find out.

I turn onto my stomach, burying my head in the comforter. The fabric muffles my frustrated scream. Cassian's vulnerable face flashes into my mind and I sit up. Enough of the wondering—I'll find out what I can for myself.

I grab the notebook off the bedside table where I left it and begin painting. I don't even bother with a mirror this time, having memorized my features by now.

As the highlights and shadows form the contours of my face, I await the familiar pulse of my skill. It begins once I've clearly taken shape on the page, but I don't give in just yet. I want to see further into the future, and to do that, the portrait must be more detailed.

Several minutes pass as I feverishly add details and shading, bringing the rough sketch to life. When I'm satisfied with the results, I let the sensation take hold. My vision blurs as the bedroom fades away.

I find myself in a dimly lit room, standing in front of the king, who glares at me. He's flanked by the farion and Cassian, whose face is impassive and unreadable.

The scene flickers, changing like flashes in a storm. I'm walking through the palace corridors, the whispers of servants following me. They appear wary, their mouths forming words like "liar" and "dangerous." My heart races as I realize they know my secret—or at least suspect it.

My vision shifts again, and I'm in a moonlit garden. Cassian stands nearby. He reaches out to me but hesitates, his face shadowed with doubt. I try to call out to him, but no sound escapes. He turns away, his expression a mixture of sorrow and determination, as if he's making a decision that will affect us both.

The room swims back into focus, the visions fading. My heart is pounding, and I try to steady it by taking deep breaths. The sketchbook is on the floor, my portrait now marred by a blotch of paint where the brush fell onto it.

I pick it up, trying to sort through the meaning of my visions. But if anything, they leave me with more questions than answers.

After putting my paints away for the night, I crawl under the covers and turn off the lamp. Darkness wraps around me like the blankets I pull tighter, still chilled by the haunting glimpses of isolation and doubt.

Tomorrow, I must speak with Cassian. The only way to prevent that horrid future is if I can convince him to keep my secret.

And I know just what to offer him in return.

Sweat drips down my forehead as I adjust my stance. "Again."

My heart pounds against my ribcage, but I keep my breathing steady. Across from me, Silas raises his sword, a determined gleam in his eyes. He lunges, our swords connecting with the sharp clang of metal. We're evenly matched, making him an excellent sparring partner.

I tighten my grip on the hilt of my sword, feeling the familiar burn in my forearms. Our blades meet again in a flurry of strikes and blocks. I parry one of his attacks, the force of it sending a jolt through my arms.

Silas steps back with a grin. "Careful, Prince. You're getting clumsy."

"Clumsy?" I sneer, wiping sweat from my brow. "We'll see about that."

Ignoring the growing ache in my muscles, I thrust forward, hoping to catch him off balance. But he sidesteps just in time. My blade whistles past him, missing by mere inches.

Silas's movements are fluid and precise, his footwork flawless. Despite my best efforts, he's always one step ahead.

I pivot quickly, shifting my weight and striking low. For a moment, I think I have him, the flat of my blade tapping against the armor of his thigh. A flash of triumph surges through me.

"Got you," I say breathlessly.

But Silas doesn't flinch.

Instead, he spins, sweeping his sword in a wide arc. Before I can react, the cold edge of his blade is against my throat. I freeze.

"Not quite, Your Highness." Silas smirks, lowering his sword. "You let your guard down."

I grit my teeth, fighting the urge to curse under my breath. He's right. My anger made me clumsy. Again.

I shake my head, rolling my shoulders to ease the tension. There's no room for frustration, only improvement. But it still stings. I should've been using my fated skill.

"Well fought," I manage.

Silas chuckles, sheathing his weapon. "You were close, though. Maybe next time you should sheath your emotions instead of your sword, Your Highness."

I'm about to make a snide remark when I sense a presence at the edge of the training yard. My head snaps up. There, standing in the shadows of the exterior corridor, is Eden. Her arms are folded over her chest, eyes fixed on me.

I wipe the sweat from my face with the back of my hand.

She shouldn't be here. Not near the training grounds. Not watching me like this.

For a moment, neither of us speaks. She's studying me—assessing, even. My mind flashes to the night before. *Is that why she's here?*

Silas notices her too and raises an eyebrow. "An audience, it seems."

I sheath my sword. "Miss Asher," I call out, my voice sharper than intended. "To what do I owe the pleasure?"

She steps forward. "I didn't mean to intrude. I was told I'd find you here."

"And here I am," I reply. "What is it?"

Eden glances at Silas before meeting my eyes again. "I wanted to discuss the details of my new position. I thought it might be best to clarify a few things."

I wipe the sweat from my palms, trying to mask the sense of unease creeping up my spine. There's something about the way she looks at me that sets me on edge.

I nod. "We can talk in the study. I'll meet you there shortly."

She gives a small nod and turns, disappearing into the palace. I let out a slow breath, unsure how to handle the lingering tension.

Silas crosses his arms. "The painter has your attention more than the sword does lately."

I glare at him but don't bother denying it.

Outside the study, I tug on the stiff collar around my neck, wondering for the hundredth time why I changed into this confining outfit. My father's voice echoes in my head, reminding me of the importance of presentation. But the collar is like a noose tightening around my throat.

Annoyed by the fluttering in my stomach, I close my eyes and recite the mantra drilled into me since childhood.

I feel nothing. I fear nothing. I am the master of my emotions.

With each repetition, the familiar emptiness settles in. Like a slate wiped clean, I feel blank. No nerves, no frustration—just a blissful hollowness. What once felt like a void, a piece of me missing, now brings a strange sense of comfort. My father trained me to embrace the detachment—to wield it as a weapon.

Emotions cloud judgment, he always said. *A prince must be untouchable.*

I exhale slowly. Nothingness is power, and now I am ready.

Pushing open the heavy doors to the study, I see Eden is already inside. She's seated near the window, silhouetted against the morning light. Her eyes flicker to me, but I don't flinch under her scrutiny. I step further inside, allowing the door to close behind me with a soft thud.

"Your Royal Highness." Though her voice is level, I sense the tension beneath the surface. She's not pleased.

Not that I expected her to be.

"Last night, you barged into my chambers as if they were your own and left without so much as an explanation."

I clasp my hands behind my back. "The reason for my visit was rather clear, was it not?"

Her jaw clenches. "You knew of my fated skill before I even confirmed it."

"I did," I say without hesitation, my voice flat. There's no point denying it.

Eden rises from her chair, crossing the room toward me. She searches my face for something. I'm not sure what she's hoping to find, but I offer nothing. Only the blank, detached mask I've perfected over the years.

"Have you told anyone else?" Her voice betrays her nerves. She's terrified that I know.

I stare down at her, unsympathizing. A muscle tenses in her jaw, her fingers curling into fists at her sides. She huffs, rolling her shoulders as if shaking off her irritation.

"I suppose not, considering the circumstances of your visit last night. Should I expect that to be a recurring event?" Her gaze is steadfast.

I step forward, using my height to my advantage. She doesn't move, looking up at me with a determined glare. "Perhaps. Your skill is rather extraordinary."

Eden's mouth flattens into a hard line. She crosses her arms, her posture stiff with resentment. "So this is about power," she states. "Like everything else."

I offer a small, detached smile. "Of course."

There's a long pause, Eden searching my face for answers once again. Finally, she looks away, her gaze settling on the window.

"You're just like him, you know."

The words land heavily, but I maintain hold over my emotions. I already know who she means. I've trained to be like him my entire life.

"I take that as a compliment," I reply evenly.

She turns her head, a strange sadness on her face. But I don't dwell on it.

"Then my request will be easy for you to accept."

A bit of surprise cuts through my calm. The sudden lapse in control allows frustration to follow close behind. I repeat my mantra, putting my emotions in check.

"And what is your request?"

Eden faces me. "I'd like to make a deal. Isn't that what your father does best?"

I nod my head in acknowledgement, but don't allow her words to stir anything within me.

"If you promise to keep my secret, I'll continue to use my fated skill for you."

"Done."

Her eyes narrow. "I'm not finished."

A muscle in my forehead twitches, though I don't feel the associated annoyance. I let her continue.

"You must also promise not to barge into my chambers unannounced again."

I take my time to answer, letting her fret over my reply. "Deal. Expect me tomorrow night." With three large strides, I reach the door.

"So soon?" Eden calls after me.

"You never specified a restriction on the frequency of my visits, only that I warn you in advance."

I leave the study before she can respond, a strange anticipation rising through my numbness.

I knock this time, adhering to Eden's request. The soft thud of footsteps grows close to the door. It takes a few seconds before it opens. As it does, I'm certain I hear her sigh.

"Evening, Wildflower."

She frowns at the nickname. Though it's late, she's still in her dress from today. I suppose she didn't want a repeat of our last nightly encounter. My neck grows hot at the thought, and I shake it away.

"Come in." Eden steps aside to let me pass.

As much as I hate to admit it, thoughts of tonight have distracted me all day. I'm eager to learn more about my future.

"Have a seat." She gestures to the armchair on the opposite side of the bed, perched beneath the room's only window.

It's the same one I sat in the other night. Although this time, she's already prepared her paints and canvas. I suppose there are benefits to scheduling things like this, though I'll never tell her that.

"So how does your skill work, exactly?" I sit awkwardly in the chair, uncomfortable with the silence.

"I agreed to paint you, not answer your questions." She stands across from me in front of an easel.

"Point taken." I decide not to push the issue. Though I technically hold the cards knowing her secret, I figure I ask enough from her as it is.

She works in silence, her lips pursed in concentration. Trying not to stare, I survey her chambers. The room is almost untouched, few signs of Eden's residency visible. A painting above the desk is new, the unfinished piece a stark contrast to the rest of the room.

The woman in the portrait bears a striking resemblance to Eden, though older and with lighter hair. Painted beside her is a man with familiar green eyes and a friendly smile. Three young children complete the family portrait—two daughters and a son. With nothing else in the room capturing my attention, my gaze wanders back to Eden.

She looks more at ease than our normal sessions. Her posture is less rigid, hair falling freely down her back instead of braided up in her usual style. If it weren't for the flick of her eyes back and forth, I'd think she forgot all about me. She appears completely lost in her work.

My gaze travels down her body, noting the way she sways slightly. Her dress shifts with the movement, just enough to reveal bare feet underneath. I grit my teeth to keep from smiling.

Glancing back at Eden's face, I find her in a rare moment of vulnerability. The end of her paintbrush is pushed against her lips, her brow scrunched together as she stares at the canvas. She glances over at me, catching me staring.

I hold her gaze.

The paintbrush jerks away from her mouth. She clears her throat, staring intently at the painting. When Eden's eyes finally meet mine, they dart away, a light blush coloring her cheeks.

"So," she begins, pausing her work. "Why is it you want to see your future so badly?"

"I could ask the same of you." My gaze shifts to the bin of crumpled portraits near her desk.

Eden's shoulders tense. She mumbles something before letting out a slow, measured breath. "If you answer my question, I'll answer yours."

"Which one?"

She shifts her weight to one leg. "Are you always this insufferable, Princeling?"

I raise my brows at the unexpected nickname. Eden notices my expression, her cheeks reddening as she realizes her impolite behavior.

"I, uh… I'm not sure where that came from. My apologies, Your Royal Highness."

A wide grin breaks across my face. "You are full of surprises, Wildflower. I suppose it's only fair you have a nickname for me, too."

Eden averts her gaze, focusing on mixing a color on her palette.

"And somehow," I murmur, "Princeling sounds more fitting than my official title."

She glances up, her blush deepening. "Are you still going to answer my question?"

"Alright, fine. I'll answer if you do."

Satisfied, she returns to her work. "Go ahead. But don't move too much."

I chuckle. "I want to know my future so I can change it."

Her eyes meet mine briefly, a sense of understanding flashing across them.

"Now you," I direct.

Eden shakes her head and swipes her brush across the canvas. "I know there is more to it than that."

"Ah, so that's how this is going to be."

She shrugs. "Better answer now before the painting is finished. After that," she looks over at me, "the deal is off."

I sigh, moving to place my head in my hands before Eden stops me with a disapproving noise.

"You must have assumed by now that the portraits are to help secure a marriage proposal," I begin.

Eden nods.

"I want to prevent that from happening."

Her brush stills. "Oh."

A range of emotions cross her face as she processes my answer. I suddenly have the urge to flee. I've never liked opening up. "So, tell me how your skill works, Wildflower."

"That's getting old, really fast." Eden brushes a loose strand of hair away from her face as she regards me warily. "I don't know how much you'll understand, but…" she hesitates, weighing her words. "When I paint someone's portrait, I see fragments of their future."

I nod, genuinely intrigued. She glances down at her hands. Some of her fingers are smeared with paint and she wipes them on her apron. I get the sense she doesn't talk about her skill very often.

"I never know what will come up or how far ahead it might be," she explains. "If the portrait truly resembles the person, I can see months, sometimes even years, into the future. If it's less accurate, I can see only days or weeks."

Eden focuses on the canvas again, resuming the painting. Her demeanor shifts as her breathing deepens. It's as if she's bracing herself to let go of her surroundings entirely.

I shift in my seat, uncomfortable with her scrutiny. "And you can't control it?" I ask softly.

"Not at all." Her gaze flicks back to me, and I'm taken aback by its intensity. "It's not like wielding a sword or enchanting an object. It's like jumping into the sea and letting the current take me where it may. I surface where I can, but I catch only glimpses of my surroundings, never knowing how far I've traveled."

With that, she applies a small stroke of paint to the canvas before dropping her arm. The effect is immediate. Her eyes glaze over like she's looking through the canvas. Her breathing hitches, and a tremor runs through her, leaving me with an unexpected surge of concern.

I'm unsure whether she's not suppressing her skill like she usually does, or if her vision is more intense.

"Eden?" I whisper, unsure if she can hear me.

She doesn't answer. Her gaze is vacant for a few long moments before she finally finds her voice.

Blinking slowly, her gaze focuses on me. "I saw a ship with orange and gold sails."

"Aetherean," I mumble, recognizing the royal colors.

"And you, standing on the docks of Scintillia alongside the king. You were waiting for someone."

"Did you see who?" I lean forward in the chair.

Eden shakes her head. "I never saw her face. But you kissed her hand."

"Is that all?"

She swallows, glancing down at her hands. "No, that wasn't all. Her high heel caught on a board in the dock, causing her to stumble. But you steadied her." Eden bites her lip before continuing. "I also saw another scene, one that felt further into the future. You were still at the docks, but the atmosphere was different."

I frown. "Different how?"

"It was quiet, both nobles and common folk gathered around. They were all watching. Some of them… they were kneeling."

"Kneeling?"

She nods. "As if they were honoring not just you, but her as well. Like they viewed her as a queen."

I lean back in the chair, unable to shake the image forming in my mind. "A queen. You're certain that's the feeling you got?"

Eden's lips press into a thin line. "I'm fairly certain. But like I said, I only see snippets. I don't know the whole story."

Unable to sit any longer, I rise from the chair. "And it's possible it will change?"

"Yes. It's possible."

For a moment neither of us speaks, her vision lingering in my mind. Eden looks pensive, as if burdened by her gift.

"Thank you." My tone is soft. "I think that's exactly what I needed."

Her shoulders visibly relax. "You're welcome."

We stand awkwardly in the room's silence before I remember I'm the one intruding on her space.

"I'm sorry, I'll get going now." I maneuver around her and toward the door.

"When should I expect you next?"

"I'm not sure," I admit. "But I know where to find you."

Before leaving, I wink, hoping to hide my growing apprehension. Eden scoffs, waving me out the door.

"Just don't forget about our deal," she reminds, leaning against the door frame.

"I'm well aware you don't have a high opinion of me, but I'm a man of my word, Wildflower."

Her face scrunches together, but not before relief brightens her green eyes. "Goodnight, Princeling."

She shuts the door to her chambers, leaving me alone in the dim hall.

The lamp near her door flickers slightly, clinging to life like my last bit of hope. In an otherwise dark stretch of future, Eden's words are the final glimmer, a spark refusing to die.

Faint and fleeting, but able to start a fire.

I turn her words over in my mind, letting the flame catch, a stubborn glow in the dark.

Something that will set my father's entire plan ablaze.

Right. Left. And left again.

I stop at the end of the hall, satisfied to see the dining hall up ahead. The palace corridors are quiet, the marble floors sparkling in the morning light.

It's the perfect time to practice navigating the palace. No spectators. No embarrassing encounters. No worries.

The clank of metal sounds nearby and I turn to my left.

Other than the guards, I suppose.

Retracing my steps, I wind back through the corridors and up the stairs, pace quickened by an empty stomach. Hopefully, my bit of morning exploration bought the servants enough time to deliver my breakfast. The buttery scent of fresh pastries curls through the air, coaxing my steps faster.

As I pass through the guest quarters, silver trays shimmer in the morning light, lined neatly outside several doors. My stomach clenches with anticipation. Maybe today they haven't forgotten me.

I turn down the final hall, already picturing the warm roll or wedge of fruit tart waiting outside my door. But the moment I see my tray, I slow, recognizing the empty dishes from the night before. Remnants of cold stew linger in the porcelain bowl, and the wineglass still rests on its side where I left it. No steam or cloth napkin. And no breakfast.

Again.

They're just running behind, I try to tell myself. *Or someone forgot.* But even the hopeful voice in my head sounds unconvinced. The other trays were full. Mine is the only one left empty.

Gently, I lift my tray, the utensils clinking as I head back down the corridor, determined to clean up after myself. Petty as it is, maybe helping out will make the servants like me more. The hollow in my stomach grumbles, but I straighten my spine. On the bright side, not being waited on hand and foot will keep me humble. Doing dishes is nothing new.

I descend the steps, careful not to let the wineglass roll off the tray. Then, I make my way to the dining hall, hoping the kitchen is nearby. Clanking dishes and murmured voices trickle toward me, a sign they're serving breakfast for everyone.

Anxiety twists my hunger into nausea at the thought of eating in the dining hall again. I recall my first day in the palace, searching through the tables for a place to sit, only to end up sitting alone. Maybe today will be different. At the very least, it can't get worse than last time.

Still holding my tray of dishes, I warily approach the door, laughter on the other side. Two servants burst through, almost running straight into me. The wineglass rolls close to the tray's edge, but I stop it before it can escape.

"Got it!" I give a relieved, if not slightly awkward, smile.

The servants, a stout woman with graying hair and a red-faced young man, do not return my smile.

"Good morning," I try again. "Do you happen to know where I should return these dishes to?"

Without a word, the woman takes the tray from my hands and stalks down the hall.

"Are you trying to make us look bad?" The man scowls.

Heat blossoms on my cheeks, and I just know my face is as red as his. "I–uh, I'm not sure what you mean. I'm only trying to help."

"An artisan carrying her own dishes does the exact opposite of help. It makes us seem lazy." He steps close enough I can see the sweat beading on his brow. "A true artisan would know that."

His meaning is crystal clear when his gaze shifts to the hourglass on my wrist. The heat crawls down my neck, and I hide my hand behind my back. He's right. Most people who have yet to ascend are relegated to servant roles, if they're even allowed to work in the palace at all.

I lower my head. "My apologies. I didn't mean to cause issues."

"You caused issues the moment you stepped into the palace."

I swallow the urge to cry. If I were feeling more myself, I would stand my ground and prove him wrong, prove I'm meant to be here. But after a week of being homesick and alone, all I can do is remain silent. His worn leather shoes squeak as he leaves, my eyes never leaving the ground. They burn, a lone tear breaking free, wetting the pristine marble floor.

I do not belong here. I'm neither an ascended artisan nor a common servant. I'm somewhere in-between—playing pretend in a world I thought I was prepared for. I couldn't even lie well enough to hide my fated skill for longer than a week.

Nothing has gone according to plan.

Before anyone else sees me, I hurry away from the dining hall, trying desperately not to cry. The halls blur together as I blink away tears, too consumed by humiliation to pay attention to my route. I try to orient myself based on the places mentioned in my brief welcome tour, but the palace is a maze, and I'm quickly lost.

Unsure where to go, I keep walking until the tightness in my throat is gone, my tears finally at bay. I pause near a window and catch my reflection in the polished glass. My face is blotchy, eyes dull. I force a smile and roll my shoulders back, trying to see myself the way someone else might.

But the more I stare, the more distorted I feel—like the reflection is no longer mine.

A second silhouette lingers behind me in the glass. I spin around, heart pounding, but there is only my shadow on the wall behind me. Blinking, I turn back to the window, but the shape remains, a dark echo clinging to my movements.

You are nothing special, just a lucky mistake, it murmurs. *A girl who paints what she doesn't understand.*

I know it's only my shadow, cast from the sunlight outside, but it feels more alive than it should.

You don't belong here, it continues, echoing my inner thoughts. *Everyone knows it.*

I shut my eyes.

You are enough. My dad's voice breaks through my thoughts, warm and steady. The words drift from memory, but they hit me as if he's standing right here.

I open my eyes. The shadowy reflection is gone.

In its place is something I hadn't noticed before—a faint blue light fighting with the sun's rays.

I turn slowly to find an enchanted lift not far down the hall behind me. Its opalescent doors flicker like moonlight through water.

As I approach, the doors open, revealing an intricately patterned platform. Polished silver vines curl elegantly around the edges, shimmering with blue light.

With a quick glance over my shoulder, I step gingerly onto the mosaic tile. A subtle vibration beneath my feet makes the lift feel like a living thing. Slowly, the enchanted platform rises, carrying me upward. Windows follow my ascent, offering a stunning view of the gardens below. As I reach the next floor, the platform stills with a gentle hum, as if pleased with its work.

I turn from the windows and exit the lift, my gaze sweeping across the wide hall before me. Elaborate tapestries line the walls, each one depicting scenes of Mentera's history—noble battles, grand feasts, and enchanting landscapes. Walking slowly by each one, I stop at the skilled weaving of a legendary battle. Silver and blue clad figures clash against shadowy creatures, the intensity of the scene woven into every thread.

"The battle that determined our kingdom's fate."

The low voice startles me, and I turn to where the farion stands a few feet away. He leans against the wall, his arms crossed over the velvet Morphi cape clasped around his neck.

"Fortunately, we chose to embrace our fated skills, sparing us from the fate of the now fallen Divinia," he continues. "Foolish people they were, not to cherish their divine gifts."

His dark eyes glimmer with curiosity as he watches me, the light from the nearby window casting shadows on his face. The farion is imposing enough at Ascension Rites, but up close, his presence is daunting.

I curtsy low, pulse racing. "Good morning, Farion. It's an honor to meet you."

"You're up early, Miss Asher." He pushes off the wall and approaches with quiet confidence.

As he steps out of the shadows, morning light catches on the silver strands threaded through his dark hair and beard. His gaze is steady—disarmingly warm, yet unnerving, as if he already knows every secret I've ever tried to hide.

I clear my throat. "I thought I'd, uh, get to know the palace better. It's easy to get lost here."

A half-smile plays at the edge of his mouth. "It is, isn't it? The corridors here were designed to be a labyrinth. Keeps people on their toes." His voice lowers. "Or away from places they're not meant to be."

My muscles stiffen, and I suddenly realize how out of place I must look exploring on my own. But the farion merely raises an eyebrow, studying me with that same appraising look. There is no hostility in it, yet there's still something else—an intensity that leaves me feeling small.

"I didn't mean to intrude," I say, gathering my composure. "I only wanted to become more comfortable with the layout."

The farion shrugs. His gaze shifts to the tapestry I'd been admiring. "No harm done. The palace has secrets, some worth uncovering and others best left buried."

He takes a step back, his gaze softening, as if truly seeing me for the first time. "I do hope you come to enjoy your new home. Change can be difficult, especially when it upsets tradition."

The shift in his tone makes me pause. His words are simple enough, yet something in his expression hints at a warning. Before I can ask, the farion straightens, giving me one last glance before turning back the way he came.

"Good luck with your exploring," he says, his voice echoing down the empty corridor.

I wait until he's gone before hurrying back towards the lift. After that encounter, exploring sounds a lot less appealing. My heels sound louder on the marble than they did earlier, every sound in the hall making me jump. I wrap my arms around myself, heading back the way I came with my head lowered.

Checking over my shoulder for anyone nearby, I round the next corner and run straight into the thick skirts of a royal gown. I'm mortified, almost too terrified to see who it belongs to.

Please don't be the queen.

"Eden!" Lyra beams, brushing away a stray curl that escaped her bun.

I breathe a sigh of relief. "Your Royal Highness. Good morning."

"Enough with the formalities. I told you to call me Lyra, remember?"

"My apologies Your—Lyra."

"I'm on my way to the Great Hall for breakfast. Would you like to join me?"

The servants' hostile stares and snide remarks flood back to me. Although I have yet to eat this morning, I'd rather not face any more of them today.

"That's very kind of you, but I'm just returning to my room." I give a slight nod, hoping to be on my way when my stomach audibly growls.

Lyra giggles. "It sounds like your stomach would like to join me for breakfast."

My face heats up in spite of myself. "Truly, it's okay."

The princess frowns, her delicate features pinching together. She regards me with a tilt of her head, understanding dawning in her amber eyes.

"How could I be so silly? Of course you don't want to endure another horrible royal meal." She loops her arm through mine before I can protest. "I have a better idea."

Her enthusiasm is infectious, a gentle warmth seeping into my chest. For a moment, I wonder if it's part of her fated skill, but I don't have long to dwell on the thought. She launches into cheerful chatter, her voice light as birdsong. With brisk, purposeful steps, she begins leading us down the corridor. The scent of baked goods grows stronger with each turn.

It's the same route I walked this morning, heavy with disappointment—but somehow, with Lyra beside me, it doesn't feel the same. Her presence soothes my frayed nerves, each friendly word chipping away at the defenses I'd begun building around my heart. I smile, grateful for her company.

The hum of activity spills into the hallway as we near the kitchen. When Lyra opens the door, a wave of warm, mouth-watering aromas envelops us. Cooks and servants bustle about as they prepare breakfast. They pause to curtsy and bow when Lyra enters, wasting no time in returning to their tasks. She greets many servants by name, navigating the kitchen with ease. We each leave with a napkin full of pastries, Lyra munching on hers before we've made it even a few steps.

"Where are you off to next?" Her words are garbled around a mouthful of muffin.

I turn away, stifling a laugh at her un-princess like behavior. "No specific plans, Your—" I catch myself. "Lyra."

She gives me a satisfied nod. "Perfect. I'd like to take you on a real tour of the palace. None of that welcome tour nonsense."

I stare blankly, surprised the princess would offer to give me a personal tour.

"Well, do you want to see all the good stuff or not?" Lyra shimmies her shoulders playfully, sending a few muffin crumbs onto her dress. She brushes them off before waving me to follow her.

"How could I refuse?"

We end the tour in the courtyard, sitting on the edge of the beautiful stone fountain to bask in the sun's warmth. I lift my face to the sky. A gentle breeze ruffles my hair, bringing with it the clink of metal against metal. The glint of steel catches my eye.

It's Cassian.

Focus sharpens his features, black hair damp with sweat as he spars with his guard.

Lyra notices where I direct my attention, clicking her tongue at the sight. "He's always out here. I bet if he could, he'd trade his Menteran skill for a Corvican one. He might be just as good as one of them, for all the training he does."

It's easy to see why Lyra would say such a thing. His movements are quick, precise, and powerful, just like the fated skills of a Corvican. Each swing of his blade flows seamlessly into the next, his footwork deliberate and unyielding. Pausing for a break, Cassian lifts the hem of his loose-fitting cotton shirt, wiping his brow. The sun glints off the lean muscles of his stomach as he turns.

I should look away, but I don't. My eyes betray me, lingering far too long. He catches me staring. His gaze, as sharp as the blade in his hand, locks onto mine.

Heat rushes to my face, and I prepare myself for what will surely follow—a smirk, a wink, anything to turn my stare into a joke at my expense. But there's nothing. No grin, no flicker of friendliness, no acknowledgment of familiarity. Just the cold, detached indifference of someone who thinks I'm nothing more than another face in the crowd.

The lack of reaction stings far more than I expected. My stomach twists as I stare down at my lap, my heart sinking with the realization I've been foolish. Stupid, even. What was I hoping for? That he'd smile, nod, or treat me as if I'm more than the girl who paints his portraits?

Of course not.

To Cassian, I'm nothing but a tool—a means to an end. He doesn't see *me,* only the skill I wield. And why would he? In this world of fated talents and hierarchy, that's all anyone sees.

Which is precisely why I hide mine.

"I don't know how you deal with him as often as you do." Lyra's words make my heart skip a beat. For half a second, I worry she knows about my secret painting sessions with the prince.

"I couldn't even get through *one* full portrait sitting with him, let alone two!" Her lips curve into a rueful grin.

My muscles relax. "I don't mind. It's my job, after all."

She's contemplative for a moment before her eyes light up. "Do you think you'll get around to painting my portrait?"

I shrug in reply. "That's up to the king, I suppose."

Lyra's face falls, but she quickly brightens again. "The king's approval? Psh. If I must commission it myself, I will. It would be an honor to be painted by someone so talented."

I place a hand to my chest. "You always offer such high praise. Thank you, Lyra."

She beams, clearly pleased.

"Come on." Lyra stands and brushes off her skirts. "There's one last stop on this tour, and it's one of my favorite places in the palace. I think you'll find it fascinating."

Curious, I follow her through the courtyard to a small building near the outer wall. The air grows warmer, the sound of hammers reaching my ears.

"Is this the forge?" I ask, surprised.

Lyra nods. "Yes. The royal forge is the best in the kingdom." She steps close, lowering her voice. "It also happens to be where many of the best-looking men work, too."

I laugh softly, shaking my head. "Is that so?"

"Oh, absolutely," Lyra teases, linking her arm with mine as she leads me into the forge. The heat intensifies, the crackle of flames and rhythm of hammers loud around us. "Now, keep an eye out. You might find your next muse."

I'm about to retort when my gaze lands on Luca, Mateo's brother. He stands near one of the central hearths, focusing intensely on a glowing piece of metal. It takes shape before him, no tool in sight.

His fated skill, I remember. *He can shape metal with his mind.*

Lyra notices where my attention has drifted and smirks. "You're looking at Luca, aren't you? I can't blame you. He's quite the looker."

"I've met him before, actually."

The princess's eyes widen. "Oh, you *must* introduce me."

"He's married."

She pouts. "Married, huh? What a shame. And how do you know him?"

"He's my best friend's brother."

Lyra's excitement returns. "If your best friend is anywhere near as good looking as his brother, I'd love an introduction."

I shake my head, amused by her boy-crazy antics. "Perhaps." I glance back over at Luca, my gaze lingering on the black butterfly on his wrist. "Do you mind if I say hi?"

"Not at all. I'll just be over here enjoying the view." Lyra squeezes my arm with a grin.

As I approach, Luca looks up from his work. He sets the bar of steel on the anvil and wipes his hands on a cloth, his movements deliberate.

"I didn't expect to find you working in the palace." His tone is as neutral as the unyielding steel in his hands.

I step closer, the air heavy with the hiss of fire and the clink of tools. "I didn't mean to disturb you. I just…" My words falter at the way his gaze pierces through me, his usual friendliness absent.

"You didn't," he replies, though his voice holds no warmth.

"Congratulations on your ascension. How has life in the royal forge been? Missing the life of a simple craftsman yet?" I'm hoping to lighten the mood, knowing Luca always liked to joke around with his brother and I when he'd visit.

"Why would I miss what is below me?"

The response chills me. "I just mean working with your father and all. I know you enjoyed the family forge."

"There's no room for what was. Only what is." His tone remains calm. "I've been… refined," he continues. "Sharpened like the blades in this forge."

I nod nervously, eyeing the weapon he's been forging. Even unfinished, its elegance is unmistakable. "The sword is beautiful," I murmur. "You certainly haven't lost your touch."

Luca watches me closely. "I always appreciated your artist's eye. You see more than most, don't you?"

The comment feels pointed, though I can't tell if it's meant as a compliment or a warning. I glance back at Lyra, but she's distracted, chatting animatedly with another worker.

I swallow hard.

"You're different," I whisper. "Are you alright? Are they treating you well?"

His lips twitch, almost into a smile, but it never quite forms. "I'm better than alright. I've ascended beyond what I was, called to a higher purpose. You wouldn't understand."

The words land heavy, and I wonder if he even believes them. There's no arrogance in his tone, but there's also no joy—only a cold certainty that makes my chest ache.

I force a smile, but inside, unease churns. "I should go," I say, stepping back toward the door.

He nods once, already turning back to his work. "The forge does not wait."

Our conversation leaves my stomach in knots. If Luca's behavior is any indication of palace life, I don't have much to look forward to.

Cassian

y tutor's droning voice grates on my nerves like nails on glass. He's been lecturing me about the history of Aetherea for the better part of an hour, and I'm no closer to caring than I was when we started. Something about alliances, trade routes, and their peculiar artistic traditions. None of it matters to me. The Aetherean King and Queen are visiting soon, and though they are my grandparents, I see no point in learning every detail of their centuries-old customs.

"Are you even listening, Your Highness?" Lorenzo snaps, his whiny tone cutting through my thoughts. Thin eyebrows draw together as he glares at me, clearly unimpressed with my lack of engagement.

"I'm listening," I lie, leaning back in my chair and crossing my arms. "Something about… their obsession with body art."

Lorenzo groans. He removes his glasses, rubbing his temples as if I'm the greatest trial he's ever endured. "If you don't take this seriously, you'll embarrass yourself—and the kingdom—when they arrive. You—"

Movement near the door catches my eye, and whatever scolding Lorenzo is spewing fades into the background.

Eden steps into the library, her expression unguarded as she admires the space. Her gaze lifts to the vaulted ceiling, lips parting in quiet wonder at the intricate mural sprawling above. She's still for a heartbeat, caught in the moment. But the spell breaks, her eyes drifting over the rows of towering shelves in search of something.

My irritation with Lorenzo melts away, replaced by a keen interest I can't suppress. Eden glides toward the far end of the library, her brown waves falling loosely over her shoulders. I sit up straighter.

What is she doing here?

Lorenzo clears his throat.

He stares indignantly, hands clasped on the table in front of him. "Your Highness, focus."

I scowl at him, ignoring his direction in search of Eden once more. But she's disappeared among the rows of books.

"I need a break." I push my chair back and rise to my feet.

"We are *behind* on this lesson!" Lorenzo protests, stepping into my path. "Please sit down, Your Highness. This is not a—"

"Lorenzo, I appreciate your passion," I interrupt, resting my hand on his shoulder. With a flicker of concentration, I tap into my fated skill. "But I think we both know the Aethereans are the least of my worries. They're family, after all." My words are sweet like honey, coating his mind with delicious detachment. "I say we've earned a midday reprieve, don't you think?"

His eyes grow dull, the sharp hazel gleam fading into a colorless haze as my influence takes hold.

"A break sounds nice, Your Highness. Carry on," he murmurs, his voice hollow.

Satisfied, I make my way toward the bookshelves Eden disappeared behind. By the time Lorenzo regains his bearings, his protests are but a distant echo. Tuning them out, I strain to hear footsteps or the rustle of fabric nearby. But this row is quiet.

My boots tap quietly against the marble floor as I maneuver through the library. A flash of green appears to my left. I peer through a gap in the books, spotting Eden in the history section. Her back is to me as she examines a row of dusty tomes.

Light on my feet, I move across the aisle to stand opposite her, only the bookshelves between us. I shadow her movements, following as she trails her fingers along the spines of several books. Finally, she picks one. As she slides it from its place on the shelf, I do the same, leaving a sizable gap between the volumes.

"Fancy seeing you here, Wildflower."

Her green eyes snap up, finding mine through the gap in the bookshelves. The book slams closed, sliding quickly back onto the shelf and blocking my view. I shove my book back and hurry down the row, intercepting her attempt to flee.

"Leaving so soon?"

"What do you want?" Her tone is curt.

"To talk," I reply, stepping closer.

"I'm busy."

She pushes past me, moving down another row.

I follow, undeterred. "Too busy to answer a simple question?"

"Yes." Her pace quickens.

"Did I do something?" The words slip out before I can stop them, and for the first time, she pauses.

Turning to face me, her eyes narrow, glinting with annoyance. "Nothing you need to bother yourself with, *Your Royal Highness*. I just have better things to do than indulge your whims."

The formal address bothers me more than I expect. I close the distance between us, my frustration bubbling to the surface. "Indulge my whims?" I repeat. "You're the one suddenly avoiding me. Forgive me if I'm curious why."

She closes her eyes for a moment, lips pressing into a thin line. I brace for her usual unfiltered honesty, but this time, she looks away, a quiet sigh slipping out.

"I don't have time for this." She turns sharply to leave, her voice clipped and resolute.

Before I can think better of it, my hand shoots out, grabbing hers. "Wait."

The contact lasts only a moment before Eden recoils. She pulls her hand free as if I burned her.

"I've seen what you do with your touch and silver tongue. I want nothing to do with it." Without another glance, she marches down the row of books.

My jaw tightens, teeth grinding together as her dismissal lingers like a slap. A fire rises in me, a mix of anger and something far more unsettling. I can't let her walk away like this. Not from me.

Two long strides close the distance. I seize her arm, tugging her gently but firmly into a quieter row. Her face flashes with fury as she jerks out of my grasp.

"Let me go," she snaps, her voice low but sharp enough to cut.

I release her, blocking her path with my body instead. She glares up at me, her cold, unyielding demeanor sending an unexplainable ache through my chest.

My mouth opens, but no words come. For once, my confidence falters, my anger dying down. What did I do to deserve this reaction? And why does her disdain unsettle me so deeply?

I clench my fists at my sides, willing myself to regain control. Emotions churn within me, relentless and unwelcome. They break through the carefully constructed walls I've spent years fortifying. Somehow, Eden slipped through a crack I hadn't noticed—hadn't even thought possible.

It's dangerous, this vulnerability. It claws at me, threatening to unravel the threads of discipline and detachment I cling to. I can't let it win. Especially not with her.

Breathing deep, I shut my eyes for a fleeting moment, as if drawing back into myself. A familiar mantra forms in my mind, each word a stone I lay to seal the breach. Lock the door. Bar the windows. Wall it all away. My emotions become prisoners in the dark recesses of my mind, buried so deep they can't reach me.

When I open my eyes, the last traces of vulnerability are gone, replaced by the cold, unfeeling precision I rely on. My voice is steady, a faint echo of the struggle she'll never see.

"Two days," I say, my tone a fortress in itself. "Same time."

Her expression twists into one of disdain. "That's what you wanted to tell me?" A sharp, bitter laugh leaves her throat. "Now who's obsessed with their future?"

She storms off in the other direction before I can respond. My chest tightens as the heat of anger rises, clawing its way to the surface. Every word of hers is like a challenge, an intentional defiance that only stokes the fire.

I chase after her, but a familiar figure catches my attention— Silas. He advances, his tall, solid frame cutting a direct path toward Eden. His eyes narrow as he assesses the situation.

"We're fine." Eden holds up a hand to stop him.

He doesn't listen. His steps remain measured, his focus locked on her. My frustration boils over at the interruption. In a flash, I grab his shoulder, my skill shifting from me to him.

"Do not intervene," I command. "Your concern is unwarranted. Trust me, you don't want to get involved in this petty quarrel. Walk away."

Silas hesitates, his eyes clouding over with a glassy detachment. Without another word, he heads back to his post, leaving me and Eden alone once more.

When I glance over, her disgust is unmistakable.

"You treat even the people you're close to that way?" Her voice is filled with scorn.

I lunge forward, closing the gap between us in an instant. My hand presses against the wooden bookshelf near her head, caging her in. My other hand hovers at her waist, just enough to keep her from slipping away.

"I do what I must," I say firmly, though the weight of her judgment gnaws at me.

Eden's face hardens. She studies me, silent for several tense moments. "You can't force me to be there," she says finally, her voice dripping with defiance.

Her words cause the breath to leave my lungs. They're a sharp reminder of her independence, her refusal to bend to me. My hand tightens on the bookshelf as I lean closer.

"You will respect your prince and remember your place, *Wildflower.*" My lip curls, my tone cold and cutting. "You're nothing but a fraud—pretending to be something you're not, growing where you don't belong. You're common. A weed." I let the word hang between us, watching the faint flicker of hurt cross her face. "And it would take nothing—*nothing*—for me to uproot you right now." My voice lowers, a quiet menace seeping into my words. "You will be there if you don't want your secret exposed."

Her eyes widen for a fraction of a second before narrowing again. "You wouldn't," she says, though her voice wavers.

I drop my arm, stepping back as the tension lingers between us like a storm about to break. "Try me," I spit.

Eden turns on her heel, her steps quick as she leaves the library without a backward glance. I watch her go, my chest tightening with every step she takes away from me. The echo of her departure rings in the quiet air, leaving me frozen in place and reeling from the encounter.

What has she done to me?

"Do you have a minute to talk? There's a lot I need to catch you up on." I gesture to one of the small tables in the corner.

He nods, flipping the open sign to closed and locking the door. "I have a feeling this will need more than a minute."

My lips curve into an appreciative grin. I wait for him to get comfortable at the table before telling him all about my new position as court artist. He listens intently, brown eyes thoughtful as I mention my conversation with his brother. I have half a mind to stop my story there, but that's not the real reason I'm visiting today. With a deep breath, I reveal my secret painting sessions with the prince, and the disturbing argument we had yesterday.

Mateo crosses his arms, his muscles stiffening when I relay the prince's callous words. When I finish, he's silent for a long moment. He drags a hand across his face with a sigh, leaning back in his chair.

"That's a lot to take in."

"I'm sorry for dumping all my problems on you. I just needed to talk to someone. And you've always been that person for me."

Mateo leans across the table, squeezing my hand in his. "Anytime. You know I've got your back. But Eden, what have you gotten yourself into? This is exactly what you were scared of— someone finding out about your skill and using it for their own gain."

I look down, ashamed. "I know. I didn't expect to be discovered so soon. The prince is more observant than I imagined he'd be."

Mateo snorts. "Thought he'd be too focused on himself to notice you?"

I shrug.

"Eden, don't you know by now how impossible you are to miss? You're one of the boldest people I know, always speaking your mind. I'm really hoping you've stayed quiet around the royals, but with your current situation, I doubt that's the case."

"It's not my fault the prince is so aggravating!"

Mateo raises a dubious brow. "Are you sure about that? You haven't provoked him with your honesty or disdain of royals?"

I bite the inside of my cheek, feeling the heat creep onto my face as I remember the many times I spoke my mind with the prince. "Point taken. Keep my mouth shut and I'll make it through."

"And Eden," Mateo's tone is serious now, "don't let some pompous royal dictate your worth."

His brown eyes are warm with sincerity, and yet I struggle to maintain his gaze. I've never been good with compliments, even indirect ones.

"Don't start acting like them, either. Sounds like my brother already has that one taken care of." The wooden leg of his chair scrapes against the stone floor as he stands. "Let me grab something before you leave."

Mateo disappears around the counter into the back of the bakery. The quaint dining space looks once again unused as I push in our chairs and wait by the front counter. Finally, Mateo returns with the distinct teal boxes of baked goods.

"Mattie, I don't need—"

"No is not an option." He holds them toward me, unwavering until I accept the gift from his hands. "Top box is for you and the prince."

I peek inside, surprised to find a diamond donut resting beside a chocolate chip cookie.

"Sweet resilience to help you endure palace life, and warm fuzzies for the prickly prince." Mateo wiggles his brows.

I nod approvingly, chuckling at the image of the stone-cold prince enjoying a happy-inducing cookie. With his attitude, I bet he's never had one in his life. "And the bottom box?"

Mateo smiles knowingly. "For your last stop before returning to the palace."

The door opens before I can even knock.

Aria wraps me into a hug, quickly followed by Soren and my dad until I'm crushed under the weight of their warm welcome.

"It's good to be home."

Dad ushers us inside and we gather around the dining area, Mateo's pastries placed like a prize in the center of the table. But they go untouched, everyone eager to hear about my new position in the palace. I relay everything that's happened so far, minus the skirmishes with the prince. I'm not sure what drama that might stir up, and I don't need more people scolding me for my blunt candor.

"I'm jealous you have a legitimate reason to stare at the prince all the time," Aria swoons, resting her chin in her hand.

"It's really not all it's cracked up to be, I promise."

Dad listens from across the table, a glint in his eyes like he can tell there's more to my story. Thankfully, he keeps his suspicions to himself.

"My turn!" Soren slams his arm down on the table, making me jump. On his wrist, a silver hourglass shines in the light.

A shocked gasp escapes me. "Soren! When did this happen?"

He leans forward excitedly in his chair. "Not long after you left. Dad let me help him with the doors he's making for the house, and it finally showed up!"

"So, you're a carpenter like Dad? But I thought we tried that before!" I think back to the many skills Soren tested in pursuit of his fatemark.

"He did," Dad clarifies. "But not with doors. It seems Soren's skill is very particular."

It's peculiar how fated skills vary, no one able to decipher what might show up next. "What can you do with it?"

"It's best if I just show you."

We follow Soren upstairs to his bedroom, where a deep mahogany door rests in place of the old, faded birch one. Motioning for us to watch, Soren places his left hand on the door as he twists the handle with his right, walking through it into his bedroom. It clicks softly closed and we wait in silence in the cramped hallway.

I glance over at my sister and dad, my nose wrinkled in confusion, when Soren's voice sounds from my bedroom to the right. He pokes his head between the door and the frame, beaming.

"How did you get in there?" I ask, utterly bewildered.

Soren looks at me like I asked the dumbest question in the world. "Enchantment, of course! Every door I craft, I can enchant with a specific location. Wherever I picture in my mind when making it is where the user ends up on the other side."

My jaw drops. "That's incredible, Soren! How far can you go?"

He leans against the doorframe of my bedroom and gives a small shrug. "It's brand new, so I can't go very far yet. What I *have* discovered is I can go anywhere through my doors, while others can only go where I've enchanted it to go."

I cross my arms, sharing an exasperated look with my sister. "And you *chose* to have your door lead directly into our bedroom?"

"What can I say? I started small, and I couldn't think of where else to go." Soren shrugs sheepishly.

I walk over, pulling him into a hug and resting my chin atop his head. "I'm proud of you, Soren. I knew you'd find your skill."

To my left, Dad grimaces. It's no surprise he's not ecstatic about Soren's new skill. I would hate to see his reaction to finding out the prince has already discovered mine.

I let my brother go and he bounds down the stairs with a cheerful farewell, intent to continue refining his newly discovered talent.

"Anything else new I should know about?" I glance between my sister and dad.

Dad gives Aria a knowing look. "I'll leave you two to chat for a while."

Aria giggles conspiratorially, pushing me into our bedroom and shutting the door. My mouth opens to ask questions, but the sound dies in my throat at the beautiful sight before me. Pinned to the dress form is a deep green corseted gown with flowing sleeves, a partially draped skirt falling from the hips.

"Surprise! I've been making another gown for you now that you must dress like an artisan every day."

I spin on my heel, crushing my sister into an embrace. My eyes grow wet with emotion as I imagine the countless hours she spent making something so beautiful just for me. "It's stunning, Aria. Your talent is beyond words, truly."

Delight twinkles in her green eyes, the same shade as mine, her full cheeks coloring with a rosy hue. She grabs my hand, tugging me closer to her masterpiece.

The dress's design beautifully combines structure and softness. Its sage-green color is light and feminine, a sharp contrast to the finely-tailored pleats that form the corseted bodice. Embroidered floral appliques add a graceful, garden-inspired touch to the shoulders. A sheer overlay extends into flowing sleeves, blending elegance with noble refinement.

My stomach twists with guilt, remembering the night I wore her Edenia-inspired gown to the royal dinner. How could I ever question my sister's creations? All the hard work and hours she pours into each stitch, crafting it for no other reason than to see me thrive.

Aria mistakes the emotion on my face for distaste, her forehead creasing with worry. "What is it? Is there something wrong with it?"

"Of course not! I'm just in awe of my sister's talent."

"Thanks, Eden, but I haven't even told you the best part." Aria steps behind the dress form, eyeing me over its shoulder. "I'm enchanting it with regality. When you wear it, you'll feel empowered, strong, and regal." She moves her head to the other side of the dress form. "And when others look at you, they'll be intimidated, treating you with the respect of a royal."

The air leaves my lungs. It's as if Aria knew just what I needed, her enchantment full of everything I've been lacking since my stay at the palace began. "I'm never going to want to take this dress off. Can I have it now?"

Aria laughs, a joyful sound that lights up her face. "It's not quite finished. I still need to layer the skirt. But I promise to send word when it's ready."

With one last hug, I head to the front door, knowing the palace—and my work—awaits me. My paintings won't paint themselves.

As I step outside, my dad's voice stops me. "Didn't think I'd let you sneak out without a goodbye, did you?"

He meets me at the door. A gentle smile softens his stern features, enhancing the wrinkles near his eyes. He carries something in his hand.

"It's always good to see you, Dad."

He chuckles. "Now," he says, his expression growing concerned, "are you going to tell me what's bothering you, or did you really come all this way just to say hello?"

My gaze drops to my shoes, the scuffed leather suddenly fascinating. He knows me too well. As much as I'd like to keep my worries to myself, Dad's advice has always been sound—even when it's hard to hear.

"Eden," he prompts, his voice patient but expectant.

I sigh. "I've been having a hard time adjusting to life in the palace," I admit, glancing at him from the corner of my eye.

His brow furrows in concern, but he waits for me to continue.

"My main task has been painting the prince, but… we don't exactly see eye to eye."

Without a word, Dad hands me a small leather journal, its brown cover worn smooth from use. "This might be even more useful than I thought."

"What is it?" I take it from him, loosening the strap and flipping through the pages. The delicate lettering is immediately familiar, recognition hitting me like lightning. "Mother's?"

He nods. "I found it in her dresser. She enjoyed writing—capturing moments as if she wanted to preserve them forever. I never quite understood why, but now it makes sense. Though she's no longer here, a part of her remains in these pages. She painted nobles often. I'm sure you'll find some wisdom in her words."

My fingertips trace the elegant loops of her handwriting, and my chest tightens. Almost ten years have passed, and yet the ache of missing her feels fresh. "I miss her," I whisper.

"Me, too." Dad's voice is soft, steady. He reaches out, tucking an errant strand of hair behind my ear. "Eden, no matter how hard things get, remember you can always rely on Delayon for strength. What others think of you means far less than who you truly are. You are royalty in the eyes of our Creator, a cherished daughter. And you'll always be a princess to me."

I step into his arms, comforted by his woodsy smell and protective embrace. As I pull away, he presses a kiss to the top of my head. "Thanks, Dad."

Tears prick my eyes, and I step outside to tuck the journal into my saddlebag. I mount my horse, and Dad steps forward to rub the mare's mane, his gaze distant yet thoughtful.

Just as I'm about to leave, he looks up, his voice carrying an unexpected note of hope. "Give the prince the benefit of the doubt," he says. "You might have more in common than you think."

His words stay with me as I ride away.

What could I possibly have in common with the prince?

Cassian

Silas's sword slams into mine with surprising force. I almost lose my grip, distracted by Eden's appearance in the courtyard. She dismounts her horse and collects something from her saddlebag.

Silver metal glints to my right. I sidestep another blow, narrowly missing the impact.

"Letting me win so easily?" Silas twists the sword in his hand, his stance confident. "That's unlike you, Your Highness."

"Says the royal guard who's trying to kill the future king."

Silas shrugs. "I knew you'd see it coming."

I smirk, advancing suddenly, thrusting my sword toward him. He skillfully deflects, but I use his arrogance to my advantage. My sword cuts through the air, sweeping down to meet his with a satisfying clang. The strength behind the blow takes him by surprise, and I deal a rapid sequence of attacks that end with our blades locked.

"I don't like losing." In a flash, I break off by raising my hilt, the metal of our swords sliding together. As my arm comes down, I trap his blade under my shoulder, pressing the edge of my sword against his wrist with a spin.

Silas clings to his weapon, gritting his teeth. I spin further, increasing the pressure until he's forced to let go. I grab his hilt with my left hand, pointing the tips of both swords at him.

He rubs his wrist. "Well played, Your Highness."

I hand his sword back and sheath my own. "That will be all for now."

Silas nods, heading into the palace as I stride toward Eden. I haven't seen her since our conversation yesterday. She eyes me warily as I approach, preparing to leave the courtyard.

"Out for a joy ride, were you?" My gaze sweeps over her riding outfit.

"Your Royal Highness." Eden curtsies. "If you'll excuse me."

I sidestep into her path, glancing behind me to ensure no one is around. She gives me a withering glare. Hurt flashes through me, but I tamp it down. Though I should let her walk away, I don't. Part of me feels more alive with her around. I crave her presence, even when I know I shouldn't.

An apology rests on the tip of my tongue, but I can't bring myself to say it. I clench my jaw, turning my attention to the teal box in her hand. "What's that?"

Her lips press together, an expression of pained tolerance. "A gift from my friend."

Eden steps forward once more and panic seizes me. This is not how I wanted the conversation to go, but all my charm flees when I'm near her. Without thinking, I snatch the box from her hands before she can leave, spinning backward.

"Hey!" she shouts. "Give that back!"

I hold it out of arm's reach, using my height to my advantage. My mind grasps at straws, searching for a reason to be around her longer. "Spar with me," I blurt.

Her eyes widen in surprise. "Excuse me?"

I grin, the idea taking shape as I lazily open the box to find sweets inside. "I challenge you to a sword fight."

"And why would I agree to such a thing?" Eden scowls, crossing her arms in a way that reveals the leather journal in her other hand.

"You must admit," I tilt my head, "swinging a sword at me sounds appealing, does it not?"

She sighs, looking up toward the palace. "I have a painting to finish. The role of court artist isn't all fun and games, unlike being a prince apparently is. Shouldn't you be preparing for the Aethereans' visit tomorrow?"

"Don't remind me." I close the box. "And it's not as if your painting will sprout legs and run away."

"What do *you* get out of this ridiculous idea? Sparring with me has no advantages."

I ponder her question, trying to come up with an excuse for such an illogical request. "The desserts. I want them."

"You're the prince! You can have any sweet you desire. Why do you need—"

Her words stop short and there's a palpable shift in her demeanor. She clears her throat.

"Fine, Your Highness. But only the cookie. And you'll have to give me a few pointers to make this even remotely fair."

A thrill runs through me. "Excellent."

Eden follows me to the sparring area. I unstrap my sword and set it aside as she places her belongings on a nearby bench. Grabbing two wooden training swords, I hand one over. She accepts it with a raised brow.

"You didn't think we'd be fighting with actual swords, did you?"

"One could hope." She swings her sword experimentally.

"Hold it like you're shaking a hand." I motion to the hilt.

Eden's brows knit together as she tries to follow my advice, but to no avail. I step closer, demonstrating with my sword. "You want to hold it higher and ensure your wrist is strong."

Eden readjusts, smacking her sword against mine, her movement choppy. I suppress a grin, but she senses my amusement.

She sighs in frustration. "This is a silly idea."

"Eden, I don't expect you to be an expert." I press the point of my sword into the ground.

Her annoyance softens at my words.

"And don't worry, I'll take it easy on you."

Her agitation returns. "Let's start already."

"One last tip." I move to stand beside her. "While your wrist needs to be strong, you can't hold your sword with a death grip, or your movements won't be fluid."

I demonstrate a sweeping motion with the wooden sword, signaling for her to copy me. As she does, her wrist falls into a weak position once more.

Instinctively, I reach out to adjust it. She flinches away from my touch, and I'm reminded of yesterday's conversation. I should be grateful she wants anything to do with me. I used one of my most powerful weapons against her—my words. Even without my skill, they hold weight. She has every right to hate me.

I back off, feeling a heat creep up my neck. "Just, um, have fun with it, I suppose. It's not every day you get to swing a sword at the prince."

She arches her brow.

"Even a fake one," I add, taking my position.

Eden follows suit, holding her wooden sword with a comical mixture of determination and uncertainty. I tap the flat of my blade against hers, signaling the start. She lunges, her movements wild but surprisingly quick, forcing me to take a step back.

"Not bad," I say, dodging another swing.

She grins, confidence flickering across her face as she attacks once more. Her form is sloppy, but there's an untamed energy behind each strike that almost catches me off guard.

Almost.

I block her next blow with ease, the sound of wood meeting wood echoing across the sparring ring.

"You're leaving yourself open," I point out, right before my sword jabs into her abdomen.

Eden spins away, her skirt flailing behind her. "You could've mentioned that *before* you exploited it."

"Where's the fun in that?" I sidestep her attempt to land a hit. "You're quick, but you're predictable. Try to mix it up."

Her response is another determined swing, this one aimed lower. I'm impressed she's already adapting, but her footing falters. I deflect, sweeping her blade away with a swift motion. She stumbles but catches herself.

"You're stronger than you look, Wildflower," I say, a note of admiration creeping into my voice.

Eden narrows her eyes, circling me like a predator, though her movements are more cautious now. I let her attack again, giving her an opening that I easily counter, spinning her blade from her hand. It clatters to the ground, and I step forward, lightly placing the tip of my sword against her shoulder.

"Match," I declare, my breathing no heavier than before.

Eden laughs, her chest rising and falling as she catches her breath. "That was as humiliating as I thought it would be." She bends to retrieve her sword.

A grin tugs at my lips. "If it's any consolation, you held your own longer than I expected."

She shoots me a look, equal parts suspicion and annoyance. "That's not exactly comforting."

She crosses to retrieve the box of sweets, handing over the cookie. I dip my head in exaggerated thanks, planning to set the treat aside when Eden lifts the donut from the box.

"The cookie is enough." I wave her away.

Eden rolls her eyes. "The donut is for me." She takes a bite.

My eyes drop to the sugar now clinging to her lips. "Eating mid spar?"

Eden licks her lips. "Sustenance for the next round. Are you sure you don't need some?" She gestures to the cookie still sitting untouched in my hand.

I take a bite, the sweet chocolate bursting on my tongue. A warmth spreads through me, filling my body with a pleasant buzz.

"Good, isn't it?" Amusement dances across her face, but I'm not sure why.

"Where did you get it?"

"A bakery in the village. My best friend owns it."

With two more bites, the cookie is gone. I lick my fingers.

Eden wrinkles her nose. "You could've at least enjoyed it."

"Oh, I did. Tastes like winning." I wink, my spirits suddenly lifted.

She ignores me, setting her donut aside. "Another round, Princeling? I quite like swinging a sword at you. Even if it's only a fake one."

"I told you it would do us some good. Especially after our conversation yesterday." The words slip out before I can stop myself, my voice sounding lighter, more carefree.

Her eyebrows raise. She takes her stance, adjusting her grip. This time, she starts the match, tapping her sword against mine. Immediately after, Eden attacks. I pivot out of the way, light on my feet. She's fast, I'll give her that.

And yet it still won't be enough to win.

After several swings and successful parries, Eden's breathing is noticeably heavy. She clenches the hilt, knuckles white as she compensates for her tired arm.

"Ready to quit, Wildflower?"

"You should know by now—I don't give up that easily."

"Ah, yes." I strike my sword against hers. "You have a habit of defying my expectations."

She swings low. I hop back, causing her to lose balance when her sword hits nothing but air. When I sidestep another attack, she huffs, clearly annoyed.

"Fight back, Princeling."

The nickname makes me unexpectedly giddy. Or maybe it's the strange warmth still coursing through me. Whatever it is, I sense our earlier tension has dissipated, making me feel light and unbothered, like I don't have a care in the world. Eden stares at me with narrowed eyes, a determined set to her jaw.

"Why so serious?" My lips form a pout in mock sadness.

Eden smiles tentatively.

I tilt my head and exaggerate my sad face.

She breaks out laughing. "You've never made a face like that before. Who knew you could be so expressive?"

While she's distracted, I extend my arm in a flash, tapping her shoulder with my blade. She jolts back, sword raised defensively in front of her.

"Well, Wildflower," I say, tapping her on the hip, "there are a lot of things you don't know about me." With a smirk, I lunge forward, knocking the sword from her hands once more. It falls at her feet.

Eden puts one hand on her hip, swiping her hair out of her face. "How about another challenge?"

"Oh? And what would that be?"

She glances at the rack of archery equipment nearby. "Bow and arrow. Winner gets a truth."

"A truth?"

She nods. "The winner must truthfully answer one question. Unless you're afraid to lose."

I snort, warmth still buzzing through me. "Afraid? Hardly. But don't cry when I win."

She scoffs, already stringing her bow.

We set up a makeshift target at the far end of the sparring ring, and Eden lets me shoot first. I land a respectable hit just outside the bullseye.

"Impressive, Your Highness," she says, not sounding impressed at all. "Care to offer a few tips?"

She draws her bow, and I immediately notice a few problem areas.

"If you insist." I step forward, lifting her elbow before shifting her foot back with the side of my boot. "You were fighting with the bow instead of working with it."

She looks at me through the drawn bow, a slight smile on her lips. "Was I?"

Her subtle confidence surprises me, especially considering her grip is too tight. But I'll keep that to myself. Wouldn't want to help the competition *too* much.

"Now let it fly," I say.

In a flash, her muscles relax, grip readjusting with a practiced ease before she releases the arrow. It flies straight, striking dead center.

"Like that?" She grins.

I blink, genuinely surprised. "You've been holding out on me, Wildflower."

"Like you said," she starts, lowering her bow, "I have a knack for defying expectations."

Shaking my head, I take another shot, though her victory already feels inevitable. When her next two arrows outmatch mine by a wide margin, I brace myself for her question.

"Truth time," she declares. "What is your fated skill, *really*?"

A sobering cold floods through me. I'm not sure what I expected, but not that. "You seemed certain about it yesterday," I deflect.

Eden remains silent. For a moment, I consider lying, but her gaze pierces through me, unrelenting.

"It's my charisma. With the right words, I can numb emotions."

Eden's expression shifts into one of understanding, quickly followed by disdain. "So that's why you can be so cruel. You detach."

I flinch at her words. "I have a habit of using it on myself, yes."

"And were you using it during our conversation yesterday? In the library?"

Though she phrases it as a question, the look on her face says she already knows the answer. I nod in reply.

Eden looks away.

She's disappointed—a reaction I'm not used to receiving. Most revere me with wonder, envy, or respect. Some even beg for the momentary reprieve from the onslaught of human emotions.

But not Eden.

"You don't understand the impact you have, Cassian." Her soft voice breaks through my thoughts.

"Your ability to silence emotion, to feel nothing, is more dangerous than you realize." She looks up at me, jaw set, gaze resolute. "Emotions make us human. I'd hate to see what we'd become without them. Please consider that the next time you go to use your skill." She gathers her things. "Thanks for the duel, Your Highness. I hope you enjoyed your reward."

The formality in her tone is back, and I sense the growing distance between us.

I grab her hand before she leaves, hoping to sustain our connection. Her gaze flits down to our hands. I let go, embarrassed by my sheer lack of control around her.

"Um, will I see you tomorrow night?"

She bites her lip, my question hanging in the air. After a long pause, she breaks the silence. "Yes."

My tension dissipates. I give her a small nod, suppressing my sigh of relief. She disappears into the shadows of the palace, and I stare after her into their depths. If I'm not careful, she'll find her way through my defenses once more.

If she hasn't already.

Cassian

Sunlight illuminates the sails, turning them liquid gold. As the ship approaches the docks, my foot taps restlessly on the stone. Father stands stoically beside me, clad in Mentera's royal colors, the seamless blend of fabric and armor intimidating yet regal. Though I'm in similar clothes, I feel much less confident, like a cheap imitation of the king.

Mother stands to my right. She gives me a reassuring smile, radiant in her home colors of orange and gold. The Aethereans' visit is one she always looks forward to, a chance to greet family and old friends. Separated by the sea, she sees them less often than she would like. I can't remember how long it's been since her last visit.

I tug my sleeve lower as ropes hit the dock with a thud. Dockworkers hurry to secure them, shouting over the groan of wood and waves. Onboard, my grandmother's silver hair is unmistakable, gleaming beneath a large gold crown. Grandfather stands next to her, his gilded cape reflecting the sun in a blinding display. They certainly know how to make an entrance.

To their left, is a man with a gold sash draped diagonally across his chest. A young woman stands beside him, her long auburn hair blowing in the breeze.

My jaw clenches. *That must be her—my potential future queen.*

Mother's gentle touch on my shoulder startles me. "Cassian, the Bendettis are a wonderful family. Alfonso has faithfully served as my father's Royal Advisor for many years. His daughter will make a fine match for you."

"Like I have much of a choice in the matter, anyway." I can't meet her eyes.

She lifts my chin, understanding flickering across her face. "I didn't choose your father, either. He's a harsh man, but I wouldn't change anything. He gave me you and your sister. Delayon has a plan for our lives; we must simply trust where it leads."

Mother adjusts the simple crown on my head, smoothing back my dark hair. "I love you, Cassian. You may not realize it yet, but you will make an excellent king one day."

Her words soothe some of my nerves. A soft smile breaks through my stoic expression, and she returns it gratefully.

"A smile suits you. You're always so serious."

"Father says—"

"I know what your father says." She glances over my shoulder at the king. "But that apathetic expression of yours won't win any hearts. Trust me."

My stomach flips. Winning hearts is the last thing I want to do today. "I can't promise any miracles, Mother."

"Says the young man blessed with charm." She leans in close. "It's a gift, Cassian. Even without your fated skill."

With a small squeeze of my shoulder, she turns back toward the dock, readopting her regal pose. I follow suit. By now, Grandfather is stepping off the ship, the others close behind.

"King Felix, Queen Brenee, welcome to Mentera!" Father says. "We hope Delayon blessed your journey."

"And blessed it was." Grandfather beams, his amber eyes creasing with warmth.

He looks younger than I remember, especially with his shoulder-length hair. His tan skin is exposed above an orange tunic, golden ink visible on his collarbones. He's the opposite of everything Father has taught me about being king—relaxed, roguish, and completely unbothered.

Grandmother is just as carefree, gold jewelry adorning her neck and chest across a flowing amber dress. Her brown eyes lock onto mine, and the gold markings on her cheekbones bloom to life.

I glance over at Father. His smile appears friendly and natural, but I know it's all an act. He has never seen eye to eye with the Aethereans. Where he is all rigidity and structure, they are creativity and freedom. But allies are allies, as he would tell me. Calling them family would mean he actually views them as such.

"Cassian, dear boy!" Grandmother wraps her arms around me, her thin arms squeezing with surprising force. "You've grown so much since I last saw you! If it weren't for you being a spitting image of your father, and that lovely portrait you sent us, I'd hardly recognize you!"

"It's good to see you too, Grandmother."

"Where's that sister of yours?"

"Lyra stayed at the castle. This is Cassian's moment, remember?" Mother smiles, holding her arms out to embrace Grandmother.

Behind them, the Royal Advisor and his daughter are making their way down the dock. Mother tips her head toward them.

"Go greet her," she whispers.

As I pass Grandfather, he pauses his lively conversation with Father to clap me on the back. I nod respectfully before stepping onto the dock. It creaks beneath me when I walk.

"Cassian Moretti." I shake the advisor's hand. "It's a pleasure to meet you, Sir Bendetti."

"And you, Crown Prince. This is my daughter, Sienna."

She curtsies, my eyes drawn to the golden swirls coiling up her arm like a snake.

My tutor's words ring in my ear, a reminder of the Aethereans' love for body art.

Before I can dwell on it, Sir Bendetti walks ahead of us, and I fall into step beside Sienna. Unsure what to say, I glance down at our feet, noticing her dainty gold heels. My heart skips a beat, and I realize I all but forgot Eden's vision.

The Aetherean woman stumbles into me, I remember.

As if thinking it into reality, I watch as her left foot catches on an uneven board. In a split second, I decide to step out of her way. Without me there to brace her, she falls unceremoniously into the glittering sea.

"Sienna!" Sir Bendetti rushes over. "Why didn't you catch her?" His deep brown eyes are alight with fury.

"My apologies, sir. I wasn't fast enough." The excuse sounds weak even to my ears.

Sir Bendetti scowls, barking at the nearby dockworkers to fetch his daughter from the water. She sputters below us, her dress floating around her like a pool of spilled honey.

I meet my father's eyes on shore, his icy glare enough to tell me I've made a big mistake. Grandfather frowns beside him, a worried Grandmother racing toward us up the dock.

But what they see as a misstep, I see as the first step toward changing my fate.

After being outside for so long, the palace feels cold. My tailcoat is draped over Sienna's shoulders in a poor attempt to keep her warm. By now, it's soaking wet, leaving a trail of water on the marble floor.

Far ahead of us, Father speaks animatedly with my grandparents, likely still smoothing over my earlier fiasco. From what I was told, they were quite excited about their match for me, gushing about her in many exhaustive letters. When my portrait was well-received, I assume Father saw the match as a wonderful way to get in my grandparents' good graces.

And now I've humiliated him.

"I apologize again, Miss Bendetti. I could've avoided your swim in the sea." I paste on a charming grin.

She purses her lips, dramatically wringing out her hair once more. Water drips onto my boots. "If only I had thought to bring you with me. We both could have enjoyed a little *swim*."

Sienna pushes my tailcoat off her shoulders. It drops to the floor at my feet with a squelch. Her dress clings to her body, the fabric almost the color of her skin. I try to avoid staring.

She scoffs. "Take a good look, Prince. If I have anything to do with it, this will be the last time you see me."

Her words don't have the intended effect as she storms off to talk with her father. Instead, I'm hopeful. *Maybe she has more sway with her father than I do.*

A servant quickly approaches, scooping my clothing from the floor. "I'll take care of this for you, Your Royal Highness. Someone will be by shortly to wipe up all the water. We are a bit preoccupied at the moment."

"Preoccupied?" I question. "With what?"

The servant girl casts a furtive glance over her shoulder. "The court artist, Your Highness."

My muscles tense. "What about the court artist?"

"It's nothing of concern," she says quickly. "We have it under control. It won't interfere with the Aethereans' visit."

I grab her wrist, hand clenched tight. "What. Happened." My voice is guttural.

"She refuses to come down from a ladder," she explains, words coming out in a rush.

"Where?" I growl, eyes narrowed.

"The Great Hall, Your Highness."

I release her, and stride toward the Great Hall with purpose. My mother calls after me, causing the rest of the group to notice my departure. But the heavy beating of my heart drowns out their questions and offended glares. *Stuck on a ladder? How does that even happen?*

I barge into the Great Hall, opening the doors before the attendants can. At the far end of the room, a tall ladder rests precariously against the wall. Eden clings tightly to the top rung, knuckles white as servants plead for her to come down. Not wanting to alarm her further, I quietly walk closer, motioning for the servants to step aside. They open their mouths to argue, but I silence them with a lifted hand.

"Always surprising me, aren't you, Wildflower?"

"Cassian?" Eden turns to look but quickly flattens herself against the ladder when it shakes beneath her.

Despite the servants' shocked expressions, her casual use of my name is electrifying.

"No, it's someone else who calls you Wildflower," I tease. When Eden doesn't laugh, I drop the joking pretense. "Now, how about you come down from up there?"

She shakes her head, voice warbling. "I can't."

"You got up there, so surely you can get down." I place both hands on the ladder, steadying it. "I've got the ladder. All you have to do is take it one rung at a time."

Eden lowers one foot, the tip of her high heel trying to find the next rung. As it connects with the wood, she puts her weight on it only briefly before her foot retreats to its previous perch.

"How long has she been up there?" I ask the nearby servant.

He shrugs. "It's been a while, Your Royal Highness."

"Why is she even up there in the first place?" I hiss.

The servant shrinks back. "She hung a painting for the Aethereans."

"Something one of you couldn't do? Her job is to make the paintings, not hang them."

The servants stare at the ground. I scowl, instructing them to hold the ladder steady as I position myself to ascend. "I'm coming up."

"What?" Eden squeaks. "No!"

Before she can say another word, I pull myself up a rung. The ladder quivers under my weight. Careful not to move too wildly, I continue until I'm only a few rungs below her.

"Can't say I expected to be staring up your skirt today, Wildflower."

She shrinks into herself, pressing against the ladder more than I thought possible. "Stop looking, then." Her voice sounds less worried than before, an annoyance taking precedence.

That's good. I want to distract her.

"How did you get yourself into this situation, anyway?" I climb another rung.

Eden huffs. "Does it matter?"

Carefully maneuvering my hands to the outside edges, I pull myself onto the rung just below hers, my stomach flush with her back. "You're right," I whisper. "Maybe now is not the time. But I'd love to hear the story when you're safely on the ground."

She tilts her head to the side. "Okay," she breathes.

Her body shakes, and I place one of my hands over hers.

"You're strong and brave." I channel my fated skill. "You feel no fear, only a peaceful emptiness."

Eden jerks her hand out from under mine. "Stop!"

My stomach drops at the panic in her voice. She's disgusted by my skill. How could I be so dense as to try to use it on her? I'm doing the very thing she warned me is dangerous—relying on my skill when emotions run high.

Taking the easy way out.

"I'm sorry."

"No, it's just—" Eden pauses. "Thank you for wanting to help me, but manipulating my emotions won't do that. I need to face them head on. I don't know if I'll ever get over this fear, but I am willing to try."

Her words strike a chord within me. I stare at her hand clenched tight around the ladder and feel a surge of admiration. "Alright. One rung at a time, then. When I move, so do you."

Eden's hand finds mine again, her trembling touch sending a shiver up my arm. She threads her fingers through mine, giving a small, firm squeeze—her silent way of saying she's ready. I lower myself with one foot, and Eden does the same, still pressed tightly against me for support. We descend without issue for several feet.

"You're doing great," I murmur.

She turns, her lips forming a tentative smile when her heel slips on a rung. My heart stops. Her balance falters, gravity tugging at her.

Then my arm darts out, wrapping around her waist and pinning us both against the ladder before she can fall.

"I got you," I say, breathless.

I'm acutely aware of how close we are. Her erratic breathing matches my own. My arm grows warm where I hold her, fingers pressed into her waist.

We stay like that for several long moments, our hearts beating in a chaotic rhythm. I attempt to steady mine, but it's almost impossible, though I'm not afraid of heights.

"Keep going," she says finally.

Our pace slows for the next few rungs. As the ground grows closer, her muscles relax, though her movements are still stiff. A door creaking grabs my attention, and I turn to where my father steps into the Great Hall. My grandparents are close behind. Eden turns to look, but I stop her.

"Focus, Wildflower. We're almost there."

She takes a shaky breath. "Why I thought climbing a ladder in heels was a good idea, I don't know."

I laugh softly, grateful her joking attitude is returning.

By the time both of our feet hit solid ground, our limbs are weary from stress. Eden swipes a hand across her damp forehead.

"Thank you." She smiles weakly, turning away from the ladder.

Her body trembles, and she seems fragile, like glass that would shatter with a single touch. Something flickers within me, a desire to pull her close once more—to hold her tight until my strength becomes hers. But the thought of her recoiling from my touch makes me take a step back.

Eden's thoughtful green eyes lock onto mine.

A wave of inadequacy washes over me, and I avoid her gaze. "I'm glad you're alright."

The loud clearing of my father's throat echoes across the hall, shattering the moment. "Cassian. We have much to discuss."

With one last glance at Eden, I follow them out of the room. If my earlier inaction with Sienna wasn't enough to sever the betrothal, my actions with Eden surely will be.

"Evening, Wildflower." The prince leans casually against my door frame, a sly grin on his face.

I suppress an eye roll, stepping aside to let him in.

"No witty remark?"

"Not tonight," I say.

We settle into our normal spots. As I begin his portrait, Cassian's gaze is questioning, and for a second, I think there's a flash of worry. I shake my head to clear my thoughts, focusing on each paint stroke as the colors build to form his face.

Minutes stretch by, but the silence feels different, a strange connection forged between us after this morning. Cassian's stone-cold stare has softened, an unexpected warmth thawing his icy gaze.

"You still owe me that story." He breaks the silence, the ghost of a smile on his lips.

"Do I?" I capture the quirk of his lip with my brush, its boyish charm dulling the harsh lines of his face.

He chuckles, a low sound in his throat that makes me pause. "It's the least you could do after I rescued you this morning."

"You make me sound like a damsel in distress, Princeling." I block out the shape of his wide shoulders, his tense muscles betraying his aloof facade.

"Weren't you?"

I look up from the canvas to meet his gaze. The worry is back, stormy eyes looking up at me through dark lashes. A muscle flexes in his jaw as he breaks his pose to lean forward.

"You aren't supposed to move," I murmur.

"I'm sure you can still finish the painting," he whispers. "I hear you're quite talented."

I bite the inside of my cheek. "I *have* painted you many times by now. I could probably do it in my sleep."

Cassian tilts his head, moonlight from the window giving him an unearthly glow. "You fancy dreaming about me, do you, Wildflower?"

Heat crawls up my neck, setting my cheeks on fire. I point my paintbrush at him. "Sit back the way you were, and I'll tell you what happened this morning."

He raises his hands in surrender before returning to his pose. "Alright, no more teasing. I'm eager to hear what made you climb a ladder not only in heels, but with a clear fear of heights."

With a deep breath, I layer in the shape of his ink-black hair. "You know I was hanging a painting for the Aethereans."

Cassian hums his affirmation.

"I did it because the other servants wouldn't."

His hand clenches where it rests on his thigh. "What do you mean, they wouldn't?"

"No matter how many times I asked them, they wouldn't help me. I knew the Aethereans were coming soon, and it needed to be hung before we received them in the Great Hall. So—"

"You did it yourself," Cassian interjects.

I nod.

He's silent for a little while longer, staring at the wall behind me. I focus intently on the portrait, unsure what more to say.

"Did they give you a reason?"

"I'm sorry?"

"For not helping you," Cassian clarifies.

"Not specifically. But—" I stop myself, not wanting to get anyone in trouble.

"Eden." He says my name like I've never heard it before, a resonant song on his lips.

My stomach flutters. He waits patiently, a gentleness in his expression that tells me my words are safe with him.

"They've never liked me." His eyes darken and I stop painting. "Many don't think I deserve the title of court artist. I'm a commoner—not even a Morphi."

His nostrils flare. "Who?"

"It doesn't matter."

"Tell. Me. Who."

The rage behind his words catches me off guard. "Why do you care?"

"I just do."

He makes no sense, his lack of explanation making me put up my defenses. "Worried the rumors will make me quit and you won't have a peek at your future anymore?"

"No!" He drags a hand over his face. "That's not it."

"Then why the sudden interest? It's not like you cared before," I mumble, adding absentminded shapes to the portrait's background.

"I don't know what changed," he blurts, turning to look at me intensely. "But something did. When I saw you up on that ladder, I couldn't breathe until I knew you were safe. That reckless, untameable spirit of yours is intoxicating, Wildflower."

The look on his face steals the breath from my lungs, his features painted with tortured desire. A shiver runs through my body. *The prince thinks I'm intoxicating?*

"No matter how many times I try to get you out of my head, you keep coming back." A lopsided grin tugs at his mouth as he exhales a quiet, disbelieving laugh. "Just like a weed."

"That's a strange way of saying you can't stop thinking about me, Princeling."

His head snaps up, a flicker of hope dancing across his face. A question lies unspoken in his gaze, dark brows lifted with surprise. I linger on the way his lips part. My heart feels like it's about to beat out of my chest, the paintbrush suddenly rough in my hands.

He's the prince, I remind myself. *He's about to be betrothed to another woman.*

I look down, breaking eye contact and clearing my throat. "Apologies, Your Highness. You're probably anxious to know if your future has changed after today's events." I glance back up, but the softness is gone—only his smirk remains.

"Right. That is why I lose precious hours of sleep to be here, isn't it?" His jaw clenches as he readjusts to find his earlier position.

I resume painting but notice he's sitting at a different angle, making it hard to finish the portrait accurately despite how many times I've painted him. "Turn toward me."

He does as instructed but loses the pose.

"No, like this." I demonstrate, keenly aware of his searing gaze. Yet even as his stare clings to my body, he can't get the pose right.

Pulled by an unexpected urge, I move to where he sits on the chair and place both hands on his shoulders to adjust their angle. His body tenses. Despite my inner voice telling me not to, I reach out to lift his chin, turning it toward me. Cassian's eyes never leave mine. I hesitate, close enough to feel his breath tickling my face.

A slow smile tugs on his lips. "Careful, Wildflower. If you play with fire, you're bound to get burned."

My breath catches. I drop my hand. As I turn away, the cool metal of his rings chills my skin, his hand finding mine.

"Why do you do that?" he asks, searching my face for answers. "Pull away just when I think you're about to be honest with me."

A soft laugh slips past my lips. "Same reason you do—to protect myself."

He tugs me closer, lips inches from mine. "What are you so afraid of?"

I hold my breath. There's power in his gaze, an intense vulnerability that threatens to pull me in and unravel me, all at once. Every fiber of my being tells me to lean forward, to press my lips to his and abandon my fears. His fingers thread through mine, moonlight shimmering off my ring.

I gasp. The image of our hands intertwined, my arrow ring glowing in the night, is the perfect replica of one of my visions. And the very fate I've been trying to avoid.

I unclasp his fingers from mine and set his hand on his lap. My touch lingers. "I'm afraid of many things. But that's for another time."

He watches me as I return to the easel, a puzzled expression on his face. With precise motions, I resume the painting and attempt to quiet my mind, separating from my emotions so I don't fixate on Cassian's features.

The rest passes in a blur, my heart pounding so loud in my ears I'm sure Cassian can hear it amidst the silence. As I paint the final details, I eagerly let my fated skill wash over me, drowning out the beating of my heart.

I'm at a dinner—royals clad in bronze and green sitting around me. Cassian is at the head of the table, a pale-haired woman by his side. He raises his goblet to say a toast when the vision ripples into another one.

Cassian's hand stretches toward a woman in a ruby gown. Her face is blurred, the details distorted as if looking at her under water. I squint at her familiar face, though it's like trying to open my eyes while dreaming, the scene only getting blurrier. Then, with a voice I instantly recognize as my own, she agrees to a deal, shaking Cassian's hand.

Shocked by the sight of me striking another deal with the prince, I lose my grip on the vision. I fight to stay in the moment, but the current of my skill takes me away until the image of Cassian fidgeting in his chair swims into focus. He slides one of his rings off and back on again, lost in thought.

For a minute, I'm transfixed, our future deal looping through my mind as I search for a reason. No logical answer emerges. I bite my cheek, forcing my thoughts back to my other vision. "Whatever you did today changed your future."

He sits upright with an expectant grin. "Really?"

I grimace, knowing it hasn't changed in the way he hopes. "Just not enough to eliminate a betrothal."

A muscle pulses along Cassian's jawline. "Why? What did you see?"

For the first time, I hesitate before revealing my vision, guilt pooling in my stomach as I prepare to reveal only half the truth. "You were about to give a toast during a meal. A pale-haired woman was sitting next to you. She looked Corvican."

"Corvican?"

"She and the other guests wore green and bronze."

Cassian stares down at his hands, fingers clenching and unclenching in his lap. The rest of my vision sits on the tip of my tongue, begging to be told.

What would he say if he knew?

My lips part, heart pounding in anticipation of telling him. But then he stands, running his hand through his jet-black hair. I press my lips together and close my eyes at my cowardice.

"I should let you get some sleep, Wildflower," he says, a rough edge to his voice that hints at disappointment.

"I'm sorry it wasn't enough, Cassian."

His blue eyes find mine in the dimly lit room, the earlier warmth dispersing into a hopeless gray. "Me too."

He walks past, and a shiver runs through me at the slight brush of his arm against mine. As the door closes after him, a surprising emptiness settles over me. If my heart weren't still beating in my chest, I'd think it left the room with him.

My lungs empty with a long sigh, and I stare up at the ceiling. Our fates are so entangled it will be all but impossible to undo— if I still want to untangle them at all.

Eden

A knock at the door jolts me awake the next morning. With a measly attempt to smooth my hair, I throw on a robe and answer it. A servant girl around my age stands on the other side. Her blonde hair is bound neatly at the nape of her neck, and an apron is tied over her dress.

"Good morning, Miss Asher. His Royal Highness, Prince Cassian, summons you to the studio for a portrait session. My name is Eliana. I will accompany you and assist with setting up."

I stare dumbfounded, trying to process her words through the haze of inadequate sleep. "I'll get ready. But your assistance isn't necessary."

"My apologies for the confusion, Miss Asher. Prince Cassian assigned me to you himself, and I intend to obey his instruction."

With a curt nod, I shut the door, throw on the first dress I find, and follow Eliana to the studio. My fingers deftly braid my tangled brown hair as we walk, drawing several strange looks from servants as we pass by. I tie it off just as the studio doors open.

"Good morning, Miss Asher." Cassian gives me a lazy grin. "I hope you had a restful sleep full of sweet dreams."

He drapes his arms over the studio chair, clasping his ring-studded hands. The leisurely pose contradicts his distinguished appearance. His black hair is neatly swept back, except for a few rebellious strands that soften the look. A simple silver crown rests on top, matching the silver details on his striking blue doublet. They shine against the deep velvet fabric like stars in the night sky.

Has he always looked this dashing?

I run a hand over my hair, suddenly wishing I'd spent more time on my appearance, even if it meant making him wait longer. "I wasn't expecting such an early morning portrait, Your Royal Highness." I busy myself with my paints while Eliana skillfully prepares the easel and canvas.

"It's at the king's behest, not mine. I could've used a bit more beauty sleep."

My eyebrows raise. *More beauty sleep? If he gets any more beautiful, I'm in trouble.*

I fight the blush rising on my cheeks, and turn to Eliana, intending to dismiss her when I pause—having an audience might keep my emotions in check.

I spin back around.

Out of the corner of my eye, I catch a quizzical look on Cassian's face as I brush paint across the canvas. I prepare for him to comment on the hideous color of the underpainting.

Except Cassian's words surprise me.

"Thank you, Eliana, for your assistance. You're dismissed until Eden completes the painting."

Curtsying, Eliana swiftly exits the studio, leaving me alone with Cassian. Though we've been alone many times, my stomach flips in spite of itself. But to my surprise, Cassian remains silent, on his best behavior while I paint.

"Is the servant really necessary?" I ask finally, curiosity getting the better of me.

"You said the others wouldn't help you, so I found one who would. You're welcome."

"When did you even find the time?"

"I have my ways, Wildflower." The nickname rolls easily off his tongue, all malice from the first time he said it now replaced with a peculiar fondness.

I wrinkle my nose, annoyed I even noticed such a minor detail.

"You still hate it, don't you?" Cassian asks, his usual charm tainted with disappointment.

My brush stills and I'm filled with a sudden clarity. Despite the circumstances of its inception, I don't hate the nickname. At some point, I grew quite fond of it—a pleasant prickle crawling over my skin each time Cassian uses it.

"I don't. At least, not anymore." I meet his gaze, wanting him to know I mean it.

"I had no idea when I first called you that, how accurate it would be."

Our conversation replays in my mind. His tortured expression is seared into my brain, a memory I don't want to forget.

Several hours later, my eyes roam the canvas, searching the finished portrait for any flaws. Cassian now watches over my shoulder, his steadfast gaze making me nervous.

"And I suppose you have an opinion as well?" I ask.

He leans forward, pointing to a specific spot. "This here needs fixing."

I squint, examining the area he's gesturing to, but everything looks perfect. "I don't see—"

My words stop short when Cassian touches the canvas, his finger smearing the still-wet oil paint.

"Cassian!" The name bursts out before I can stop myself. Formalities forgotten, I glare at him.

He raises a brow, his mouth curving into that insufferable half-smile.

I quickly compose myself, remembering my renewed vow to keep my distance. "I apologize, Your Royal Highness," I correct, forcing the title out. "I was simply surprised by your... interference with my work."

Cassian's laugh is quiet but clear. His relaxed demeanor gnaws at me, as if he didn't just ruin a portrait that took hours.

"Have you no respect for my craft?" I snap.

His smile fades, replaced with a sincerity I hadn't expected. "Of course I do. I'm sorry, Eden."

Hearing my name from his lips quells my sudden anger. His gaze, as cold and piercing as ever, locks onto mine. For a moment, it's as though he's seeing more than I want to show. I tear my eyes away, unnerved by how easily he affects me.

"Perhaps," he says, his voice a murmur just for me, "I wasn't ready for the portrait to be over."

My skin tingles. His words are laden with a meaning I don't dare acknowledge—one that feels more real in the light of day. Some small part of me is relieved, validated in knowing he meant what he said last night. His confession wasn't just a product of the day's events and the romantic moonlight glow. But I stop myself before my emotions entangle me further. I refuse to let him charm me, to let the future I've seen come to pass.

Cassian watches me closely, waiting for me to respond.

I grab my paint palette and dip my brush into the correct shade to repair the damage. "You ruined it," I say, my tone challenging, "so you must fix it."

I extend the brush toward him.

His head jolts back, and he recoils, holding up both hands in defense. "I don't know how to paint! That's what I hired *you* for!"

"Then now is the perfect time to learn," I reply, meeting his gaze with a smirk of my own—a mirror of his usual expression.

He hesitates, staring at the brush as if considering my offer. Then he chuckles, shaking his head. "The portrait would be beyond repair if I tried."

I hold my ground. "I'm not asking," I insist, still holding the brush out to him.

He looks at me, amusement dancing in his ice-blue eyes. After several long moments, he reaches out, taking the brush. "Show me what to do, Wildflower."

Gently, I position the brush in his hands. "Unlike your swords, a paintbrush is a delicate, finicky thing. You must hold it firmly to apply pressure to the canvas, but not so tight that your hand shakes."

He presses his lips together, brows furrowed in concentration as he touches the brush to the canvas. I try not to laugh at his comically intense focus. With a painfully slow movement, he swipes the paint across the ruined spot, leaving a defined line on the portrait.

Cassian panics. "I told you I'd ruin it!"

Laughter bubbles out of me, startling the horrified look right off his face.

"What?" he asks, my laughter making him smile.

"Who knew you'd give up so easily, Princeling?"

"You really trust me to keep painting?"

"With my help, I do." I point to the canvas. "Put your paintbrush back up there."

He does as he's told, and I place my hand over his. With circular movements, we blend the line into the rest of the painting to seamlessly cover the flaw.

"It just takes patience and a careful touch," I say.

Cassian stares down at our hands.

I let go, realizing my mistake. "Well, uh, it's almost done," I stammer. "A portrait of this level will show me more than I could see last night. You *do* want to know your future again, right?"

"Not the future," he says softly. "Just you."

I fumble for a reply, shocked by his continued honesty. "Me?"

"It's not fair you get glimpses of my future all the time, but I hardly know anything about you." He holds out the paintbrush. "So, Eden Asher, tell me a secret."

I reach for the brush, but my fingers pause just before touching his. "There's not much to tell."

"I don't believe that," he says. "Not for a second."

His gaze conveys an unexpected warmth, a sincerity that breaks through my defenses. Our fingers graze as I take the brush from his hand. My pulse flutters.

He leans in. "Why are you afraid of heights?"

Cold floods through me. I shudder involuntarily, a sour taste in my mouth. I try to swallow.

"My mother," I say. "She… She fell to her death."

Cassian freezes, his expression changing instantly. "Eden… I'm so sorry. I didn't know."

I nod, trying to keep the image from rising. It presses forward anyway, the horror of her crumpled body flashing through my mind like it was yesterday. I blink fast, but my eyes burn.

Cassian reaches for me, slowly, as if he's not sure how much space I need. Then, his arms wrap around me, and I don't pull away. His warmth is grounding, the scent of thyme and leather comforting my frayed nerves. I let myself lean into him.

"She died when I was ten."

"So young," he murmurs.

Something about the way he holds me, the tenderness in his tone, draws the full truth from me.

"It was my fault." My voice cracks.

Cassian pulls back enough to see my face, brows furrowed. "What do you mean?"

"I saw it happen," I whisper. "It was my first vision. The next day she was gone, and I couldn't stop it."

His eyes widen. "Eden…"

"I told her, but I don't know if she believed me. I should've said more. Maybe she would still be alive."

Cassian shakes his head. "You were ten. Ten. You had no way of knowing it would actually happen. You didn't cause what happened to her."

"But I saw it and couldn't change it. I was useless."

He reaches up, brushing a tear from my cheek with the backs of his fingers. "You were a child," he says. "A terrified little girl with a gift no one could've expected. What happened wasn't your fault, Eden. Not even close."

His words wrap around me, words I never knew I needed to hear.

"You don't understand how many times I've replayed that vision," I confess. "It haunts me."

Cassian leans in, forehead gently pressing to mine. "Then don't let it. You are so much stronger than you realize, Eden. You don't have to keep carrying that guilt."

My breath catches. I meet his gaze, feeling seen in a way I haven't for some time. His hands are warm against my arms, grounding me in the moment. I draw back, eyes dropping to his lips, heart pounding.

Tentatively, I lift my hand to his jaw, tracing the familiar line I've memorized from every painting. His breath hitches, and mine follows.

And then the door bursts open.

We jump apart.

King Leopold stalks into the room, his expression one of fury.

"So, this is how you spend your painting sessions, is it?"

Cassian's demeanor shifts immediately. His muscles tense, face growing vacant. He stares at the ground, cowering in front of his father like a scorned child.

"Speak, boy!" the king roars.

"No, Father. It's not what it looks like."

"Oh? And how is that? After your display in the Great Hall yesterday, I don't see how it couldn't be. She was worth destroying your potential betrothal and bringing shame to your grandparents. This painter," the king looks at me with disdain, "clearly means *something* to you."

"No."

The word is sharp and decisive. I try to meet Cassian's eyes, to gauge whether he means what he says, but he refuses to look at me.

"She means nothing to me, Father. I swear."

My eyes sting, but I hold back my tears.

The king sneers. "Your words are hollow. Whatever she is to you is over now. There will be no more fun and games with the help."

The king's words feel like a slap to the face. It's as if I'm nothing more than a lowly plaything for the prince.

"It's unbecoming of the future king, especially for someone soon to be engaged. Start spending your time with people more befitting of royalty." The king points to the door. "Now, go. I'll deal with you later."

Cassian does as he's told, fleeing the room without so much as a glance in my direction. King Leopold walks closer, his previous rage replaced with an eerie calm. I fight the urge to retreat.

His hand settles gently on my shoulder, chilling blue eyes pinning me in place. A strange pressure pulses at my temples, like something unseen is pressing inward. My body tenses. Every instinct screams at me to run. But I'm held captive by his presence.

I don't dare defy the king.

And then, the feeling vanishes. His hand lifts from my shoulder, his attention shifting to the portrait.

"You're a talented painter, Miss Asher." A smug smile forms across his stony face. "Stick to what you're good at."

My hand feels empty without the familiar weight of my ring. I curl my fist, trying for the thousandth time to recall where I last had it.

In two weeks, Father's dragged me to more places than I can count, keeping me busy with his ridiculous tests. Ever since my grandparents cut their visit short, he's been relentless. Eden's portrait barely dried before he sent it off to Corvica, and of course, they responded with unnatural speed, eager to discuss terms in person. Now Father is intent on ensuring I don't ruin yet another betrothal.

A wave of shame crashes over me. But not about the betrothal—about the way I left things with Eden.

Habitually, I move to spin my ring, forgetting its disappearance once more. I sigh and internally vow to scour my room again in hopes of finding it. Perhaps I'll have enough time to pay Eden a visit as well. It will put my mind at ease to reassure her I didn't mean what I said.

"Cassian."

My father's voice cuts through my thoughts, drawing me back to the board meeting. I sit up straight. "Yes, Your Majesty?"

"I asked you how the preparations for the Corvican's visit are going? We wouldn't want a repeat of last time."

I bite my tongue and force a smile. "Good, Your Majesty. Lorenzo has been diligent in refreshing my memory on their customs and traditions as of late."

"Enlighten me."

I fold my hands in front of me. Farion gives an encouraging nod from across the table. The other nobles eye me expectantly.

"The Corvicans pride themselves on their physical prowess, mastering the art of swordsmanship and combat at an early age," I say. "They are manual laborers—a majority of the population blessed with physical abilities."

Disgust darkens my father's face. "I hope your tutor has taught you more than basic concepts even a child would know."

Farion catches my eye, subtly tapping his ring finger as a reminder of my betrothed. I clear my throat.

"Yes, Your Majesty. King Valter's grandfather led the charge against the Divinians. His inhuman strength in combat secured the victory over the encroaching darkness of the Fateless kingdom. His daughter, Isabel, follows in her great grandfather's footsteps. She is a fierce warrior with the ability to perceive an enemy's next move before it happens. Her fated skill is a harmonious blend of Corvican and Menteran, making her an excellent candidate for our future queen."

Farion nods in approval and I turn to the king. A slow grin spreads across his face.

"So you *have* been listening. Isabel's skill is a close-kept secret only those deemed worthy know. As is yours." He gives me a pointed look. "She shall not know about your skill until a ring is on her finger, understand?"

I nod. "Yes, Your Majesty. Our skills are advantageous only when kept secret."

A secret I've already shared.

Eden's face appears in my mind, her delicate features marred by disdain when I told her about my skill. Somehow, in mere seconds, she cut through the walls of pride I spent years building. Instead of envying me or falling at my feet in wonder, Eden was disappointed—disgusted, even. To her, my talent is not something to revel in. And I haven't seen my skill the same since.

The king regards me with calculated interest. I fight to keep my collected facade, not wanting him to catch on to my thoughts. If he knew I told her, he'd be furious. But before he can say another word, the doors creak open.

It's Lyra.

She curtsies politely. Her amber eyes find mine from across the room. "Apologies for the interruption, gentleman, but the queen requests the prince's presence."

Father narrows his eyes at his daughter.

"I wouldn't keep her waiting long," Lyra adds, unwavering under his scrutiny.

Relieved to get out of the board meeting, I stand with a bow and follow my sister out of the room. The telltale clank of Silas's armor is close behind as I trail after her down the hall. Only once we turn the corner do I speak.

"Did Mother really send for me?"

Lyra grins. "No. I just know how busy you've been and assumed you could use a break.

My shoulders sag with relief. "Have I told you that you're the best sister ever?"

She stops, dramatically turning to face me. "I'm sorry, could you repeat that?"

"Always a sucker for compliments." I shake my head, chuckling under my breath.

Lyra puts her hands on her hips. "Watch what you say, dear brother, or I will waltz you right back into that meeting."

I hold up my hands in surrender. "That won't be necessary. I will gladly say you're the best sister however many times you'd like."

"Just once is good. I already know I'm your favorite, even if you rarely admit it with words." She loops her arm through mine, tugging us down the hall once more.

Grinning, I walk in step with my sister, aimlessly following her lead. After the countless tutoring sessions and surprise check-ins from my father, it's nice *not* to think for once.

"How are things with Eden?"

Lyra's question makes my stomach drop. "I'm not sure what you mean," I hedge.

"Cassian, you can't possibly think I haven't heard about the ladder incident."

The ladder incident? Is that what they're calling it now?

"Ever since, you've been brooding more than normal."

"Brooding?" I question, looking back at Silas for support.

He simply shrugs, unable to hide his amused expression.

I turn back to my sister with a huff.

"Yes. Brooding." She purses her lips. "Now, don't feign ignorance with me. I could tell you liked her from the moment you hired her as our court artist."

I sigh. Nothing gets past my sister's keen eyes. Unsure what to say, I let my moments with Eden play through my mind. An unbidden smile stretches further across my face with each one, until my heart constricts at the thought of my parting words. *She means nothing to me.* I close my eyes against the memory.

"Fine, don't tell me," Lyra says, mistaking my uncertainty for unwillingness. "But if it's any consolation, Eden is just as melancholy."

My head snaps toward Lyra. She grins at my sudden interest, leaning close.

"She's painting in the studio," Lyra whispers. "I'm sure she wouldn't mind a visitor."

My gaze flicks back to Silas. "Any chance you can help me lose my perpetual tail?"

Lyra's amber eyes shine with glee. "Hoping for some alone time with Eden?"

Heat crawls up my neck at the thought, but I remain silent. However appealing that may sound, I have other plans in mind— plans my sister doesn't need to know.

She takes my silence for affirmation, patting my arm with a devious grin before strutting toward Silas. I follow her lead, walking back to where he stands in the hall. As she latches onto him, I edge my way out of his view, and bolt around the corner.

Silas's frustrated sigh echoes after me, but I'm already too far gone for him to catch up. And I expect he won't know where I'm headed. It's the only place I have yet to search for my ring.

The door handle turns with ease, thankfully not locked. I shake my head at Eden's trusting behavior and slip quietly into her room. It looks almost the same as it did two weeks ago. Her bed is neatly made, a notebook on her bedside table the only item out of place. It's open to a specific page, a familiar portrait watching me approach—mine.

The thought of Eden staring at my portrait makes my heart skip. I flip through several pages, admiring the variety of paintings and sketches throughout. Turning back to my portrait, another nearby notebook catches my attention. It's the same one Eden held the day we sparred. Curiosity getting the better of me, I open the journal to find pages of swirling script.

Eden's diary?

Thumbing through it, I notice the dates atop each page are old. I find the latest entry and read a small snippet. It isn't Eden's journal—it's her mother's.

I shouldn't be prying into something so personal.

But as I go to close it, a word roots me to the spot.

Farion.

What would Eden's mother have to do with Farion?

With a quick glance at the door, I begin to decipher the cursive, silently promising to read only this entry. But all I catch is the mention of a portrait session before footsteps approach.

Frantically placing the journal where I found it, I scan the room for a place to hide. Under the bed?

I crouch down to assess.

Too small.

Behind the door?

Too risky.

I turn to the window, noticing the excessively draped curtains.

That'll have to do.

Wrapping myself in the thick fabric, I will my heart to beat quieter as the door to Eden's room opens.

"It's fine, Eliana," Eden says, her voice growing louder as she approaches my hiding spot. "I just need to grab something. It'll be perfect for what I'm trying to paint."

I hold my breath, listening as she rustles through a drawer nearby. Being so close but unable to say anything is torture. My fingers graze the velvet drapes, itching to push them aside—to catch a glimpse of Eden. But I'd rather not explain why I'm hiding in her room.

"Found it!" she says triumphantly, the curtains moving as she walks past.

When the door closes, I suck air into my lungs, unraveling myself from the suffocating drapery. *Search for your ring, and then get out*, I remind myself, heart still pounding from the unexpected encounter.

After several hurried minutes of searching with no luck, I decide to leave before Eden comes back again. As much as I'd like to visit her in the studio, there's something else I need to do first.

"Finished so soon with the queen?" Farion stands from his writing desk, lips curving into a knowing smile. "To what do I owe the pleasure of the prince's company?"

"You make it sound as if I never visit," I say as I enter, casually eyeing the space. Though I've been here many times, it's as if I'm seeing it anew. The large portrait on the wall immediately stands out.

"Lately, you haven't." Farion motions me toward the immaculate sitting area.

I sprawl across the couch, knocking a pillow onto the floor and earning a disgraced look from Farion. Everything in his room has its place. His perfectionism is what makes him such a good Ascended One. Grabbing the pillow, I set it back in its rightful spot. "There. Perfect once more."

Farion shakes his head at me. "Speaking of perfection."

"Not this again." I bury my head in my hands.

"You have yet to become a Morphi."

"As you like to remind me frequently," I mumble.

"I'm only looking out for you, Cassian. Ascending is a necessary step to becoming king."

"It's not that easy."

"But it could be." Farion leans forward in his chair. "You simply need to prioritize using your skill."

I sit up. "Trust me, I do. These days my emotions just get in the way. With my father always over my shoulder, I only make it through the day when I use my skill."

"Not solely on yourself—on others."

"Why?" I argue.

Farion's gray eyes flash with irritation before his usual poised demeanor returns. He runs a hand over his manicured beard. "What's changed? You never questioned it before."

The blank faces of Lorenzo and Silas surface in my mind, their soulless eyes haunting me. Before Eden, I didn't think twice about using my skill. But her visceral reaction to it has changed me more than I realized.

But I don't dare say that aloud. Instead, I stand in front of Farion's portrait, staring at the swirling signature in the corner—Adelaide Asher.

It's clear where Eden gets her artistic talent from. Farion's portrait is exquisite. The longer I stare, the more I notice how little his likeness has changed in all this time. He still has the same salt and pepper hair, his face surprisingly youthful for his age. But what really unsettles me is the look in his eyes. Just like Eden, her mother captured Farion's essence through his gaze—the slight wrinkles at the corners unable to hide the cunning gleam in the colorless gray orbs.

"Magnificent, isn't it?" Farion stands beside me, his sudden proximity shocking me out of my intense focus.

"You haven't changed," I remark. "How do you manage it, running the Mimicry and all?"

He regards the portrait thoughtfully. "Perspective."

His response clicks into place like the last piece of a puzzle. I've known for some time my views have shifted. And now I realize it's all thanks to a new perspective in my life, one untainted by royal life.

Farion turns toward me, interrupting my revelation. "But not all perspectives are helpful." His stare cuts through me and I feel exposed, as if he can read my thoughts. "Something you seem to be experiencing now."

I swallow my nerves and give him a wry grin. "I'm glad you agree your perspectives can be unhelpful, Farion."

He is unamused, my attempt at humor falling flat.

"Cassian." Farion's tone is serious, brows drawn low over his eyes. "I told you growing close to her would be a mistake."

Sweat prickles my palms. "With who?"

"Miss Asher."

My mouth goes dry.

"She may bring a new perspective to your life, one that feels foreign and exciting, but it is not one a king should pay heed to. Distance yourself from her before she unravels you further." He stares at the balcony with a faraway look. "If she is not dealt with, your future could be ruined."

A future I've never wanted.

I follow his gaze, staring through the ornate doors at the view of Scintillia below. A whispered idea forms in my mind, and I glance back at the painting. Eden said her mother fell to her death. And the last entry in her diary was before a portrait session with Farion.

Could Farion have killed her?

I shove the thought away as quickly as it forms. It's absurd. Though cunning, Farion would never do such a thing. He's more my father than the king, always showing me kindness and understanding. Raking a hand through my hair, I thank Farion for his advice and hastily part ways.

But not before I look once more at his balcony. The thought of Eden's mother hurtling to her death sends a chill up my spine.

Paint swirls in the jar, overtaking the turpentine's clarity like the thoughts muddying my mind. It's been two weeks since I painted Cassian's portrait and yet I can't stop thinking about him. I make myself sick, wanting someone so impossibly out of my reach.

I jam the brush against the bottom of the jar with force, sending another stormy gray tendril coiling to the surface. Each plume of paint purged from the brush is like a thought freed from my mind.

"Miss Asher, you're ruining the brush," Eliana chirps, her face pinched with worry as she leans closer.

I blink, noticing the turpentine is now a dreary brown. The brush's drowned form drips into the jar as I lift it, hairs bent and frayed—a visual representation of my nerves since the king's scolding.

"Sorry," I mutter, dropping the paintbrush back into the murky depths.

Eliana takes over, cleaning the rest of the brushes. I collapse into a chair and study my latest work—the Menteran shoreline commissioned by one of the nobles. It turned out nice. Less refined than my usual paintings, but that's only from a lack of practice. Landscapes aren't my specialty, but of course, no one in the palace knows that—except Cassian.

There I go again. Cassian, Cassian, Cassian.

I groan into my hands.

"Are you alright, Miss Asher?"

"I told you, Eliana, please call me Eden."

She smiles politely. "Sorry, Miss—Eden."

I contemplate what to tell her as I wipe my hands on the rough fabric of my apron. I don't want to confess I'm falling for someone I can't have—someone I barely know. "I've been under some stress lately, is all. I appreciate your concern. You've been an immense help these past weeks."

"After the last kingdom's visit, it's only natural to stress over the Corvicans' impending stay."

My head jerks up. "The Corvicans are coming?"

"Oh, I assumed you'd heard, given how close you seemed with His Royal Highness."

I grimace, folding my arms over my chest. "Right."

Eliana senses my discomfort. In her haste to apologize, she knocks over the jar of turpentine, a dark pool of solvent spreading over the table. I jump to my feet, grabbing the nearest paint rags to assist in the cleanup. Together, we slowly eliminate the mess. But the table is still slick with oil, its surface impacted by only a seconds-long encounter.

Like Cassian's impact on me. The feeling of his body pressed to mine atop the ladder flits through my mind. In that moment, I knew he'd affected me in a way I couldn't describe.

I shake my head to clear my thoughts and accidentally run my sopping rag straight into Eliana. Solvent runs down her arm, covering her fatemark with an oily sheen. *What could her skill be?* But the question remains unspoken, silenced by the sight of her fatemark dissolving off her wrist.

I stumble backward, my hand shaking as I point at the fading mark. Our eyes lock. Then she grabs a rag and covers her wrist, stepping back.

"Eliana, what was that? Are you okay?"

She shudders, lips pressed tight to suppress a sob.

"Please, you can't tell anyone," she whimpers.

My heart sinks. "Tell anyone what?"

She remains silent as she wraps the rag around her arm.

"Are… Are you a Fateless?" I stammer, fearful of her answer.

The word spurs her into action. "I beg of you, please don't turn me in," she pleads, a tear sliding down her cheek. "You know what they'll do to me."

I picture her beaten and bruised, paraded in front of a crowd before being publicly executed. The kingdoms are not kind to Fateless. They are our enemy. Those born without a skill are tied to the darkness and cursed by Delayon—a threat to our way of life.

But I see no threat in her glistening hazel eyes.

Don't believe everything you're told. My mother's words drift back to me, crisp amidst the fog of memory. *Just because someone is different, doesn't make them any less worthy—any less human.*

The memory of her voice, melodic in my ears, gives me the clarity I need. "I won't," I whisper. "I promise."

Eliana falls to the ground at my feet, clutching at my ruby skirts. "Thank you, Miss Asher. Thank you."

I crouch beside her, wrapping her into an embrace. "There's nothing to thank me for. You are no less worthy of a beautiful life than I am. I could never take that from you."

She's sobbing now, her body sagging against me. "I should've known to trust Delayon. He told me you were special."

Goosebumps tingle up my arms, my hairs standing on end. *Delayon told her? No one has ever described such an intimate relationship with our Creator.*

"Eliana, what do you mean, Delayon *told* you?"

She pulls away and wipes the tears from her face. "Oh, I don't mean audibly." Her hand covers her heart. "I mean in here. I get these impressions, these feelings, and I just know it's Him. It's hard to explain."

I wrap my arms around myself, still feeling a chill. Eliana's words send questions buzzing through my mind. But for some reason, I can't bring myself to ask.

As I enter my room, my mother's words still echo in my mind. Longing to hear her speak again, even if only through words on a page, I grab her journal from my bedside table. Its haphazard position makes me hesitate. *Did I leave it like this?*

A chill runs down my spine. I haven't even opened the journal since my dad gave it to me. There's no way I left it like that. I survey my room, looking for other items out of place. But there are none. Breathing deep, I push aside my paranoia and flop into the chair by the window.

The one Cassian sits in for our late-night portraits.

I smack my hand against my forehead. "Stop thinking about him!"

Shifting in the seat, I attempt to get comfortable, but something prevents me from doing so. I reach between the chair and my leg, shoving aside the fabric of my dress. But it's not my skirts causing the issue. Cold metal chills my fingers.

Cassian's ring.

Despite my better judgment, I slip it onto my thumb, its weight a reassuring presence. The ring is still a bit big, and I spin it on my finger. It's a relaxing sensation. I understand why Cassian does the same when he wears it.

Could he be the one who came to my room?

My heart skips a beat at the thought. I look around once more for any sign of him, my eye catching on the curtain to the right of the chair. Its usual elegant folds appear disturbed. Strange.

I settle back into the chair, dismissing all thoughts of Cassian as I open my mother's journal. Her swirling script is comforting, each page detailing painting sessions and daily activities. Scrawled throughout, I find her wisdom like bits of buried treasure. For each painting session recorded, I notice a pattern—she often left a poem hidden in the frame of each one.

Hope swells in my chest, and I rush over to the unfinished painting hanging in my room. Carefully lifting it off its hook, I turn it around and run my hand along the wooden frame. There, on the bottom right, I find a small piece of paper nestled between the frame and the canvas. Without her journal, I never would've noticed it.

Excitement buzzes through me as I eagerly unfold the paper, mindful not to rip it. Written on the yellowed slip is a poem.

> From the very beginning, it was love at first sight,
> But the thought of losing you gave me such a fright,
> So I guarded my heart,
> Thinking I was smart,
> Until I could no longer refute,
> My feelings were absolute.
> Meeting you was a sign,
> Fateless or not, you were fated to be mine.
> I'm forever grateful to be your wife,
> Blessed to be living such a beautiful life.

The last two lines blur together, one word making my blood run cold.

Fateless.

I reread the poem, hoping I missed something that will quell my growing fears. But it's clear my mother wrote this for my dad. Could he really be a Fateless? I return to the journal, scouring the pages for mentions of my dad. The first one I find is embedded in an entry about the painting of a merchant.

His eyes still follow me, as if I painted them onto my mind instead of the canvas. He should've been happy, having hired me to commemorate his ascension as a Morphi. But there was no joy in his gaze, only an unsettling emptiness like he lost something. Maybe Aldo is right. Our fated skills might be more dangerous than we realize.

Her words are reminiscent of things Dad has said to me—always worried about me using my skill. But that's not enough to confirm he's Fateless. I flip through the pages, finding several more mentions of my dad warning mother about using her skill. Each time, she brushes it off, justifying her choice by claiming it's what's best for her family.

And the more I read, the deeper the doubts take root. I keep looking, not knowing how many more entries I must read for reality to sink in. But the journal ends, her last entry stealing the breath from my lungs.

Eden found her skill today.

The room blurs as that moment flashes through my mind like a waking nightmare. But I can't stop reading, wanting nothing more than to escape my perspective of that day, to view it through the eyes of the person I admired most. It may finally set me free from my guilt.

She's a painter, like me, and her skill is just as powerful, if not more so. But her vision today scared me. And I made her a promise I'm not sure I can keep. But how do you tell a ten-year-old that you can't promise not to die? It's a fate none of us can escape.

When I told Aldo, he was angry, saying he knew I shouldn't have taught her to paint. As if he knew she'd be an artist just like me! But we both knew this day would come—the day one of our children found their skill. Aldo and I have always had different perspectives on the matter, but now we must decide which one we will instill in our children.

But if Eden's vision is accurate, I might not live long enough for it to matter. I can only hope she wasn't. She's only just discovered her ability, after all.

I slam the journal closed, hot tears making the rest of the entry unreadable. My breathing grows shallow, chest tightening as my emotions build. The walls close in around me and I feel suffocated. I need to get out of here. To be far away from this painting and the reality of this poem. To forget what my mother wrote, if only for a little while.

With no destination in mind, I flee my room, heading aimlessly down the hall. But even here, my panic follows me like a wolf hunting its prey.

I clutch my chest, trying to keep my tears at bay.

My dad is a Fateless. He's been lying to me my whole life.

My thoughts run wild and a lone tear escapes. I stumble down another hall.

My mother lied too. She knew. And neither of them trusted me enough to say anything.

I suppress a sob, steadying myself against the wall. The labyrinth of palace corridors is disorienting. Vision blurred, I walk faster, searching desperately for a way out.

"Miss, are you alright?" A boy swims into focus, his youthful face wrinkled with worry.

His unexpected kindness sends me over the edge, my tears spilling over uncontrollably. "No. I'm sorry. Please help me get out of here," I plead, not caring how disgraceful my behavior is.

He takes my hand, his touch gentle, and leads me through a small side door. We descend a narrow stairwell and take a right, toward a hall that ends with a set of ornate glass doors.

"Here, Miss. The gardens always help me clear my head when I've had a long day."

"Thank you," I whisper, already feeling lighter at the promise of fresh air.

He nods wordlessly, heading back the way we came as I step through the doors. The sun is warm on my skin, and I can finally breathe. But the ache in my throat is yet to leave. I search the gardens for a place to cry in peace, and spot a tall hedge maze a few steps to my right. A peaceful fountain sits at its center. It's perfect.

It doesn't take long to find my way to the middle, the trickling sound of water guiding me easily through the maze. My tears feel further away, the fresh air and sunshine easing my tension.

Behind the fountain is a gazebo, embellished with flowering vines. As I walk closer, a shadow takes shape through the fountain's flowing waters. Curious who else is out here, I tentatively continue, stopping short as the person materializes in front of me.

Cassian.

He stands inside the gazebo, arms resting on the railing as he stares into the distance. I'm grateful his attention is elsewhere. Part of me wants to confront him—to make him understand the power of his words. The other part of me wants to run, knowing the fragile state of my emotions can't handle another rejection, another reminder that I mean nothing to him.

My tension returns and I give in to my fear. Now is not the time to talk to Cassian. But in my hesitation, Cassian turns his head, dark brows raised as he registers my presence.

"Eden?"

I turn on my heel, the sound of his footsteps on the gravel fast approaching.

"Eden!" he calls after me again.

I walk faster, silently berating myself for choosing such a brightly colored dress. The ruby red practically screams, *"Look at me!"* Why couldn't it have been green? Or blue? Maybe then he wouldn't have spotted me so soon.

I hurry toward the exit.

"Wait!" Cassian shouts.

And the maze heeds his command. The hedges shift before my eyes, growing over the exit in seconds and sealing me inside.

Cassian

Eden spins toward me. A grin curls my lips knowing I finally got her attention. But it stops short at the look on her face. She's furious, ablaze in a red gown. Her frustration ripples in my direction, its intensity catching me by surprise.

"Let me out!"

I frown. "What do you mean?"

"I know you did this. Now, let me out."

Her eyes are rimmed with red, as if she's been crying. I step closer. She takes a step back.

"What are you accusing me of?" I grit my teeth at her reaction.

"Trapping me in this maze," Eden replies. "You wanted to talk to me, and of course, the prince *always* gets what he wants."

Her bitter tone grates on my nerves. All my excitement at seeing her is now gone. "Leave if you're so disgusted by my presence!"

She crosses her arms. "And how am I supposed to do that when you sealed off the exit?"

It takes a moment to process her words. But then it clicks. I look to my left and right, inwardly groaning as the maze shifts around us. This can't be good.

"It wasn't me—" I cut myself off as I realize it technically was. "Or at least, not intentionally," I amend.

Eden regards me with a slight tilt of her head.

"The maze feeds off the emotions of its occupants." I watch her reaction closely.

"It's enchanted?"

I nod. "My father designed it to help me practice my skill. The only way out is by calming your emotions."

Eden laughs, a short, biting sound that echoes around us. She throws up her hands in dismay. "That's just great! Exactly what I needed right now."

She spins in a circle, inspecting the maze. As she does, I notice a familiar ring on her thumb, the sunlight reflecting off the engraved silver.

"Is that my ring?"

Eden stops, looking at her hand as if surprised it's on her thumb. Without hesitation, she slides it off and throws it toward me. I barely manage to catch it, not expecting that reaction.

"It fell between the cushion and the side of the chair," she says. "The one place you didn't think to look, huh?"

My stomach drops. *She knows?*

"The journal. And the curtain," Eden explains, correctly interpreting my surprised expression.

I clear my throat. "Sorry."

"No need to apologize. I should know better by now. I mean nothing to you, so why would my privacy? Sneaking into my room is the perfect way to get what you needed without disobeying the king. You wouldn't want to run into the plaything you so gracelessly discarded."

Her words are a knife to my heart, the hurt on her face twisting it further until I feel like throwing up. What I said impacted her more than I realized. And she interpreted my busyness the last two weeks as avoidance.

I curse myself for being such a fool. "Eden, I didn't mean it. And I wasn't avoiding you! With the Corvicans coming, these last—"

"Save it. No more excuses. I don't know if I can trust anything you say anymore."

Eden stalks in the opposite direction, disappearing into the maze. Hollowness spreads through me, though I'm not using my skill. Somehow, I've done it again—proven I'm unworthy of her affection. A chasm of despair threatens to swallow me whole.

And for once, I let it.

I stumble toward the fountain and sit on its edge.

You're not worthy of love. You sabotage everyone you get close to, a voice whispers in my ear. *You can't do anything right. You're a disappointment to the king. To Farion. To your mother.*

To Eden.

I slide the ring off my finger and back on again, but the motion does nothing to calm my nerves. After all my searching, I finally have it back, but it's useless. A sudden wave of rage makes me rip it off my finger and throw it across the center of the maze.

It lands almost soundlessly on the gravel, disappearing among the rocks.

My hand feels empty once more and I immediately regret it. Gravel crunches beneath my feet as I rush forward and drop to the ground, hands skimming the sharp stones in search of the ring. After several panicked seconds, I find it, posture slumping as I slip it over my knuckle. I stay on the ground. The voices in my head grow louder, drowning each other out until I want to scream.

But someone else beats me to it.

I turn toward the source of the frustrated yell, watching Eden emerge into the maze's center once more. She kicks the hedge with another shout of dismay. Her shoe disappears into the greenery, and she drops to the ground, arm wading through the branches to retrieve it.

A breathy laugh rises in my throat. We look absurd. Two adults, sitting on the ground, lost in a maze because we can't control our emotions.

Before long, laughter is bubbling out of me, a maniacal sound that draws her attention. At this moment, I'm grateful I made Silas wait outside the maze.

Eden stands, shoving her shoe back on with a scowl, clearly assuming she's the sole source of my laughter. She stomps toward another path, and I jump to my feet, running toward her, all thoughts abandoned in favor of doing something.

Anything.

"Let me help," I plead.

A piece of hair has escaped her bun, damp with sweat. She peels it off and wipes her brow with the back of her hand. "I don't want your help."

"It's hot. The longer we're out here, the worse it will get. I can help."

"Cassian."

Her use of my name gives me hope.

"You've done enough." She walks past me into the gazebo.

I follow. "I'm sorry, Eden. I really am. Let me make it up to you."

She refuses to look at me. I move closer to where she leans against the railing.

"Just leave me alone, Cassian. I'll figure it out." Eden turns away, heels clicking on the wooden floor as she leaves.

I lunge forward and plant my hand on the post in front of her. She stops, head level with my arm.

"Hear me out. Please?"

Eden turns her head toward me and my pulse jumps.

"I can get us both out of here," I promise. "I just need to use my skill."

Her expression grows cold, and she ducks under my arm, escaping into the maze in a flash of red.

I chase after her. "I know you hate it!" I yell. "But it's the only way. That's the whole reason my father designed this maze."

"And I have faith there's another way out!" She yells back without turning around.

"There's not!"

I catch up, following close behind as she winds through row after row of hedges in search of an exit. Several right turns later, we reach a dead end.

"I told you."

Eden glares daggers at me before walking back the way we came.

"You really want to be stuck in here all day?" I walk behind her, uncertain why I'm still trying.

She doesn't respond.

"At least say something, will you?"

Eden stops abruptly and I barely keep myself from running into her.

"Say what?" She turns to face me. "That I'd rather be stuck in here all day than accept your help? That your words hurt me in a way I can't describe? That back there," she points toward the gazebo, "I dared to believe you would change—that you would apologize and own up to your actions. That maybe, *just maybe,* you'd actually be vulnerable with me?" Her breathing is heavy now, eyes shining with tears. "But no. All you want is to leave the maze, and me, behind."

My heart breaks. "Is that why you were crying earlier? Because of me?"

She lets out a strangled laugh. "Of course you think that. Because everything is always about *you.*"

Eden starts to leave, but I grab her hand. "Wait."

She looks down at our hands with a resigned expression. "I'm done waiting, Cassian. Stop making me stay when you're unwilling to face the truth."

I stare at her hand in mine, fear telling me to let go, to let her walk away. What if I'm vulnerable with her and she thinks I'm weak? If she breaks through my walls again, I'm not sure I'll be strong enough to build them back up. It will leave me exposed.

And yet the thought of losing her feels ten times worse—a piece of my heart missing forever.

I tighten my grip.

She looks at me, a glimmer of hope returning. I pull her into me, wrapping my arms tight around her. "You're right," I whisper into her hair. "It's unfair. All I've done is take from you, Wildflower. It's time I finally give something back."

Her arms, frozen with shock at her sides, now return my embrace. She buries her face in my chest, her breathing hitched from crying. I hold her, my heart still torn in two, knowing some of her tears are because of me. Because of what I've put her through.

"I'm sorry," I murmur. "I'm so sorry."

She sniffles. Her crying slows. And still, I hold her.

"If I'm being honest, you scare the hell out of me, Wildflower."

"I do?" she loosens her grip to look up at me.

"Yeah. You are the opposite of me and everything I aspire to be—bold, free, and undeniably yourself." I cradle her face, brushing a tear away with my thumb. "From the very first time you painted me, I knew you were different. And I haven't been able to stop thinking about you since. You make me feel truly alive."

She looks away, blushing. "Enough about me. You're the one I know nothing about."

I let her go, raking a hand through my hair with a sigh. "Right." I contemplate where to start. "Does your fated skill ever weigh you down? Like it's more of a curse than a gift?"

Something flashes across her face, and I know I hit a nerve. She nods imperceptibly.

"I didn't realize until recently—and with your help—that I've felt this way my whole life. Knowing I'm expected to ascend is such a burden. Why do we have to work ourselves to the bone to prove our worth?"

Eden is silent for several long seconds. "I assumed it was because we must be perfect for Delayon. If he's a perfect creator, we must become a perfect creation. But lately, I'm not so sure. True perfection seems unattainable."

"Exactly. No matter how hard I try, I'll never be perfect. It's impossible. Take my father, for example. He's a Morphi, a supposedly perfect creation, and yet he's anything but." I stare down at the ground, preparing to admit to Eden what I've only ever said to myself. "I don't want to be like him."

"Then don't." Her reply is immediate.

I feel more validated in seconds than I have by some people in years. "It's not that simple."

"Couldn't it be? Traditions can be changed."

Her positive outlook sends a wave of appreciation through me. This is why I can't let her go. She makes me dream—to consider things I didn't think possible.

"Some traditions are easier to change than others," I say.

"One step at a time, then." Eden smiles, wiping the last of her tears. "Sorry, I'm a little emotional."

"Don't apologize. I'm sorry for assuming it was about me. I can be a bit conceited at times," I admit, giving her a rueful grin.

"A bit?"

I shake my head, feeling lighter, like a weight has lifted off my shoulders. "At least I'm self-aware."

"Sometimes."

"I'll work on it," I reply with a smirk. "Starting with a humble request for your help."

Eden raises a brow.

"Search for the exit with me?"

She sighs. "Alright, Princeling." Eden leads the way, and I fall into step beside her.

"So why did you walk into the maze, anyway?" I ask, curious how she ended up here.

"I made an unsettling discovery and needed to clear my head." Eden heads left, trailing her fingers along the greenery as we walk. "And you?"

"You might not believe me, but for the exact same reason."

She turns her head in surprise. "Really? And what did you discover?"

I picture the balcony in Farion's room and the entry in her mother's diary. *Do I tell her?*

Eden senses my hesitation. "There you go again, not wanting to be vulnerable."

My jaw tightens. "It's not that I don't want to tell you. I just don't want to worry you over something that's pure speculation."

Her expression shifts, growing more serious. "I can handle it."

I rub the back of my neck. Telling her means opening a door that can't be closed. She'll want to figure out the truth, and I'm not sure I want to know. What will I do if my theory is true?

"If you're worried I'll think it's ridiculous, don't be." She leans in, her voice softer now. "Even if I do, you won't be seeing me as often, anyway. I hear you'll be engaged soon."

My stomach clenches. "It seems I never had control of my fate, after all."

I feel sick thinking about our time together coming to an end. But without the portraits, there's no need. My father will ensure it. And with the Corvicans arriving soon, even the late-night paintings will be nothing more than a memory.

But not if she needs me for something, I realize. If I know Eden, she'll be determined to uncover the truth herself, a task that's much more doable with my help.

"Did you know your mother painted Farion's portrait the day she died?"

Eden stops walking. "What?"

I clench my fists, questioning whether I made the right decision. "I saw Farion's name in her diary and read the last entry." Eden's silence is heavy. I press on, words coming in a rush, worried she'll walk away before I can finish. "I was curious, so I went to Farion's room to see the painting. At one point, he stared out the balcony with this faraway look on his face and—" I pause, not wanting to tell her what he said.

"And?"

"I had the split-second thought that he could've killed your mother."

Her face grows pale. "Why would you think that?"

I spin my ring. "I don't know. You said your mother fell to her death and the last entry in her diary was before she painted Farion, so I just connected the two."

She purses her lips. "While that's an interesting theory, it's highly unlikely. He's the Ascended One! And my mother's body was found in the marketplace, not the palace grounds."

Heat creeps up my neck. I nod and give a dismissive wave of my hand. "Forget it," I say, resuming our walk through the maze.

"But her body could've been moved," Eden suggests, voice thoughtful. "Tell me more about Farion. Why would he have any reason to kill my mother?"

For several feet I'm silent, gathering my thoughts. Farion has been nothing but a diligent advisor and friend. So why did I have that thought?

"He's a perfectionist," I begin. "And a meticulous planner. It isn't like him to kill without reason."

Eden walks silently beside me. She spins a strand of hair around her finger, processing my words.

"Could it have been an accident?" I ask.

"Then why would he cover it up—move her body and act like it never happened?" She notices my unease. "Assuming he actually did it, that is."

"Right."

We're quiet once more, neither of us having the answers. Another hedge shifts nearby. The idea of Farion being a murderer is clearly unsettling us both. As we walk, I contemplate what reason Farion would have to kill an artist. What would have made her a threat?

"What was your mother's fated skill?"

Eden slows, realization dawning on her face. "She could see the darkest secret of the person she painted."

Despite the heat, I shiver. "And if Farion realized she had knowledge like that, it would be motivation to kill her."

"A secret dark enough to kill for…" Eden murmurs, talking more to herself than me.

Every interaction I've had with Farion is now tainted. The sharp gleam in his eye, once a mark of cunning wit, now seems darker—the gaze of a killer. *What is his secret?*

"You said the portrait is in his room?" Eden's question draws me from my thoughts.

"Yes, why?"

"I'd like to see it."

This is it. This is the reason she would need me.

"Alright, but you'll need my help to get into his room. What are you hoping to gain from seeing it?"

"Her last words," she says.

I freeze, momentarily falling behind. When the shock wears off, I have to pick up my pace to catch up to where she's taking the next left in the maze. "What do her last words have to do with the painting?"

"That was part of my revelation today," Eden says. "I found out she hides poems in the frames of her paintings. She might have left one in Farion's portrait, too."

"And if she did, they would be her last words," I finish for her.

"It's worth looking." Eden locks eyes with me, gaze steady. "Will you help me?"

"I know you, Wildflower. If I don't, you'll try it anyway."

She tilts her head. "True. But with your help, I'm much less likely to get caught."

"And I have the perfect idea." I hold out my hand.

"Which is?"

"The Corvican dinner. Farion will be there, and his room will be empty. I'll ensure it's unlocked and his attention is elsewhere."

She shakes my hand. "A deal it is, then."

Our hands linger, neither of us quite willing to let go. My pulse thrums in my ears. The first time we struck a bargain, I only considered myself—grasping for control instead of embracing the fall. But this time, I'm leaning into my emotions, to the possibility of what could be, even with the risks.

The rustling of leaves interrupts the moment, and we both turn as the maze shifts. An exit reveals itself at the end of the row. A way forward. A way out.

I exhale, and something inside me settles into place. This is how I will keep my promise to give instead of always taking. Not in grand gestures or more desperate confessions, but in small choices. I will prove—one moment at a time—that I can be more than the villain of my own story. That I can become worthy of Eden's company.

"A deal it is, Wildflower."

Cold palace air chills my skin, a blissful retreat from the blistering Scintillia sun. I stand inside as Cassian continues to a different entrance. He catches me watching and lifts a brow as he walks past. I roll my eyes, turning around as Lyra enters the hall. It appears I've exchanged one Moretti sibling for the other.

"There you are!" the princess calls, practically floating toward me with glee. "I've come to get the juicy details."

I fight to keep the blush off my face. She doesn't know about our time in the maze, does she? "Good afternoon, Your Highness." I curtsy.

"Please stop with the formalities, Eden! We're friends."

I rise, her kindness never failing to make me smile. "And that means a lot, Lyra. Thank you."

"So?" She gives an impish grin, amber eyes sparkling.

"I'm not sure what juicy details you speak of."

Lyra pouts. "You didn't get a brooding visitor in the studio?"

Immediately, I know she means Cassian. He did look rather brooding when I found him in the maze. "None," I reply. "Now, if you'll excuse me, I really must be going."

"Where are you off to in such a rush?" Lyra follows me down the hall as I make my way to my room.

"I plan to visit home."

"Oh, take me with you! Please?" She grabs my arm, leaning her head on my shoulder. "The palace has been boring as of late. You can introduce me to that handsome baker friend."

"Are you always this boy obsessed?" I speak without thinking.

Lyra jolts upright, eyes narrowing.

"Forgive me," I say. "I didn't mean to offend you."

The corner of her lip twitches and she bursts out laughing. "I'm teasing! Your boldness is refreshing. Even though I don't know you that well, I consider you one of my only real friends… And I apologize if I come off a little dull. Boys are all my ladies-in-waiting like to talk about."

"You don't have many friends?" I exclaim, as if it's the most absurd statement she could make. "But you're the princess!"

"Being a princess doesn't equate to being popular. In fact, it's quite the opposite. We have servants, sure. And we attend fancy balls and meet other nobles. But I wouldn't call any of them my friend. Royals aren't afforded that luxury."

Her words paint a rather dreary picture of life. I can't imagine not having any real friends. My thoughts shift to Cassian, and it suddenly makes sense why he is so friendly with his guard.

"So?" Lyra prompts, tugging on my arm. "Can I come?"

I sigh. Though I'm going home to confront a painful truth, Lyra's enthusiasm is contagious, lightening my mood for the task ahead. I would also hate to crush her spirits, preferring to stay in the princess's good graces.

"Yes, Lyra. You may join me."

She squeals with delight.

"But I can't promise it will be very exciting," I warn, trying to prepare her for our simple lifestyle.

Lyra swats the air. "Don't worry, Eden. Anything outside the palace is exciting in my eyes—an adventure into the unknown."

Lyra's horse crosses the wildflower field first. I'm seconds behind her, our laughter stolen by the wind as we race to my house. I kick my heel into my mare's side, clicking my tongue to urge her into a faster gallop.

"Come on, girl," I murmur into her mane.

As we gain on Lyra, I croon, "That's it!"

Lyra glances back, her navy skirt billowing in the wind. With a devious grin, she picks up speed, flying past my house to solidify her win before expertly circling back to meet me.

"Better luck next time, Eden," she says as we trot to the front door.

"Your riding skills are formidable."

She beams, rubbing her horse's side. "Thank you. It's one of my favorite pastimes, though I never get to ride very far. This was glorious."

"It was rather fun, wasn't it? Other than my defeat." I stare at her horse, barely winded compared to mine. "Are you sure you don't have an enchanted horse?"

"A princess never tells her secrets." Lyra laughs, her once immaculate crown of raven hair now wind-blown, strands flying free from her braid.

She looks radiant and unrestrained. Head high, eyes gleaming, she sits astride her horse with effortless grace, her smile unguarded. She tilts her head back, letting the sun warm her face.

I slide off my horse and tie the reins around a nearby tree in the shade. Lyra follows suit, feeding the horses carrots as I knock on the front door. Muffled voices come from the other side seconds before it swings open.

"Eden!" Soren barrels into me.

"You've grown since the last time I saw you! How is that possible?"

He grins and flexes one arm. "Gained some muscle, too. Crafting doors is hard work!"

I ruffle his hair, mussing his chestnut waves even more. Soren ducks away from me and fixes his appearance as Lyra comes to the door. He clears his throat, a slight blush coloring his tan skin.

"Good day, Miss. I didn't realize Eden brought a visitor with her."

Aria pokes her head out the door. "A visitor besides Eden?" She inspects Lyra's outfit, the wheels turning in her head as she assesses their craftsmanship. She drops into a curtsy. "Your Royal Highness."

Soren bows hurriedly, his blush deepening. "Apologies, Your Royal Highness. I didn't recognize you."

"No apologies necessary."

"Lyra, this is my brother Soren and my sister Aria," I introduce.

They usher us inside, and Lyra surveys the space. I suddenly feel smaller. I'm painfully aware of how worn and modest our cottage must seem compared to the gleaming elegance of the palace.

"Your home is lovely," she murmurs. "It has such a warmth to it."

Her fingers trace the wall near the stairs where our dad marked our heights through the years—a tradition my mother started. As she admires the cottage, Aria and Soren embrace their roles as hosts, fetching glasses of water for us and bowls for the horses. Soren heads outside as Lyra wanders into the living area. I help Aria clear the table, watching warily as Lyra stops in front of the family portrait.

"An Eden Asher original, I presume?"

I nod.

"Your family is beautiful." Lyra leans closer to study the painting. "Will I get to meet your mother and father as well?"

The shuffling of papers stops. Aria's face pales.

"Our mother passed away almost ten years ago, now," I say.

Lyra's head whips toward me, her posture straightening. "I'm so sorry. I didn't know."

"It was a long time ago."

"And still, you never forget a loss such as that."

The room goes quiet, heavy with memories.

Aria breaks the silence. "I'll go get Dad."

She walks to the backdoor and leans outside, her words muffled as she tells Dad I'm visiting with a royal guest. The princess joins me at the dining table as Dad steps inside.

"Greetings, Your Royal Highness! Eden." He nods at the both of us, swiping sawdust off his apron before hanging it on the hook by the door. "I'm sorry I'm not more presentable at the moment."

"We came unannounced. It's no worry at all," Lyra reassures.

"Even so, give me one moment and I'll get cleaned up."

Dad heads upstairs, leaving us alone with Lyra once more. We clear the rest of the table, but not before Lyra snags one of Aria's sketches.

"You must be the talented dressmaker."

Aria's eyes flick to me, and she gives a small smile. "My sister has been talking about me, has she?"

"Your dresses speak for themselves. I'd love to commission one from you."

Her stack of fabric teeters perilously as her focus shifts to the princess. Aria lowers her head. "I'd be honored, Your Royal Highness!"

"Splendid! Now, shall we sit?"

"Hopefully you aren't on a schedule," I say, pulling out a chair next to Lyra. "I'm not sure how long our visit will take."

She leans back, all traces of her royal posture gone. "I don't mind. It's nice to be away from the palace."

"You don't have duties to attend to?" Aria interjects. "My apologies if that's rude to ask, but I've always wanted to know what it's like to be a princess."

Lyra stares into her glass of water, watching it ripple as she taps a finger against the side. "The life of a princess isn't as glorious as it appears on the outside. There are many days where I wish I'd grown up like you—free to make your own choices away from the confines of the palace."

Soren reenters the cottage, shattering the vulnerable moment. "The horses are refreshed and ready for the journey back."

"What responsible siblings you have," Lyra says, her tone much lighter than before.

"Only when guests are around." I prop my head in my hand.

Aria scoffs. "Next time, I won't bother getting you water."

I chuckle, appreciating the comforts of home. Even with the princess in our midst, I'm at ease, not worried about prying eyes judging my every move. It gives meaning to Lyra's wish to live like us.

"Where's Dad?" Soren asks.

"Cleaned up and ready to entertain our guests!" Dad's deep voice booms as he reenters the dining area. "You should stay for supper."

"I'm not sure we have time for that, Dad." I watch his smile falter and feel even worse about the conversation I must have with him. "But we'll see. I just really need to speak with you."

Dad's brow creases with curiosity. "Alright. What is it you want to discuss?"

I sense Aria and Soren's eyes on me. Standing, I move closer to Dad, not wanting to be overheard. "Not here."

"We have guests, Eden."

I glance at the princess, unsure what to do. I knew letting her come would make the situation more strained than it already would be. But there's no changing it now.

"Please?"

A flash of worry crosses his face. "Of course."

Lyra leans back in her chair, looking up at my dad and I. "Leave the entertaining to me," she whispers.

I give her an appreciative nod, my earlier regret transforming into relief.

"I'd love an official tour of the cottage!" Lyra announces, standing suddenly.

Soren's eyes sparkle with excitement. Aria glances warily at Dad and me.

"It would be my pleasure to show you our humble abode, Your Royal Highness," Soren replies with a dramatic bow.

I suppress a laugh. Soren is clearly smitten with the princess, though being the same age as me, she's too old for him. *And a royal, at that,* I think, my mind returning to my affection for Cassian. I shoo the thoughts before I get carried away.

"Wonderful. Start without us. We'll join you in a moment," I reassure them, walking toward the back door with Dad.

But another knock at the door stops us in our tracks. Before anyone can answer it, Mateo walks in, arms full of bakery boxes.

"Baked deliciousness has arrived!" he declares, his back to us as he closes the door. "Though Eden probably smelled me coming from a mile away."

"Well, I'm not sure what's in those boxes, but something delicious has certainly arrived," Lyra murmurs.

My eyes bulge and I kick her leg without thinking. She gives me a scandalous grin.

"What? It's true."

I cover my face, embarrassed by the princess's boldness.

Mateo almost drops the boxes when he turns around, face reddening at the sight of Lyra. He clears his throat. "Uh, I'm sorry. I didn't know you had another guest as well."

It takes a moment longer for him to recognize her, scanning her appearance before stopping on her raven-black hair. He bows.

"Your Royal Highness. Not the guest I would've expected Eden to bring home."

Lyra turns to me with raised brows. "Oh, and why is that?"

"She doesn't have the best manners."

"Mattie!" I scold, rushing over to grab boxes out of his hands. "You are embarrassing me," I whisper.

"Sorry. I'm awkward around pretty girls."

I roll my eyes. "Not in the bakery, you're not."

"The princess is different!"

"Well, you're just in time for the cottage tour." I place the boxes on the table. "Supper won't be necessary with all the treats you brought. Feast away but save some for us."

Mateo's head whips toward me. "Where are you going?"

"Out back for a quick conversation, that's all."

His lips press together, and he jerks his chin toward the princess. He raises his shoulders as if asking what he's supposed to do all alone.

Lyra, watching more closely than expected, laughs softly. "The handsome baker is scared of me, is he?"

Mateo blushes once more. He rubs the back of his neck. "No, not at all, Your Royal Highness. I'm just unprepared to entertain such an esteemed guest of the Asher family."

"Please, call me Lyra. I'm not as stuffy as most other nobles."

Seizing the moment, I slip out the back door, urging Dad to follow while everyone remains caught up in conversation. The air outside is crisp, carrying the scent of sawdust and fresh earth. Birds chatter in the trees, their songs a soft contrast to the muffled voices drifting from inside.

The workspace is a familiar sight, dominated by a large workbench pushed against the cottage. Its ragged appearance is evidence of years of craftsmanship. A half-finished table stands at the center, curled wood shavings still clinging to the base. Carved into the grain on one side is the beginning of an intricate pattern. Dad has always been an artist in his own right, though his medium is wood rather than paint.

Further out, where the sun catches on golden flecks of dust in the air, a large slab of wood rests on sawhorses—Soren's latest project. Careful measurements mark its surface, evidence of the patience and dedication he's pouring into his skill.

This place has always felt safe, filled with the steady rhythm of carving blades and the scent of varnish, not unlike my oil paints. But after what I'm about to say, it may never feel that way again.

I turn to face my dad, taking in the worried crease of his brow, the quiet patience in his gaze. He looks every bit the concerned, devoted parent. And yet he's keeping something from me. Something that could tarnish everything.

I swallow hard. I don't want to ruin this moment—this cherished visit home.

But I need to know the truth.

"What's wrong, Eden? Is it the prince again?" Dad swipes wood shavings off a chair, pulling it out and motioning for me to sit.

I shake my head. "No. That's… resolved itself."

Dad frowns, taking the seat for himself. "So, what's troubling you?"

My stomach twists. I let out a long breath. "I read mother's journal."

"Good, I'm glad," he says. "Did you find some helpful advice?"

"I learned she hid poems in all her paintings."

Dad stares out at the wildflower field. "I recently discovered that as well. It was a part of herself she never shared with me, so I've only read the ones from around the house."

"I found one she wrote to you." I watch him, noticing the way his muscles tense.

"Where?"

"In the family portrait she never finished."

His head slowly turns. "The one from the attic?"

I nod. "Mother described you in a strange way."

Shadows darken his eyes as he furrows his brow. But there is no sign of recognition, no confirmation he knows what I'm talking about. Despite my best efforts to stay realistic, to protect myself from the inevitable reality, a flicker of hope lights inside me. I take another shaky breath, finding the slip of paper folded in the pocket of my skirt. "Is there something you need to tell me?"

"Eden, I'm not sure what you mean. What did your mother's poem say, exactly?"

"See for yourself." I hand him the poem, unable to look away as he unfolds it. A range of emotions dance across his face while he reads her words.

"Dad." My voice breaks, barely more than a whisper. The words lodge in my throat, heavy with fear. But I force them out. "Are you actually a Fateless?"

"No." He sighs. "That's not what your mother meant, Eden. I had no idea she even wrote this. But I have a fated skill. I've used it." He holds out his left wrist to expose his fatemark.

I squint at it, worried it will suddenly disappear like Eliana's. "And it's real?"

Dad's brows knit together. "Yes, of course it's real. Why would you ask that?"

"That's a conversation for another time." I lean against the closed door, relief swirling through me. "So, if you have a fatemark, why would mother refer to you as a Fateless?"

"She probably wrote this around the time I was questioning the fated skills. They've never sat right with me, and I hit a breaking point, mentioning to your mother I might stop using mine."

My worry returns. *Stop using his skill? Is that why his business is failing?* But I don't interrupt.

"This feels like her way of supporting whatever decision I made." Dad stares down at the poem in his hands. "But she was gone too soon, and I would never have known any of this without you finding it. Thank you for being brave enough to share this with me." He looks up with a sad smile. "What else do you want to know?"

"Did you actually stop using your fated skill?"

"Not completely," Dad says. "When your mother died, my grief was obvious. But I kept my guilt hidden. I felt, and still feel, responsible for her death."

"How would you be responsible?" I ask, bewildered by his confession.

His eyes drift to his workbench, unfocused, as if the memory is etched there. "Do you remember her supply case?"

"Yeah, the one you made for her. I loved that thing. What happened to it?"

"I have often wondered that myself. I hoped one day it would be yours. I would have loved to show you the secret compartment I designed."

I blink, stunned. "There was a hidden compartment?"

He nods once. "With a weapon inside. Just in case." Dad's tone grows more serious. "I thought it would keep your mother safe. And I *told* others it would. They may not have known exactly how, but they knew I made it—the *craftsman* whose work heightens the quality of its purpose." Dad scoffs.

I furrow my brow, unsure where he's going with this.

"After her death, people started whispering, saying I must be cursed." A half-hearted, broken laugh slips past his lips. "And I believed them. So I stopped using my skill and told myself I'd live like the Fateless. Like it was some kind of penance. But I wasn't strong enough. I needed my skill to finish commissions and bring in coin. And every time I used it, I hated myself a little more."

"Dad, you're not cursed."

He shakes his head. "Don't you see her death is my fault?"

"No, it wasn't." I hesitate, my fingers curling into my skirt. "If it's anyone's fault, it's mine."

"Eden…" A heavy breath escapes him. "I thought you let go of your guilt a long time ago?"

"I tried, but I couldn't handle it on my own." I look down, watching as the wind scatters wood shavings across the dirt. "I needed you. Soren and Aria needed you, too. But you were drowning in your own grief and burying yourself with work. Or were you just hiding?"

His face crumples. "Eden—"

"Never mind, don't tell me. All I know is you weren't there when we needed you most. You let fear win. And I had to bury my guilt to keep our family together. So when you scold me about living for the future, don't forget you're still stuck in the past."

A tear slips free, my chest heaving from ten years of silence. Ten years of being strong for everyone else, of swallowing my grief and playing parent, of pretending I didn't miss him too.

And now, I'm losing him all over again. I couldn't see it before—who he'd become. I was holding on to the father I remembered, the father I needed. But looking at the man in front of me, that illusion is shattered. He's an imposter, a faceless, defeated figure in the portrait of my life.

Dad stands, reaching for me. "I was trying to protect you—"

"No. You were protecting yourself," I say, another tear slipping out. "And it cost all of us."

He drops his hand, pain distorting his features.

My eyes burn. "Did you think I wasn't strong enough to handle it? That I wouldn't understand how you felt?"

"No, Eden," he says. "It's because of your strength that I allowed myself to fall apart. I see so much of your mother in you. But that is not an excuse for what I did. I see how wrong I was."

"More wrong than you know. Because when we lost Mother, we lost you, too." I blink away my tears.

"Eden…"

I shake my head, my hand motioning for him to stop. The wind picks up, fluttering the hem of my skirt. "I need time. And space."

He nods soberly. "Whenever you're ready, I'll be here to talk. No more hiding."

With one last breath of fresh air, I gather my composure and step back inside.

Thankfully, the tour has moved upstairs. Dad hovers in the doorway behind me, but I don't look back. If I do, a fresh wave of tears is sure to follow.

"Happy thoughts, Eden. Happy thoughts," I murmur, taking a deep breath.

Voices filter down the stairs and I follow them. I find everyone crowded in the room Aria and I share, admiring her work.

"Eden, there you are!" Aria beams. "I was just showing them the dress I'm making. I haven't made much progress since the last time you visited. The skirt is giving me fits."

"And I was just asking if I could have it instead," Lyra adds, running her hand over the corseted bust.

I paste on a smile, hoping my red eyes will go unnoticed. "Who am I to deny the princess what she wants?"

"I'm just teasing! This dress is clearly made for you. It will bring out your eyes."

Aria launches into another idea, holding up various sketches and designs for the princess. As she does, Soren snakes his way around them to stand beside me in the doorway.

"What were you talking to Dad about?"

I hug him to my side. "Nothing you need to worry about. I saw your work in progress, though. Think you could link it to my room in the palace? I'd love to visit more often."

Soren scrunches his brow in thought. "I'm not sure. I've only ever enchanted doors with places I've been before."

I ponder his words, piecing together the constraints of his skill. "I have an idea."

Maneuvering through everyone, I gather some of the painting supplies I left behind. Mateo watches me from where he sits on my bed.

"What are you doing?"

"I'm going to paint something for Soren."

Mateo jumps up and follows Soren and me down the stairs. I lay out my supplies on the table and start painting a picture of my bedroom in the palace. Soren watches with confusion for several moments.

Once the underpainting is complete, understanding dawns on his face. "You're a genius, Eden!"

"If it works. I'm not painting a masterpiece—it's only a sketch."

"But I think it will be enough."

Mateo leans in and grabs a donut. "I'm lost," he says, words garbled around the food in his mouth. "Someone fill me in."

"You're lucky the princess isn't here to witness *your* lack of manners." I shake my head.

Mateo gulps down another bite with a shrug. "I'm still surprised you brought her home. Last time we talked, her brother threatened you. Now you're best friends with his sister?"

"Threatened?" Soren's eyes narrow.

"It's nothing. I took care of it." My voice is harsher than intended, Mateo withering under my glare.

He mouths a silent sorry, knowing I didn't want to get my siblings involved.

"So are you going to fill me in, or what?" Mateo asks, trying to distract Soren from his previous comment.

With one last questioning look, Soren sighs and explains my plan. I continue painting, my room in the palace quickly developing on the page.

Moments later, Mateo clarifies, "If I'm understanding correctly, we'll get to visit you in the palace whenever we want?"

"In your dreams. That kind of power is strictly off-limits to amateurs like you," I tease, unable to hold in my laughter.

Mateo retaliates with a series of jabs to my side, only increasing my laughter until it infects both him and Soren.

"Stop!" I protest breathlessly, shielding my side from further attack. "You're going to ruin the painting!"

Mateo ceases with a triumphant grin, raising his hands in surrender. "Sorry. I *would* like to see your room in the palace. Please continue."

I shake my head with a smile, returning to the painting. If this works, it opens up a world of possibilities.

Dust dances through the air. Golden rays of light illuminate its path, finally floating free from the heavy book now resting in my lap. I watch the specks until they disappear into the shadows. My eagerness from before is quickly disappearing. A part of me no longer wants to know more about the Fateless, though it's within reach, scrawled on the pages in front of me.

A shaky breath sends more dust flying off the book. Divinian history is rarely studied in Mentera. I open to the first passage. Black ink lettering stretches across the yellowed pages, faded in various places.

The Divinian Kingdom was known for its peculiar rejection of fated skills, standing alone as the birthplace of the Fateless. Ruled by the Amato family, its people were diverse but untrained, forgoing the divine gifts that shaped the other three kingdoms. For years, they coexisted peacefully, until their dangerous ideals threatened to distort the Creator's sacred design.

To preserve the divine order bestowed by Delayon, the kingdoms of Mentera, Aetherea, and Corvica united against Divinia, determined to extinguish the corruption before it could spread. Bereft of fated skills, the Divinians fell swiftly, their kingdom erased before their influence could take root.

Yet, whispers persist. The Fateless still walk among us, remnants of a forsaken kingdom, carrying their heretical beliefs and spreading their lies in the shadows.

I lean my head against the bookcase, staring up at the mural on the ceiling. So far, the book has told me nothing I don't already know. It's hard to comprehend a kingdom so radical. What is so enticing about it that people still choose to be Fateless? Even Dad considered it.

I flip to the table of contents, looking for intriguing chapter headings. One focused on the Edenia flower catches my attention and I turn to the noted page.

A careful sketch of the flower dominates the yellowed paper. Scribbled around it are notes detailing the various parts. But other than the diagram, the chapter is smudged beyond readability, as if someone spilled water over its contents. The ink has bled through the pages, ruining the information within.

What monster is in charge of preserving the history books? Their condition is disgraceful.

Turning to other sections, I find the condition is the same throughout. Only a few chapters are unmarred. I shut the book with a thud and set it aside, intent on reading more in the comforts of my room. As I stand, I brush the dust off my skirts and return to searching for more books on Divinia's history. There are very few.

I collect a couple more, adding them to my stack before lugging them all to the folklore and poetry section. Perhaps there will be something more interesting in the texts not considered history. I'm hoping to find the infamous story the Divinians believed. For as much as their ideals are mentioned, they are never explicitly written in any history books. It's likely for fear of perpetuating their ridiculous ideas. But knowing what my mother hid in her poems, I still have hope.

The books here are thinner, their spines cracked from frequent use. Elegant script marks each one with titles like *The Lost People* and *Fated Whispers*. They're penned by well-known Menteran poets—none of whom would've written about Divinia.

My arm grows heavy from the weight of the history tomes, and I readjust my grip. Crouching to view the lowest row of books, a faded wine cover catches my eye. Written in white text across the spine is *The Vanished Kingdom*. I don't recognize the author, a sign I may have stumbled onto something.

Crushed between two large poetry anthologies, it takes a bit of effort to slide the book off the shelf. Gingerly, I set it atop my stack and hold it open with my free hand.

Before I can read a word, it's yanked out of my grasp.

The books teeter perilously from the sudden movement, and I wrap both arms around them. I scowl at the book thief, their tall frame silhouetted by the sunlight.

"And what books might the Lady Asher be interested in?" The voice is low and teasing.

Cassian.

As my eyes adjust, his perpetually ruffled hair and lazy attire come into focus. He flips through the book, a smirk slowly curving his lips as he reads its contents.

"Poetry?" He raises a brow.

"Yes. May I please have it back?" I reach for the book.

Cassian holds it out of my reach. "Not so fast. I want to talk to you." With a quick glance around the library, he grabs my hand, tugging me toward the history section.

"I was just here," I complain, clutching my books as we come to a halt.

"Then you know it's rarely used." He slides a finger along a nearby shelf and blows the dust in my face.

I swipe a hand through the air, only stirring it up more. "What did you want to discuss, Cassian?"

He steps closer, and my heart skips. "Our plan has a hitch," he whispers.

"Is it one that we can fix? The Corvicans will be here by the end of the week."

"That's why I'm coming to you, Wildflower. I thought you'd have a creative solution." He sets the poetry book on my stack. "I can't get Farion's door unlocked."

"But that's one of the main things you promised to help me with!" When my voice stirs up the dust in the air, I tone it down an octave. "If the prince can't even unlock it, how can I?"

He spins one of his rings. "You are my last resort."

"What kind words," I retort. "Tell me more, Princeling, and maybe I can help."

His mouth twitches as he regards me with amusement. "As you wish. His door seems enchanted to lock whenever he's not present. And none of my keys work."

I shove my books into his chest. He accepts them with a questioning look.

"The least you can do while I help brainstorm is hold these ridiculously heavy books."

He adjusts his hold on the stack with a laugh, a low and throaty sound. "Fair enough. Although you're the one who chose so many."

I suppress an eye roll and lean against the bookshelf, twirling a strand of hair in thought. "An enchanted door makes me even more suspicious."

"My thoughts exactly. Maybe I should search for the poem. It's not like I haven't been in his room many times before."

"No." My answer is immediate. "Isn't he always in the room with you?"

Cassian nods.

"Then you'd get caught."

"I'd find a way. Or make up some excuse. It might be our only option."

I push off from the bookshelf, pacing in the small space. "There has to be another way into his room, regardless of his enchanted door."

Cassian watches me pace. "I can't believe he's had an enchanted door this whole time, and I hadn't noticed."

I stop. "An enchanted door."

"Mm-hm."

"How did I not think of this sooner?" I mutter, remembering Soren's skill.

Cassian tilts his head, waiting for me to explain, but I pause, not sure I should put my brother in the same situation I'm in. If I tell the prince his skill, he could use my brother the same way he's been using me—for personal gain. As much as I've come to trust Cassian, I won't do that to my brother.

But he doesn't need to know who the creator is.

I look over at Cassian. "I know someone who enchants doors with locations."

"And that helps how?"

"We'd be able to enter Farion's room through a completely unrelated door."

His brows scrunch together. He shifts the stack of books to his other arm. "I'm not following."

I pull a book from the shelf and place it in front of the empty spot it created, its cover outward. "This is the enchanted door we make." I do the same with a book on the opposite shelf. "This is Farion's door." I rotate the first book as if it's opening like a door. "When you use the enchanted door, instead of going into this room," I gesture to the space between the books, "you end up in that room." I cross to the other shelf and push aside the book to reveal another empty slot.

"Clever. But how would we get a door into the palace without people asking questions?"

"Through another enchanted door that leads to my chambers."

Cassian's jaw drops. "Say that again?"

"Another door. Leading to my chambers. That's enchanted."

"Eden!" He steps closer, voice urgent. "You realize that's a major security risk, right?"

My brows knit together as I consider his words. It hadn't crossed my mind how someone with ill-intent could exploit Soren's door. "I hadn't thought about that."

"How long have you had this enchanted passage?"

"It's not actually done yet. At least, I don't think so." I stare down at the wood floor. "I'll cancel it. I'm sorry. It was a silly idea."

Cassian lets out a long breath. "No, it's smart. It will work. But I need to know where this enchanted door is."

My muscles tense. I can't tell him it's in my family cottage. It will be a dead giveaway. Excuses flit through my mind, none sounding solid enough to convince the prince. And then I realize I don't need one at all. Enchanted objects are bought and brought home from the marketplace every day.

"I had it installed in my cottage. I wanted my family to visit more often."

Cassian's expression softens. "I suppose that *was* one of your requests when I hired you, wasn't it?"

"That it was, Princeling."

"Alright. What do you need to get this enchanted door started? And can it be made in time?"

"I think it can be done. But we'll need one more painting session," I say.

Surprise flashes across his face along with a hint of something else—excitement, maybe. "And what will you be painting?"

"Farion's room."

"How soon?"

"Tonight?"

Cassian closes the distance between us and places the books in my arms, his mouth next to my ear. "See you then, Wildflower."

My stomach flutters from his closeness. Then he steps back, leaving me alone in the history section with one last glance. I stay there until my heart returns to normal. Even then, I wait until he's likely a safe distance away, not wanting to be caught around the prince. With the books clutched tightly to my chest, I make my way through the library and into the hall.

There's no sign of Cassian. For a moment, I wonder where he ran off to next, but my thought is cut short when I run straight into someone's firm chest. My books fall to the floor.

"I'm terribly sorry, sir." I bend down to retrieve them, cheeks hot.

"Still not used to navigating the palace halls, Miss Asher? You should know by now how easily they conceal those walking within." Farion's deep voice sends a chill through me.

I look up. For having just run into someone, his face is deceptively calm. "I'll take care to walk with more caution next time, Farion."

Farion lowers himself in front of me, helping to pick up the remaining books. "Divinian history? That's an interesting topic of study for an artist."

A wave of apprehension sweeps through me. *What do I say?*

"Our last conversation must've sparked your curiosity."

I take a deep breath and try to relax. "Yes, the tapestry's history still intrigues me. It's a fascinating story."

Farion hands me a book. I accept it with my left hand, but he doesn't let go. He fixes his gaze on my fatemark, cold and calculating.

"Over half gone. Impressive. But there's still plenty of work to be done to become a Morphi." He releases the book. "Don't let your fascination with the past interfere with your true priorities. With all the drama you've caused, you'll need the status to stay working for the Morettis. I'd hate to see you replaced so soon." His smile is kind, but there's a threat in his words.

I stand as he does, my posture rigid. "I appreciate the words of warning, Farion. It's always been my goal to ascend."

Farion nods, touching the black cape around his neck, a symbol of his own ascended status. "As it should be."

I curtsy in reply. His gaze follows me until I round the nearest corner, intent on reaching my chambers as fast as possible. Another moment in his presence and I'm sure he would sense my plan with Cassian. The Ascended One is known for his keen observation.

Several servants pass me in the halls. They avoid my gaze, none of them returning my polite smile. If I were a Morphi, they'd treat me differently, showing me respect instead of pretending I'm invisible.

I should be much closer to ascending by now, but I let myself get distracted. Somewhere along the way, my goals became clouded with temporary concerns and unexpected encounters. Namely, the prince. Once Cassian helps me get into Farion's room, I need to refocus my efforts on ascending.

Frustrated with myself, I walk the rest of the way to my chambers with my head down. It's not until my door closes behind me that I finally relax. The chair by the window calls my name, and I set all but the poetry book on my desk before sitting.

As I open it, the creak of the spine and the yellowed pages allude to the book's age. I skim through the first few poems, finding nothing of interest. Thumbing through the rest of it, I see a page with a folded corner, the poem's title intriguing me.

The Vanished Kingdom—the same as the book.

Made from the dust, we are a cherished creation.
Beheld by our Creator with much adoration.
Filled with His undeniable truth and love,
We lived contently with our minds on things above.
But then the world corrupted us,
Fostering distrust,
Tempting us to make a deadly exchange,
To welcome a change,
That ultimately led to becoming estranged.
With our connection to the Creator severed,
His kingdom was no longer treasured,
Vanishing from our minds,
As we latched onto the beliefs of mankind.

The poem isn't what I expected, referring to a heavenly kingdom rather than a physical one like Divinia. And yet it still feels poignant, somehow connected to the Divinian ideals.

The beliefs of mankind, I repeat, my mind stuck on the poem's last line. Divinia is infamous for rejecting fated skills, so is that what the author is referring to? Are they trying to say our beliefs about fated skills are not from Delayon, but from men? It doesn't make sense.

I stare at the wall, working through the layers of meaning. The poem contradicts everything I've been taught to believe. Our origin story, recited from the Royal Codex at the monthly Ascension Rite, directly attributes our skills to Delayon, not mankind.

But before I can dwell on it any longer, the door to my room swings open to reveal an unexpected visitor.

"Soren?"

He hollers triumphantly at the sight of me. "It works!"

"Your door? You finished it?"

With a quick glance into the hallway as if to confirm he's actually here, Soren closes the door. "Not exactly."

"What is that supposed to mean?" I set the poetry novel on the desk beside the others.

Soren meanders through my room, taking stock of all the furniture and decor. "It's almost done, but I wanted to see if our plan would work before trying it on another door. I always forget my skill is not as limited when I'm the one using the door. So I used the one I already made to come here." He peeks his head into my bathroom. "You know, the door to my bedroom? All I had to do was picture this room based on your painting, and just like that, I'm here!"

"Smart thinking, little brother. I'm glad my idea worked."

"Me too. This could change everything!" Satisfied with his tour, he makes himself comfortable on my bed, bouncing a little as he sits. "I could get used to this."

I sit next to him, and the bed sinks further under our weight. "It is pretty nice, isn't it?"

"Bigger than mine and Aria's bedrooms combined."

I shove him. "You're forgetting someone."

"Am I?" He taps a finger against his lips.

I glare at him.

He laughs. "It's not my fault you're not living in the cottage anymore. You've been upgraded to a swanky place in the palace."

Soren's assessment makes my current position finally feel like reality. All this time, I'd seen this place as temporary, still clinging to the life I had back home. But my brother is right. It's been almost a month living at the palace. Perhaps this life *is* my future. Unless, of course, I'm replaced, as Farion suggested.

"Sorry to disappoint you, though." Soren's apology breaks through my reverie. He picks at the dirt under his nails. "With not finishing the new door yet."

"Actually, I'm glad."

His head jerks up, brows furrowed. "Why?"

"A change of plans. Something time-sensitive came up, and I was hoping you could enchant the door to go somewhere else."

"Where?"

"It doesn't matter."

Soren crosses his arms. "The person creating the door should at least know where he's enchanting it to go."

"For your sake, it's best you don't. All I can tell you is that it has to do with our mother."

His eyes widen. "Our mother?"

I nod. "So, will you do it?"

Soren stares at the family portrait on the wall, deep in thought. "Okay." He gives me a rueful grin. "Aria won't be pleased I'm the only one who gets to visit you, though."

I laugh. "You can still make the door we were originally planning, just after this other one is done. When it's ready, you can bring it through the same one you used today. It's the easiest way to get it here. As for Aria, tell her she'll have to be patient."

Soren flops back onto the bed, his dark brown hair splaying across the silk comforter. "Speaking of Aria, she finished that dress she was making. She'll be mad I forgot to bring it with me."

My jaw falls open with indignation. "And you didn't think I would be?" I poke his belly, the beginnings of tickle torture. "I've been waiting for that dress!"

"Stop," Soren wheezes, squirming away from me, breathless with laughter.

I lay beside him on the bed. We stare up at the canopy, relaxed in the comfort of family.

"It's nice to see you again so soon." I press my cheek against the comforter to look at him. "I really miss you guys."

He turns his head to face me. "We miss you, too. Dad the most, I think. He's been acting weird since you left the other day."

My stomach clenches. I still feel bad about how I left things with him. He's only ever wanted what's best for me, but it still doesn't excuse what he did. "While we're on the topic of visiting home, how were you planning to get back?"

Soren squints, blinking rapidly. "Wow, that was a major oversight on my part. No enchanted door means I'll have to go home the old-fashioned way—walking."

"Then it's a good thing you could pass for a servant boy. Other than your clothes, I guess. We wouldn't want the guards asking questions about how you got in undetected."

"So what do you suggest?"

"Follow me."

I lead him to the servant door and down the narrow stairwell.

"Up ahead are the doors to the garden," I say. "When you get outside, take a right and follow the path to the front gates. Walk with purpose, as if you belong, and no one should bother you."

"What about the guards?" Soren asks.

"If they question you, tell them you're running an errand to the marketplace."

Soren salutes me. "I've got this, Sis."

I scoff at his confidence but pull him into a hug before he leaves. "Come back through your door tomorrow. The painting should be done by the afternoon."

My brother nods before heading outside. I watch him until he disappears, my heart full from his visit. Without my siblings, I'm not sure who I'd be. They ground me, tethering me to home—constant reminders of where I belong and why I fight.

A timely reminder.

I've spent too long letting my focus drift, letting *him* blur the lines of what I came here to do. Cassian is a distraction I can't afford. Not when the path to becoming a Morphi is narrowing by the day. Not when my family's future is on the line.

I've made enough mistakes as it is. It's time to remember who I am, and why I wanted this title. Because no prince—no matter how he makes me feel—can be more important than that.

Cassian

"For once, I get to sit on the artist's side," I say, dragging the cushioned armchair away from its usual spot by the window. It settles into the carpet with a soft thud. I shimmy between it and Eden's desk chair, careful not to bump the easel as she gets ready to paint.

"But don't think I'm going to let you touch this painting." Eden spins the cap onto one of her paint tubes.

"Watch what you say, Wildflower. *You* need *me* for this painting."

"Only your mind." She tilts her head. "No touching or painting required. We both saw how that went last time."

"Hey, you were the one coaxing me to paint in the first place." I lean forward in the chair. "I never forget a challenge."

Eden is quiet for a moment, exchanging her tube of paint for her palette of colors. "I couldn't forget that day if I tried." She grabs a brush, swirling it through the dull yellow as if in a trance.

A pit forms in my stomach. I'm still only beginning to realize the impact of my words, and the depth of the hurt I've caused her. I want to apologize again—to tell her I truly didn't mean what I said. But I can already feel her pulling away.

She stands with her back to me, wedged between the chair and the easel. Her posture is rigid, muscles tense. With stiff movements, she spreads the yellow paint across the canvas, its pristine white surface aging in seconds.

It's clear she harbors a lot of feelings about that day.

And she has every right to.

Tension coils in my gut, sharp and unwelcome. I've failed Eden once. I won't fail her again by staying silent.

"Wildflower," I murmur. My heart pounds, anticipating the cold look on her face when she closes herself off—when I disappoint her.

She turns her head. Pain flickers across her eyes, their normally bright sage hue turned gloomy with memory.

"I know my words aren't worth much anymore, but I need you to know I'm sorry." My voice softens. "You didn't deserve what I put you through. And I won't pretend a promise will fix everything. So I won't just say it—I'll prove it. Day by day."

Eden's lashes flutter downward.

She can't bear to look at you, a voice whispers in my head.

The thought makes my chest tighten.

But then her gaze lifts again, meeting mine. It lingers, taking me in as if it's the last time she'll see me. "Thank you, Cassian."

For a second, she looks almost sad. Then it's gone, replaced by a bright, easy smile. The shift is so fast it throws me off. Was she ever upset at all, or was it just in my head?

"Let's get started on this painting, shall we, Princeling?"

Her cheery tone relieves my worry. The tightness in my chest gives way, and I can breathe easy once more. "Anything for you, Wildflower."

She shakes her head. "Alright. Close your eyes."

I oblige, unable to keep the grin from my face.

"Picture standing in the doorway of Farion's room," she instructs.

The furniture takes shape in my mind, set in their perfect positions around his room.

"Tell me what you see," Eden says.

"A four-poster bed is directly in front of me at the far end of the room."

Her brush rasps against the canvas.

"To my left is a sitting space. There are two chairs across from a couch. A marble coffee table is between them." I pause, giving her time to paint. "To my right is a desk. It's separated from the sleeping area by a large fireplace along the right wall."

I open one eye to peek at her progress. Her current sketch is a very spacious room, not sectioned off as much as Farion's. "The sitting space juts out more, which creates a wall here," I point to the left side of her canvas, "where your mother's portrait hangs."

Eden adjusts the painting. "And where is the balcony?"

"On the far-left wall in the sitting room."

She takes a rag, wiping away the yellow paint to create a door shape in seconds. "Other windows?"

Careful not to touch the wet paint, I point to several other areas along the wall. "And the space with the bed is pushed back more. A bit bigger, too."

Eden's eyebrows raise. "Quite the room, he has."

"He's the leader of the Mimicry. But it's still nothing compared to mine." I wink.

She chuckles. "Only the best for the future king."

"Don't remind me. I'd trade rooms with you if it meant I didn't have to take the throne."

"Excuse you, I rather like my room." Eden surveys the small space before landing on me. Her skirts brush up against my knee. "It's cozy."

"No complaints here."

She rolls her eyes. "Alright, focus. Back to the painting. What color are the walls?"

"Gray."

"Very descriptive." Eden's tone is dry. "There are many types of gray."

"I'm not an artist, Wildflower. I don't know. It's just gray."

She huffs and starts mixing a color on her palette. "Warm or cool?"

I close my eyes and picture his room. "Warm?"

Eden puts a bit of yellow, blue, and red into the mess of paint.

"Well, not those colors!"

She glances up from the palette. "This is how you make brown, Cassian. I'm assuming the color you're trying to describe is taupe."

She continues mixing, the paints swirling together to form the exact color I pictured. It glides onto the canvas, Farion's room continuing to take shape.

"Are you sure your skill isn't True Color? That was impressive."

"How do you think I've been able to hide my fated skill all this time? I had to get good at color mixing if I wanted to convince anyone." She fills in the walls, adding other colors periodically to create a convincing sense of space.

"Sitting on this side is much more fun," I mutter, in awe of her talent.

Eden focuses. I stay quiet. The only sound is the faint scratch of bristles sliding against the canvas.

Despite my ineptitude, she continues to ask me to describe the colors of each part of the room. Sometimes, I'm more accurate than others, but she assures me it just needs to be close, not exact.

At some point, she sits. Her profile is now at my level, and I find myself staring more at her than the painting.

"Why do you hide your skill? You could be the most sought-after artist in all of Mentera."

"You should be the first to understand; power and fame aren't everything," she replies, her eyes never leaving the canvas.

"I suppose. But very few people think that way. There has to be more to it."

She paints the fireplace. Reds and yellows dance in tandem to form the illusion of flame. For a moment, I think she's ignoring me. As she finishes the last flame with a quick swipe of her brush, she leans back, assessing her work.

"My mother's death was the catalyst." Eden glances at me before busying herself with mixing another color.

If it weren't for our recent theory about Farion and her mother, I wouldn't understand what she means. But with Farion's room in front of me on the canvas, it's easy to picture a portrait gone wrong—a murder to silence someone with a powerful skill.

The hair on my arms stands on end. The more I think about it, the more I want answers. And the more I question what Farion is capable of.

"Tell me, Wildflower." I wait until she looks up from her palette. "Does our plan scare you?"

She doesn't hesitate. "No."

Her confidence is fitting. Eden is every bit as stubborn as her nickname suggests. Though I thrust her into an unfamiliar place, she's been nothing but herself, determined to flourish on her own accord. I stare at her, taking in the resolute set of her jaw, the defiance in her lifted chin. Lamplight casts sharp shadows across her face.

If she's afraid, she doesn't show it.

I admire her tenacity. "In moments where I least expect it, you continue to prove your fearlessness," I say.

Eden looks away with a breathy laugh. "Trust me, I'm anything but."

"Then, tell me. What else scares you?"

She frowns. "For someone who supposedly dislikes small talk, I see only evidence of the contrary."

I quirk a brow at her deflection. "I'd hardly call this small talk."

She avoids my gaze, concentrating on the painting.

I hook my foot under the leg of her chair and pull her closer. Eden glares at me. I laugh as I place one hand on the back of her chair. "Don't tell me, being vulnerable is one thing you're scared of, too. We keep finding things we have in common."

"Is that so?"

My eyes drop to Eden's pursed lips. "Like right now. I want to be vulnerable, but you don't. The roles have reversed."

"It's not you who's being vulnerable. Once again, you're asking me to be."

"Fair." I hold her gaze. "How about I share something I'm scared of first? Deal?"

"We always seem to make deals with each other, Princeling."

I fall back into my chair, raking a hand through my hair with a sigh. "You're right. I really am just like my father."

Eden sets her supplies aside. "I didn't mean to hurt you when I said that." She looks away sheepishly. "Or maybe in the moment I did. You *were* about to blackmail me."

"I deserved it." I tilt my head back to stare at the ceiling.

If I'm already becoming my father, what does that mean for my future? He built his legacy on control, bending others to his will like pieces on a board. And I—I've been doing the same. I forced Eden into a corner, used her secret against her, and played the very game I swore I wanted no part of.

But I don't want to be like him.

I exhale sharply and stick my pinky in the air. "One last deal, or how about a promise, to make no more deals?"

She links her pinky with mine. "No more deals."

The mood lightens, her green eyes full of mischief. Eden tugs on my pinky, pulling me closer. Her voice lowers to a whisper. "Plus, I hate to break it to you, but I already know what you're scared of."

I smirk. "Oh, and what's that?"

"Me."

"You got me there, Wildflower. Everything about you is a puzzle, and I don't like the unknown."

She releases my pinky with a soft smile. "You'll figure me out eventually. I'm nothing special."

"I disagree. You are extraordinary." I tuck a strand of hair behind her ear. "So why are you always trying to hide from me?"

Eden closes her eyes for a long moment. "You forget who we are. I am a common-born artist. And you…" Her chin dips. "You are the Crown Prince of Mentera, soon to be betrothed to the Corvican princess, and destined to be king."

Panic blooms within me. "That doesn't matter."

"But it does, Cassian."

"Does it matter that I don't want any of that?"

Her eyes find mine. "Of course. But it doesn't change reality. We both need to accept who we are to each other—or rather, who we cannot be."

I drag my hand over my face. "You sound like my father and Farion."

"They're not wrong."

A muscle tics in my jaw. "What have they been saying to you?"

"Nothing I didn't already know." Eden picks at the flaking wood on the arm of the chair. "I appreciate you keeping my secret. But after this last painting—after I find my mom's last words— we have to stop deluding ourselves. You'll be engaged by then, and I will become a distant memory."

I'm at a loss for words. She's right. My fate hasn't changed, and Eden won't be a part of my future. Not in the way I want. I stare numbly as she returns to the painting. It seems I'm destined to always have my choices made for me.

Cassian

y stomach twists into knots. The crowd's cheers swell around us. Princess Isabel's hand in mine feels wrong. I glance at her, my eyes catching on the bronze tiara nestled into her intricate white-blonde braid. She is the perfect picture of a queen.

She smiles down at the crowd, the announcement of our engagement exciting the masses. Then Isabel's gaze finds mine, her green eyes familiar and foreign all at once. Though a similar shade to Eden's, hers are fierce and sharp, full of a warrior-like edge.

"We thank you for celebrating with us," my father says. His deep voice echoes through the Chrysalis as the newly-ascended Morphi leave the balcony.

The cheers and clapping die down, the crowd quieting in anticipation of the ceremony's end. Except my father does not initiate the creed and wave farewell. He nods to a servant, and they disappear down the stairs.

Apparently, there is more in store for today's ceremony.

"Delayon has blessed us this month. Not only with three new Morphi and your prince's engagement, but by exposing the darkness in our lands." The king stretches an arm toward the side of the balcony, where five people are led out in chains.

A collective gasp runs through the crowd below. I watch with uncertainty as the chained people are lined up on the balcony's edge. With the Corvican royals as our guests, I should've expected Father to make this Ascension Rite unlike any other. He lives for the spectacle of his own dominance.

"Before you, stand five Fateless. Thanks to your dedication to protecting our sacred way of life, we exposed these individuals for their treachery." He lets his words sink in. "And today, they will get what they deserve."

Isabel squeezes my hand, but I don't share in her excitement. As I stare at the Fateless, all I see are their trembling, battered bodies. My father must've had them punished another way first.

Fateless executions aren't uncommon for the Ascension Rite, but this one is different. The air is charged with something darker and more dangerous.

My father steps closer to the balcony. "Today, we seek justice for Delayon's kingdom."

"Justice!" the crowd chants.

"We restore order to our nation!" the king continues.

"Order!"

"And we fight to protect divine truth."

"Truth!" the crowd roars.

Worked into a frenzy, the crowd chants the three words like a mantra. Isabel joins them, her voice added to the throng. I find my voice as well, chanting like I've done countless times before. But with each repetition, the words taste more sour in my mouth. I stare at the Fateless, some young and some old, and wonder if what we're doing is really divine justice. How could these five chained people be a threat to our nation? And how could I have never questioned it?

Out of the corner of my eye, I see the stoic forms of my mother and sister, their mouths unmoving. Beside them, the Corvican royals are vigorously shouting. My father turns away from the crowd and beckons Valter, the Corvican King. He pays no mind to his wife and daughter's lack of participation, focused only on the sword being unsheathed from King Valter's side.

My father silences the crowd with a wave of his hand. "As a symbol of our strengthened union with the Corvicans, King Valter has offered his sword for the ceremony."

King Valter balances the sword on his palms, holding it up for all to see. The emerald-encrusted bronze hilt gleams in the Chrysalis's light. "Forged by our divinely skilled blacksmiths, this blade is imbued with Delayon's power. May it root out the darkness in these individuals and rightfully preserve justice, order, and truth."

He passes the sword to our executioner. I swallow the bile that rises in my throat as the Fateless kneel. This execution is more elaborate than any we've done before. I can only assume the deadly potions of our healers were not showy enough for my father.

Not on a day where he seeks to cement his authority.

The executioner moves to the first kneeling Fateless—a young woman with wild curls. She raises her head, defiantly meeting the eyes of the man about to end her life.

"May Delayon have mercy on you all, for you know not what you do."

Fury flashes across my father's face, enraged by her boldness—her willingness to utter words in the face of death. In that moment, I can't help but see her as a reflection of Eden.

And then the sword is plunged through her chest, the sound of steel through flesh chilling me to the bone. She sags forward. I want to look away, but I can't, my eyes frozen in place as her body begins to shrivel. Her skin shrinks, muscles tightening as the sword drains her life. When the executioner removes the sword, she's nothing but withered, blackened skin and bone.

The man chained beside her begs for his life. He crumples to the ground, sobbing incoherently.

"The darkness is exposed!" King Valter shouts.

"Justice, order, truth!" the crowd replies, eager for the next execution.

I stare out at the masses, unsettled by their hunger for blood. Somewhere among them, Eden sits with her family. *Is she chanting with the rest?*

My gaze sweeps over the sea of faces until I spot pockets of stillness—groups less frenzied, untouched by the same thirst for vengeance. That's where I imagine Eden would be.

Another blood-curdling crunch reaches my ears. I let go of Isabel's hand and force myself to watch as the executioner systematically ends another life.

This is part of my future. It will be my duty as king to continue to uproot the Fateless. But I will never do it this way. I may be cold-hearted, but I'm not inhumane. If I had a say, the Fateless executions would cease altogether.

Despite my many attempts, it is yet to happen. Father hates my idea of rehabilitation. It's another reason he thinks I'm weak, pushing me to use my skill and master my emotions. For if I feel nothing, I can easily do what I must, even if it means killing people bound in chains.

As the executioner steals the fourth Fateless life, I turn to where Farion stands resolutely at my father's side. He is eerily still, though his eyes betray him. They are bright and animated, locked onto the dying Fateless. He's just like the rest of the crowd, finding pleasure in their deaths. It's one more whispered doubt that threatens to shatter my perception of him. Maybe he *did* kill Eden's mother.

Beside him, the king steps forward. He stops the executioner from killing the final Fateless. "To end our ceremony, on a day of much celebration, it is time for you to get a glimpse of your future king's power."

My blood runs cold. I look over at Farion, but he simply gives me an encouraging nod. Isabel is expectant at my side. Father urges me forward and I move to stand beside him, muscles tight with apprehension. "What are you doing, Father?" I hiss. "I thought our skills were best kept secret?"

"Using your skill today won't reveal its source—only its power. I want you to show them what you are capable of. Make them fear you."

I want to argue, to tell him I've never killed anyone with my skill before, that I'm not even sure it's possible. But his gaze is cold and unyielding. He will spare me no sympathy. This is another one of his tests. If I fail in front of the Corvican royals—in front of my future subjects—I will embarrass the Moretti name. The whole of Mentera is watching me now. This is everything my father prepared me for since birth.

My hand shakes as I reach forward, hovering just above the shoulder of the last Fateless. She whimpers softly, the Chrysalis quiet as they all wait for me. All I have to do is touch her and call on my skill, manipulate her emotions to the brink of death, and move on.

But my gut is screaming no.

I can't do this.

I won't.

All month, I've been doing everything in my power to change my fate. I made a vow to myself that I wouldn't become my father. So why am I still trying so hard to please him? Why should I continue to cower at his feet? My choice today could prove to Eden I've changed—that I won't bend to my father's will anymore. More than that, it could prove it to me.

My fingers curl into a clenched fist. "I will not," I whisper, just loud enough so he can hear me.

The king smiles, one I know all too well. It masks his inner rage, smoothing over the lines of his face into one of pleasant conversation, giving the onlookers nothing to question. "This is not a choice, Cassian. You will."

I pull my hand further away from the Fateless woman. "I know this is not the place to question your judgment, Father, but I cannot do what you are asking me."

His blue eyes darken. He closes them for a fraction of a second before wrapping his arm around my shoulders. Unlike me, he's a true master of his emotions, caging his rage beneath the carefully crafted facade of the nation's beloved king.

And there, building behind my eyes, is the familiar pressure of his skill. I scramble to dispel my thoughts. I can't risk Father connecting Eden to my change of heart. But in the frenzy of my emotions and the watchful crowd, I'm not sure I quieted my mind in time.

After several long seconds, the probing tendrils of his skill retreat, his expression unchanging as the pressure dissipates.

"Ah, I must apologize," he says, addressing the crowd with practiced ease. "It seems your future king is shy." Then he glances at me, as if my actions are endearing rather than infuriating. "We'll work on that."

A chorus of affectionate laughter ripples through the crowd as though we aren't standing mere feet from four dead and withered bodies. My stomach clenches, an ugly, sickening sensation crawling up my spine. Revulsion curls through me like a slow poison and it takes everything in me to stay standing. I look over the balcony and feel nothing but disgust for the very people I'm destined to rule over.

"Do not think this is the end of our conversation," the king says through his smile, low enough only I can hear. "Now, stand beside your bride and watch as I do what you could not."

He releases me, and I stagger backward. Isabel regards me with disdain. Farion refuses to look at me. But on my mother's face, I find a small piece of solace. Through her queenly expression, she affords me a slight nod and a genuine smile.

She's proud.

My heart swells. No matter what awaits me after this ceremony, I know I did something right. I finally made a choice for myself instead of someone else. And that is worth every ounce of my father's fury.

That feeling is what I cling to as my father drives the Corvican blade into the Fateless woman's chest. It's what I hold onto as my father finds satisfaction in her withering form. And it is what anchors me as I finally see him for the monster he has always been.

"It is finished!" My father's triumphant cry tears through the silence. He raises the bloodied sword over his head.

The people roar with delight.

"With your continued dedication, we will root out the evil, one Fateless at a time. But we must remain vigilant. Mentera is only strong when we stand together against the lies that threaten our future." He places his left arm in front of his chest, signaling the start of our creed.

"Fated to serve," I say in time with hundreds of voices. "Fated to fight. Fated to fly."

This time, I say the words not for the kingdom, but for myself. I will fight until I'm finally able to fly free from this cage.

eremonies like today's have always been hard to sit through, but today it was unbearable. As I watched the murders, all I could picture were the many Fateless lives taken in front of a cheering crowd. How could I have been so blind to such senseless killing my whole life?

I hug my sister to my side as we shuffle through the crowd to exit the Chrysalis. Another row descends in front of us, joining the line. We step forward to close the gap before the many other rows continue pouring out. If we let them all in, we'd be waiting all day. I'd rather not be here when they haul the withered bodies away.

Several minutes later, our line converges with another, and I spot a familiar face.

Eliana.

Her eyes are swollen and red from her tears. When she sees me, she pauses, ducking her trembling chin in a grateful nod. I return it, heart aching at the sight of her. This is exactly what she was afraid of. I can't imagine being forced to watch the manifestation of your deepest fears.

I look behind me at the balcony, suddenly thinking of Cassian. Despite the public display, I know the king was angry with his son's defiance. But as Cassian stood up to him today, a surge of pride rushed through me. I just hope it doesn't get him into too much trouble before tonight's dinner. We need everything to go smoothly to get into Farion's chambers.

Warmth on my shoulder startles me, and I turn to where Dad stands behind me with a concerned expression. His hand retreats now that he has my attention.

"Looking only makes it worse," he says.

I turn away. "I wasn't. Not at the Fateless, anyway."

He follows me and Aria through the front doors, Soren already a few paces ahead. Free from the constricting crowds, he falls into step beside me, and Aria moves to walk alongside Soren.

"I'm sorry," I say. "And I forgive you."

Dad's boots crunch against the loose rock as we descend the many steps from the Chrysalis. "Eden, I understand why you were mad, and I wish I had done things differently," he says. "Your forgiveness means more than you could know."

I watch him closely, the morning sun highlighting the strands of silver flecked through his brown hair. He smiles, his eyes creasing, and I can see the relief that flashes through them. In a matter of days, he appears more aged than I thought possible. Soren is right; worry is getting the better of him lately.

"But I *am* sorry for how I left things. I know I hurt you." The more I speak, the more the burden of the past ten years lifts from my shoulders. "And I understand how suffocating it feels to blame yourself for Mother's death."

Someone from behind us barrels past, annoyed with our slow pace on the stairs.

Dad pulls me to the side where a resting spot is chiseled out of the cliffside. "But that is not an excuse for what I did. I realize that now. And I am so, so sorry, Eden. You didn't deserve that. You needed me, and I let you down."

"You're here now." I squeeze his hand before letting go. "And I want to keep it that way. You might not be a true Fateless," I continue, voice low, "but your doubts could still get you in trouble."

"I'm not worried about what happens to me," Dad says. "It's always been about you and your siblings. None of you need the burden of my shame and fear. I couldn't ask you guys to bear the weight of that." He lowers his voice. "And the king has no tolerance for anyone who even considers the Fateless ideals. I didn't want you all to lie for me or be punished for my beliefs if I was caught." He cradles my cheek. "I could never forgive myself if I let something happen to you—to Aria or Soren. I promised your mother I'd keep you safe."

Sadness darkens his eyes before he looks away, staring down at his hands with a sigh. "And yet I still wasn't the father you needed." He finds my gaze again. "You have grown into such a strong young woman, and I couldn't be more proud. I'm sorry for relying on your strength and not seeing your struggle. I promise to do better."

I surge forward, wrapping my arms around him.

He holds me tight, pressing his cheek to the top of my head. His chest shakes with quiet sobs. We stay like that for a long time, his fatherly embrace reaching the parts of me I buried a decade ago, comforting the little girl who just needed her dad.

As he holds me, I'm overcome with gratitude. My dad is not perfect; he doesn't always make the right decisions, but he loves me. And he helped shape me into the woman I am today. How could I let my anger blind me, and risk losing him all over again?

"I thought I'd lost you, Eden. You have that same wild energy as your mother, short-tempered and willful to a fault." He lets go to stare down at me. "Which is why I knew you needed space. When you were ready, I had faith Delayon would bring you back to me."

I sniffle. "And here I am."

Dad looks over at the crowds still flowing down the stairs. Their shadows shift on the cliff behind him, the jagged rocks distorting them into strange, dancing shapes. I wipe my damp cheeks where tears made their escape. "I suppose we should attempt to catch up with Aria and Soren."

"They're probably wondering if the crowds swept us out to sea," Dad jokes. "But Eden, whatever else you want to know, I'll tell you. No more secrets."

My fingers find my arrow ring, sliding it over my knuckle in a repetitive motion, a habit I no doubt picked up from Cassian. I consider what more my dad could tell me, and I'm not sure I need to know. What happened is better left in the past, swept aside by a wave of forgiveness as we look forward to a different future. "I don't think I need to know, Dad."

His head tips to the side. "Alright, but I'm always willing to share."

"One day," I say. "But for today, I just want to be with my family."

"Who are you and what have you done with my daughter?" He frowns comically, eliciting laughter from both of us.

"Maybe exactly who you always hoped I'd become; a woman who's learned to live in the present." As I say it, it feels even more true. The past month replays in my mind—all the times I remained present in the moment instead of consulting the future with self-portraits. Court life is changing me more than I realized.

Or perhaps it's more related to a certain smug prince.

"I am so incredibly proud of you, Eden. I hope you know that." Dad squeezes my hand. "I love you, princess."

"I love you, too."

Sunlight scorches the workspace behind the cottage, heat rising in waves. Soren's finished door is warm to the touch, its mahogany stain almost a perfect match to the palace doors. With my guidance and his impromptu visit, Soren finished the door in a remarkably royal fashion. Other than the less ornate handle, it will fit right in with my chambers.

"It's perfect," I say.

"Good, because it's not changing now. Why did it have to be so specific again?"

"You saw my room; I wanted it to match." I turn to where Soren stands in the last bit of shade. "And I don't need people asking questions about why I have a different door in my bedroom."

"Makes sense. When do you want me to bring it through?"

"Give me time to get back to the palace and into my room. Maybe an hour?"

Soren gives me his signature salute. "No problem, Sis. I'll see you then. It shouldn't take me too long to install."

He assesses his work, lost in thought as he calculates the installation process. His arms are crossed, biceps more pronounced than I remember. He looks taller, too.

"When did you get so grown up?"

He laughs, running a hand through his too-long hair. "You miss a lot when you live away from home, I guess."

I walk over and pull him into a hug, my chest tightening when I can no longer rest my chin on his head. "That's why you're still going to make the other door we planned."

"Sure thing." Soren pulls away, but I tighten my hold.

"Too grown up to hug your sister now?"

He reaches an arm around to poke me in my armpit. I jump back and he grins at his victory before sticking his tongue out. With a laugh, I ruffle his hair in retaliation. "I may not be around as often, but you'll always be my little brother. And I'll always love you, okay?"

"Today's ceremony made you all sentimental, didn't it?"

"A little, yeah. But I mean it. I don't want you to think that because I moved to the palace, I left you behind or forgot about you. You, Aria, and Dad are still my family. You are my world."

His expression softens. "I know. I love you, too, Eden."

We head back into the cottage where Aria and Dad sit hunched over their tasks at the dining room table. They look up at the sound of the door creaking closed.

"Door to your liking?" Aria sets her needlework down. "Poor Soren has been slaving over it for the last several days."

I shove Soren's shoulder. "So that's what you've been saying about me? That I'm some horrible taskmaster?"

Soren scurries behind Aria before I can deal another blow.

Aria chuckles. "He just likes to complain. We all know he enjoys crafting."

"It's a good thing he does, because I hear you're impatiently awaiting his next door. When that's done, you'll finally get to visit me in the palace."

"And how come I haven't heard of this door until now?" Dad raises one dubious brow.

"It's nothing to worry about, Dad. I, for one, can't wait to finally visit you! That reminds me…" Aria gives Soren a vicious side-eye. "Let me go get your dress since *someone* forgot to bring it to you."

Aria jumps out of her seat and nearly knocks Soren over. As she climbs the stairs and collects the dress, I reassure our dad that this new door is safe.

"Sanctioned by the prince himself," I say.

"Glad to hear you're getting along with him now."

"Something like that." I lean over to hug him. "Bye, Dad."

"Bye, Eden. Come home whenever you need. We'll be here."

Aria bounds down the steps with a basket in her hands and I meet her at the front door. Nestled within the pliable basket, the dress is carefully folded and wrapped in cloth.

"I wanted to make sure it wouldn't get dirty on the journey back. But take it out and hang it right away when you get there. Otherwise, it will wrinkle terribly." She hands me the basket.

"Thank you, Aria. I can't wait to wear it." I hug her, careful not to squish her gift. "It's always good to see you. I love you."

Aria squeezes me. "I love you. Hopefully, we'll see you soon."

"Get Soren working on that door." I wink.

Soren hears me from the dining room and waves me off. "Bye!"

With one last farewell, I close the door on my family and start the walk back to the palace.

A soft knock on my bedroom door makes me jump. I'm not expecting anyone, and the Corvican dinner should start soon, so it can't be Cassian. Fear coils in my stomach. Tentatively setting the Divinian poetry book aside, I stand from my chair and press my ear to the door. They knock again, more urgent this time.

I twist the handle and open the door with bated breath.

"You had me worried, there, Wildflower." Cassian has one hand pressed to the door frame, leaning into it.

I breathe a sigh of relief. "Cassian."

"Were you expecting someone else?" His smirk lasts half a second until he takes in my appearance, his mouth parting, icy eyes darkening. My heart flutters as his gaze rakes over every detail on Aria's gown.

"Now I feel incredibly underdressed." He glances down at his loose-fitting cotton shirt and black trousers.

I laugh, hoping to fight off my blush as I step aside to let him into my room. "I hope you aren't planning to wear that to dinner."

"Of course not. My father would have my head." Cassian grimaces. "This was the only opportunity I could slip away to see you. I never need as much prep time as the ladies. Give me five minutes to throw on the rest of my outfit and I'll still look dashing; don't worry."

I cross the room to where he stands, aware of his eyes as they linger on my every move. A blush heats my face. "I wasn't expecting you."

"You really thought I wouldn't check in before our plan?" He looks almost hurt.

"You're a busy man." I shrug.

"Not too busy for you."

My blush deepens.

A satisfied smile creeps onto his face. "I can't help but ask, Wildflower. Why are you so dressed up? I'd give anything for you to come to dinner with me, but I know that's not possible." His smile stretches wider. "You have more important matters to attend to."

The fabric is cool to the touch as I smooth invisible wrinkles in the skirt. "It's enchanted to make me feel empowered, among other things. I figured I could use more of that feeling tonight."

Cassian rubs the back of his neck. "Please tell me one of its other enchantments is invisibility, because you are not sneaking anywhere in that dress." He steps closer. "The second someone sees you, they won't be able to look away."

"Then it's a good thing I don't have to sneak at all." I raise an arm toward my new bathroom door.

Soren was right on time, installing the door with ease before slipping out of the palace like a seasoned pro. Since then, I've been restlessly waiting as the hours crawled by.

"How does it work?" Cassian turns to examine it, his back now facing me.

I inhale sharply. A deep red line stains his cotton shirt, spreading slowly like watercolor bleeding across a page. "Cassian!"

He jolts around, eyes wide with panic. "What? What did I do?"

"What happened to you? You're bleeding."

He presses his lips together and reaches a hand around to touch his back. It comes away wet with red. "It's nothing, I'm sorry. I'll go now. Stick to the plan, and I'll make sure Farion stays at dinner all night."

Cassian bolts for the door.

I follow him, placing my hand over his to stop him from turning the handle. "Don't go. Let me help you."

He stares down at our hands, his breathing measured. His muscles tense beneath my palm.

"Please, Cassian."

Slowly, he turns, his eyes trained on the ground. It's not until I tighten my hold that he finally looks up at me, features open with vulnerability. He clings to my gaze like it's the only thing holding him together—like my presence is the first sliver of light in a lifetime of darkness, and he's afraid if he looks away, he'll be lost forever.

It's a look that shatters my defenses and pierces straight through my heart, tethering us together with an invisible thread.

A look that somehow breathes life into me and steals it away at the same time.

As he gazes at me like I am his whole world, I realize he has become mine. I am utterly his, our fates hopelessly intertwined and out of our reach, held by the hands of fate as our illusion of control is finally shattered.

I reach for him. He inhales, dark lashes fluttering against his pale skin. My fingers brush through his raven hair and trail down to cradle his face. He leans into my touch.

"You don't have to face this alone, Cassian."

He takes a shaky breath. "I didn't want you to see me like this—weak and defeated."

I move my other hand to his face, capturing his glassy gaze with my own. "You are *not* weak. It took incredible strength to stand up to your father today."

Cassian stills. His jaw tenses, pupils wide as his stare sears me like a brand. A dizzying current races through me, my skin suddenly electric where I touch him. Warmth blooms from my waist where he places his hand, fingers curling into the fabric of my dress, pulling me closer. Our breaths grow shallow. My pulse pounds in my ears.

I should let go, step back and break the spell of the moment, but I don't.

He inches closer, eyes searching mine, seeking an answer as he waits for me to make a choice. They are the blue of an ember that threatens to light a fire in my soul. All I have to do is step closer—let the heat of his gaze spark the stirrings of my desire and send a wildfire through my very being, burning its way through me until he's left a permanent mark on my heart.

But then I will lose the last bit of control I still have. My fate will be permanently tied to his.

So I let him go and step out of his arms.

The intensity in his gaze disappears like a candle snuffed in the wind. He straightens, exhaling slowly.

"I suppose it's good that one of us can restrain our impulses." He smiles, staring at the ground for a moment as he collects himself. "I have no control around you," he murmurs.

"I thought you were the master of emotion."

He laughs. "I blame the dress."

I playfully push him away.

"Shoving an injured man?" Cassian's signature smirk returns. "How dare you."

"Let's get you fixed up then——before you really do have to go to dinner dressed like this." I take his hand and pull him toward the bathroom.

Before we can enter through Soren's new door, Cassian plants his feet, preventing me from moving further. I glance between him and the door, unable to keep the smile off my face.

"It won't take us to Farion's room, if that's what you're worried about. What kind of enchanted door do you think I had installed?" To prove my point, I push it open and reveal the bathroom. "See?"

"Right. I don't know what I was thinking. That would be a pointless door if it only had one function." He grins sheepishly. "How do you activate the enchantment, then?"

I step into the small space, beckoning him inside as I search for bandages. "You place one hand flat on the door and envision your destination as you open it."

Cassian steps through, eyeing the door frame as he does. "Interesting."

"Take off your shirt," I instruct.

"So demanding, Wildflower."

I purse my lips. "Do you want my help or not, Princeling?"

He chuckles before removing his shirt in one fluid movement. A slight gasp escapes him as the cotton rubs against his back. I try not to stare when I take the shirt from his hands and run cold water in the basin. Red bleeds into the water when I submerge it. I swiftly work out the stain as best I can.

Cassian leans against the counter, his back reflected in the mirror to display a mosaic of raised, red slashes of skin. The light shines off the welts, and I imagine the pain he must have felt as the strap connected with his body. Blood still seeps from the gash in the middle of his back, the skin so raw from his beating it split open.

"How do you endure what he does to you?"

Cassian crosses his arms over his bare chest. He turns to stare at his reflection, following the angry red welts down the length of what he can see. "At some point, I got used to it. I even believed the pain was actually making me stronger, like my father said it would."

Pink-tinted water drips into the sink when I wring out his shirt. "When did it start?"

"The year after my fatemark showed up."

"But you must've only been a child!" I drape his shirt over the tub with force, taking my anger out on the soaked fabric.

"It started with small things like a slap to the wrist. He didn't use a strap until I was a teen."

"That doesn't make it right. He should never treat you this way." I wet a rag with cool water. "I'm sorry you've had to suffer his wrath all these years."

Cassian turns, bracing himself on the counter as I touch the rag to his skin. Gently, I wipe away the blood, aware of his vice grip on the counter's edge, his knuckles turning white. He makes no sound as I wrap him with cloth bandages to prevent additional seeping.

"All done."

He turns to face me. "Thank you."

"Of course." I stare at him, marveling at the strength he has despite having endured such awful treatment. "It was the least I could do. I don't know how you're going to withstand sitting in a chair at dinner."

He shrugs. "I'll manage. It helps that it serves another purpose, too. Although I can only do so much to keep you safe from a completely different wing in the palace. It shouldn't be hard to get out of his room, but make sure no one sees you."

"Don't worry, Cassian. I'll listen for noise before I leave, and the door will lock behind me. No one will know I was there," I reassure him.

"I still wish that dress made you invisible."

A smile quirks the corner of my lips. I hand him the damp cotton shirt and watch as he gingerly shrugs it on.

"I'm sorry. Your shirt is a lost cause."

"I have plenty more." He regards me with a tilt of his head. The look from before returns to his face, igniting the blue of his eyes with appreciation. "Stay safe, Wildflower. I'll see you after dinner, and I expect a full account of your adventures." Cassian steps closer. "Sneaking around the palace is much more fun than sitting at dinner."

"Fun is not the word I would use. All I want is to get in and get out. Trust me, Cassian, you aren't missing much."

He closes the distance between us, and my breath catches when his forehead touches mine. It's a small but intimate gesture, his closeness sending a shiver through me.

"I'll be missing *you*," Cassian says.

My cheeks feel hot. "You're a shameless flirt."

His breath tickles my forehead as he laughs, lingering for a moment longer before stepping back. "Always." He leaves with a wink.

I catch a glimpse of his retreating form in the mirror, knowing he's gone when the door clicks softly closed. For several minutes I just stand there, waiting for my breathing to return to a normal rhythm. After the fluttering in my stomach settles, I step close to the mirror, checking my appearance to prepare for what's coming.

The dress's enchantment is subtle; a buzz of confidence thrums through my veins, making it easier to stand with my shoulders back, head held high. Mixed with the feelings from my encounter with Cassian, and I feel ready to take on the world. I meet my green eyes in the mirror.

"I can do this."

When enough time has passed that I'm sure the dinner is well under way, I leave the bathroom and close the door. The wood is smooth to the touch as I place my left palm on its surface. I close my eyes, the shapes and colors of Farion's room overtaking the darkness of my mind to form a clear picture of my destination.

I turn the handle and step through.

arion's room is just as pristine as Cassian described. The pillows in the sitting space are perfectly placed, his desk chair pushed in—even his bed looks as if he never sleeps in it. All is quiet except for the crackling fireplace. Its warm glow melds with the sliver of waning sunlight that escapes the balcony curtains. It's strange he keeps the fire going in his absence, especially on a hot summer night like tonight.

I creep forward in the dim light. A shiver runs through me when I meet the eyes in Farion's portrait. It's unmistakably my mother's work, her rendering style evident through the absence of visible brushstrokes. An ornate black frame adorns the edges, carved with thorny vines and swirling patterns.

With trembling hands, I lift the painting and set it gently on the ground with the back of the frame facing me. My flowing skirt rustles softly as I crouch down to get a better look. Thankfully, the canvas frame is still exposed.

Although nothing is immediately visible, I know its secret. I run my fingers along the inside of the wooden canvas frame until they catch on the corner of a folded piece of paper. Anticipation and relief fill my chest; I'm happy my suspicions were correct.

Careful not to stretch the canvas, I hook the paper with my fingernail and inch it up until I'm able to pull it free. It's more yellowed with age than I expected, the paper stiff yet fragile as I unfold it, eager for another taste of my mother's words.

A log collapses in the fireplace with a sizzling crackle. My heart lurches. Instinctively, I turn toward the door, but it remains closed, and I am still alone. With my breathing now heavy, I scold myself for being impatient as I refold the paper and tuck it into the bodice of my gown. *Get in and get out. That's what I promised.*

I focus on the reassuring flow of confidence emanating from my dress until my heart beats normally again. Still hyper aware of each sound in the room, I return the painting to its spot on the wall, taking a few extra seconds to ensure it's straight. A crooked painting would be a dead giveaway of an intruder in a room this immaculate.

The low roar of the fire covers what small sounds I make on the way back to the door. I glance behind me, casting an observant eye around the space for any other signs of disturbance. As I do, a glint of gold on Farion's desk makes me pause.

It's the Royal Codex.

A thrill runs through me at the thought of being so close to such a precious book. I've only ever seen it from afar, perched on its stand as Farion reads from the Chrysalis's balcony. But here it is, within arm's reach, beckoning to be opened.

I release the door handle and move to stand over the Codex. It's beautiful, the brown leather cover decorated with gold lettering and designs. Carefully, as if one touch will set the whole thing on fire, I trace the first letter of its title. I blink to make sure it's real, awe overtaking my wariness. With a furtive glance over my shoulder, I open the book, the spine cracking with age. Though the table of contents is full of interesting chapter headings, I'm on borrowed time, and there is one thing I've always wanted to see.

The Origin of Fated Skills.

I turn the pages with careful precision, aware of each noise and bend of the paper. I'm grateful the story is at the front. If I had more time, I'd read every word, memorizing the way it looks written on the page, claiming it for myself after years of only ever hearing it read aloud. But I don't. Instead, I skim through it, surprised to find ink-drawn images accompanying the words. Each one is reminiscent of the stained-glass windows of the Chrysalis.

But it's the end of the story that surprises me the most.

It's gone; a jagged tear runs horizontally through the heart of the page. I flip through nearby pages as if the missing piece will be tucked just within. It's not. How could this happen? And in the hands of someone as particular as Farion, no less.

My stomach drops, and I run a finger along the feathery edges of the tear. The ending is my favorite, the part where our skills are described as gifts from Delayon, designed to make us more like our Creator. To find out the written words are missing feels like I've been lied to my whole life. Who's to say the ending hasn't changed, the years of repeating it by word of mouth causing slight misinterpretations?

I sigh, knowing I've wasted more time than I should have. With one last flip-through, I close the Royal Codex and place it back on Farion's desk. The floor creaks as I return to the door and press my ear against it, listening for footsteps or murmured voices. When I hear nothing but the fire behind me, I turn the handle to leave.

But it won't budge.

Everything goes silent except for the click, click, click of the locked door handle as I try to twist it in vain. Spots swirl across my vision, a barrage of panicked thoughts muddling my focus. *This isn't supposed to happen. The door shouldn't be locked from this side— our plan was perfect.*

Or so we thought.

And now I'm locked inside Farion's room.

My hands are clammy where I still grasp the handle. I don't know what to do. All rational thoughts have fled my mind, replaced by a heart-pounding panic that makes the room's pleasant warmth suddenly suffocating, like the fire is stealing all the oxygen from the air.

I stumble into Farion's desk, chest heaving as I try to calm myself down. *Think, Eden. You can do this.*

Aware of every sound I'm making, I carefully rummage through the drawers in search of a key or anything to help me escape. When I come up empty, I feel under the drawers and around the sides, straining to find a hidden space or something tucked out of plain sight.

Nothing.

As a last resort, I search the small top drawer again, reaching my hand to the very back. My fingers skim across papers and various knickknacks until they stop on the feeling of cold metal. My heart skips. I latch onto it, pulling it into the firelight.

It's a letter opener.

I let out a breath, sliding to the floor in a puddle of green silk. As I twist the letter opener in my hands, the silver metal reflects the last burnt-orange rays of sun. Despair creeps in like the somber shades of dusk beginning to overtake the sky.

The sky.

Adrenaline fuels me to my feet and I shove the letter opener back in the drawer before rushing to the balcony. I fumble for the handles through the thick curtains and fling open the doors without another thought.

Cool evening air whispers across my skin, carried by a strong breeze that ruffles my skirts. Indigo waters stretch endlessly in front of me, dappled with orange as the sun slowly slides behind the waves. For a moment, I'm in awe, the beauty of the scene luring me closer to the edge.

I look down.

The world spins, everything too small and far away. I grip the stone balustrade as my knees threaten to collapse beneath me and my breaths become shallow gasps.

In through my nose. Out through my mouth.

I repeat it until the storm inside me quiets, drawing strength from my dress's enchantment. When I finally turn from the view, my breath catches—the only way out is a thin stone ledge stretching from Farion's balcony to the room nearby. The distance isn't impossible, but it's further than I'd like. Thankfully, there are vines growing up the stone near the middle. They appear sturdy enough to offer a reassuring grip for part of the way.

Flickering firelight calls me back inside, urging me to spare myself from facing such a treacherous escape. But then this will all have been for nothing. Any hope I had of keeping my role as court artist—of proving my worth as a Morphi and working for the royal family—will disappear. They'll dismiss me without a second thought.

Or worse.

I swallow the bile that rises in my throat. It's not a trivial offense to sneak into the Ascended One's room, let alone install an unsanctioned enchanted door within palace walls.

Scaling a building, it is.

I'm careful not to turn around or look down as I close the balcony doors and edge closer to the balustrade. A strong breeze swirls around me, a reminder of my surroundings I didn't need. One arm outstretched over the balustrade, I search the wall for handholds. Dread pools in my stomach as my skin slides across nothing but meticulously smooth stone.

I check that the paper is still folded and tucked safely in my bodice. The assurance of its presence—evidence my trip was worthwhile—sets my mind at ease enough to take the first step toward escape. I maneuver so I'm sitting on the balustrade and raise one leg over the side to straddle it, still facing the wall. I've never been more grateful for my sister's love of slitted skirts.

My foot barely fits between two of the balusters, their decorative pillar shapes not designed to be used as footholds. But their grip on my shoe makes my footing feel solid. Before more doubts take hold, I shift my weight and lift my other leg over.

Deep violet sky stretches before me, my new position offering a full view of the balcony and sea beyond. I look down at my hands and squeeze my eyes shut, already repeating my mantra to maintain control of my breathing. One wrong move and I will end up like my mother. Her death loops through my mind, an unwelcome visitor threatening to rip away my control.

"I will not suffer the same fate," I say.

The air moves as if responding to my declaration. It sways my skirts toward the wall, urging me to step sideways, to keep going. It's odd, the wind. What I thought would make my escape more hazardous is proving to be a comforting presence, a stark contrast to the panic caused by the rapidly fading light. My escape is already almost impossible, but it will be insurmountable in the dark.

I pull my foot from between the baluster and take a tentative step onto the ledge. There is room for only half my foot, and the pit in my stomach grows.

"Delayon, give me courage," I say, more for myself than out of a genuine belief he cares to help me with my daring escape.

And yet another light breeze swirls around me, nature's reply sending bumps along my arms. Its chill mingles with the tingle of enchanted confidence and eases my sense of nausea. With a shaky exhale, I push off from the balustrade and place my other foot on the ledge, palms flat against the wall as I fight to maintain balance. No turning back now.

My flat-soled shoes slide easily along the smooth stone ledge—too easily. With each step, my anxiety builds, fighting to rise above my enchanted feelings. I move with purpose, not wanting to be stuck on this ledge longer than necessary. The vines approach, nearly in reach, and I lift my foot to take a larger step, desperate for something to hold on to.

My hand closes around one of the calloused stems. Relief floods through me until my foot slips on the smooth stone.

I'm going to die just like my mother.

Gravity claims my shoe, threatening to tug me down with it. I cling to the vines, praying they will hold my weight. It takes all my strength to keep from falling. My right foot is halfway on the ledge, body now diagonal as I heave myself flat against the wall so my bare foot can reclaim its hold on the ledge. When it does, I seize the vines with my other hand, adrenaline surging as I pull myself upright.

Everything goes dark as I squeeze my eyes closed to block out the world. But my mind is worse than reality, running rampant with vivid images of my mother's death—the feeling of falling, green grass rising to meet me, contorted limbs, pale skin. I suck in a breath. It's not enough, and I take another, and another, each breath fighting with the other until I can't breathe at all.

"Help me." The wind snatches my whispered words.

Fatigue and fear are closing in on me. Spots swim across my vision. The promise of safety slips away, the neighboring balcony suddenly so far away. Why did I think I was strong enough to do this? I'm not. I never have been. I should've been more prepared, should've painted a portrait and used my foresight. Maybe then, I wouldn't be in this situation.

I've allowed myself to get too distracted, focusing only on painting portraits for Cassian, helping change *his* future instead of my own. And for what? It hasn't changed, anyway. It's done nothing but make things more complicated for me. This whole time I should've focused on myself, stuck to the plan, and worked solely towards perfecting my craft and ascending.

Tears blur my vision, and I blink them away. Living in the present—ignoring my divine gift to see the future—suddenly seems like the silliest thing I could've done. Maybe I'm not as changed as I thought I was. Court life has made me weak and impulsive, overly sensitive to my emotions and swayed by feelings that don't even make sense.

Now is not the time to have an emotional breakdown, but I'm a ball of nerves. I don't know how to stop the torrent of thoughts that will send me spiraling to my death if I can't get them under control.

I redirect my focus to the constant thrum of confidence, trying to recapture the feeling I had when I first stepped on the ledge. But it eludes me, the enchantment not enough to overpower the black cloud of fear hanging over me.

The gentle rustle of the breeze through the vines distracts me from my thoughts. A leaf tickles my hand.

"Hello, wind." It's ridiculous to talk to something that won't respond or lift a finger to help. And yet it somehow calms my nerves. "It would be great if you could just lift me to the edge," I mutter.

The cool air stirs the flowing sleeves of my dress and sends a chill along my arms. Leaves rustle again, a chorus of hushed whispers that makes me feel less alone. I inhale sharply.

Maybe I'm not alone.

"Delayon?" I murmur tentatively.

Nothing answers, not even the wind, but I press on, reminded of Eliana's personal relationship with our Creator. If she can talk to Him, why can't I?

My muscles strain from balancing. If I don't get past this paralyzing fear, I truly may fall to my death.

Out of desperation, I cry out, "Give me strength. I can't do this on my own. I don't know how. I need you."

A faint wind tickles my skin. *It's Him.*

As if pleased by my revelation, the wind blows past me, stronger this time. My hair stands on end, a pleasant tingling on the back of my neck.

"I trust you, Delayon."

A sense of peace washes over me, a gust of wind all but pushing me sideways, lending me enough strength to take another step. And then another. And another.

The vines will end soon, and I will no longer have a handhold, the thought making my panic flare up.

"I trust you," I repeat, refusing to let it take hold.

As the vines end, the wind gives me one last push. My bare foot grips the ledge better than my shoe ever could, and I'm almost grateful for slipping. I never would've taken my shoe off otherwise.

With renewed confidence, I step past the vines, hands braced against the stone wall as I continue toward the balcony.

I'm almost there!

Hope surges through me, fueling the last few steps until my hand closes around my ticket to freedom. The stone balustrade is reassuringly solid in my hands.

"Thank you, Delayon," I say, fitting my feet between the balusters before lifting myself over one leg at a time.

When my feet hit the stone floor of the balcony, I sink to the ground, muscles weary. The sun is but a sliver of light above the sea, a blazing orange that reflects across the waves. It's like a gift from Delayon, the light suspended above the water until He knew I was safe.

"Thank you," I whisper again, watching the vivid sunset fade into a sapphire-blue night littered with stars.

It's breathtaking. How could I have taken the sky's beauty for granted all these years? "You're quite the artist," I murmur, finding myself talking to Delayon even as I stand to leave.

As my fingers slide over the ornate metal handles of the balcony doors, a spike of panic surges through me. Worry darkens my thoughts, my mind turning through possibilities and solutions before I even know the outcome. What if it's locked? What if I conquered my fears just to still be trapped?

A faint breeze tickles my skin, drawing me back to the present. I take comfort in its presence—a reminder I'm not alone. "Please let this door be unlocked."

The handle twists open.

My knees threaten to buckle from relief once more, but I keep going before the last of my adrenaline fades. I'm still not out of the woods yet. I close the balcony door and quickly cross the room, my one bare foot sounding loud on the cold wood floor. The room is sparse, only a few necessary items making it a livable guest area. I don't linger on the decorations, heading straight to the door, grateful the handle appears unenchanted.

I lean into the wood, listening for sounds on the other side. When there are none, I open the door, a gentle vibration in my palm as the handle unlocks. I lock it behind me and make quick work of my walk to the main level.

All that's left is to retrieve my shoe.

Several servants pass by on the way, but they pay me no mind, busy with preparations for our Corvican guests. I'm grateful, but still paranoid someone will notice my bare foot through the slit of my gown.

When I reach the doors to the garden, the night has darkened further, light-sensing lamps now lit along the paths. Crickets chirp, pausing their song when I draw too close. I send a silent thank you to Delayon that no one else is taking a nightly stroll through the gardens.

As I near the landscaping beneath Farion's balcony, my shoe takes shape in the grass, the soft satin glowing in the moonlight. I veer off the path, blades of grass tickling my bare foot. When I slide the shoe back on, warmth cradles my skin. It helps chase away the chill of the night.

Above me, flickering light draws my attention to Farion's room. My neck cranes to see up that high, mouth parting in horror as the true peril of my escape sinks in.

Moments ago, I stood on that very ledge. A ledge that looks impossibly small now, barely visible in the pale light of the moon. Gravity's pull still lingers; that brief, heart-stopping fall is something I won't soon forget. The balcony that almost claimed my life may very well be the same one that claimed my mother's. I wrap my arms around myself.

Before the images of my mother's death resurface, I turn away. My fingers find the slip of paper still tucked in my bodice. I want to read it now, to know what my mother wrote, not realizing they would be her last words. But I wait. The safety of my room beckons me, and I quicken my pace through the gardens on my return.

When I reach the arch leading into the inner courtyard, a voice reverberates off the stone. I recede into the shadows, pressing myself flat against the wall, unable to tell where it's coming from. My heart thunders in my chest. The voice grows louder, words distorted, and I wedge myself into the corner, praying I won't be found.

"Delayon, please hide me," I whisper.

Stone crunches underfoot nearby. I cover my mouth to muffle my breathing.

"Who were you talking to?"

31

Eden

he familiar timbre of Cassian's voice makes me weak with relief. A smile tugs my lips as I slide a shoe around the corner, just as another voice responds.

"Only the shadows of the night."

Farion.

I shrink into myself, remaining hidden while straining to hear the conversation.

"And what do the shadows have to say?" Cassian asks, sounding no closer than before.

They must have stopped somewhere in the courtyard.

"A great many things," Farion replies. "If one knows how to listen."

"I'm tired of listening. I've been listening all night."

"Is that why you followed me out here? For the fresh air and quiet?"

Cassian sighs. "Something like that."

Immediately, I know he's keeping his promise, watching Farion's every move to ensure he doesn't interrupt our plan. Cassian has no way of knowing I made it out already. And yet I'm still not safe, only feet away from being discovered by the very person I robbed. Cassian is protecting me just like he said he would.

"You seem distracted, like your mind is elsewhere." Farion's perceptiveness is unsurprising.

"Can you blame me?"

It's Farion's turn to sigh. "He wouldn't do such things if you stopped disobeying him. What were you thinking, Cassian? In front of the Corvicans and the whole of Scintillia, no less?"

Farion knows?

Anger seeps into me, jaw clenched on Cassian's behalf. How dare he blame Cassian for his father's actions? If anyone should have compassion, it's the Ascended One, the closest person to Delayon. But there is none in his voice.

"Your father is simply preparing you for the throne. You must learn to handle these things. It will be easier once you ascend, once you receive the divine clarity you are destined for. Only then will you understand his ways. The king can see past human emotion." Farion's boots scuff on the stone, perhaps shifting closer to Cassian. "And so can you, if you only embrace the skill you are gifted with."

"You always come back to that." Cassian's voice is tense. "As if my skill will solve all my problems. I don't believe that anymore."

Farion is silent. I want to peek around the corner and see what's happening but can't risk getting caught. After several long seconds, he finally speaks.

"I warned you Eden would be your downfall."

Me? My breathing stills, muscles tensed as I await Cassian's response.

"She is anything but. Eden is the only thing in this palace that brings light to my days."

"You think that now, but I assure you, young prince, that will change. She only wants you for your power."

It takes everything in me to stay wrapped in the shadows, voice silent. *He's wrong,* I want to scream. *Your power means nothing to me. I only want you.*

I bite my cheek, fists clenched.

"That's not true." Cassian's voice doesn't waver.

My heart swells, joy flowing over me. *He knows.*

"Eden is nothing like the rest of us. She sees the world differently, embracing emotion instead of locking it away. We can all learn from her perspective. Even you, Farion."

A harsh laugh cuts through the night. "You trust the perspective of a simple painter over that of the Farion? She isn't even a Morphi! The crown prince, in love with a common painter."

In love? The thought makes my heart skip a beat, hands tingling. But it's short-lived, Farion's next words filling me with an icy dread.

"I should have dealt with her sooner. You are already wrapped around her finger and don't even know it."

Boots tap on the stone. Farion must be leaving.

"She doesn't need to be *dealt with*." Cassian's footfalls follow. "And I'm not wrapped around her finger. You're not listening!"

"No, *you* are not listening." Farion's voice is a low growl. "By tomorrow morning, Eden will be gone, and you will return your focus to your betrothed, where it rightfully belongs."

The door creaks. I wait in silence, hearing nothing but the wind and distant crickets. Then, the scuff of a boot. A frustrated sigh, and the clatter of a rock against the stone courtyard. Cassian is still outside.

Do I go to him? Wrap him in my arms and reassure him everything will be fine? No, that would be a lie. I have no power over the Ascended One or the king. If they want me gone, I'm powerless to stop it. And I have no way of knowing who else is watching from inside. If they see me with Cassian, it will only fuel the fire.

So I wait.

I press my head to the cool stone and wait for him to leave, my heart aching, throat constricting with the onset of tears. This isn't how this night was supposed to end. I'm a coward, facing my fears one second only to hide the next, unwilling to comfort the person I've come to care for most.

What is there to lose?

The thought gives me pause. My inner voice is right. If I'm leaving tomorrow, what harm is there in going to Cassian now? I can reassure him he's right about me. Show him I care only about him, not his power, not the throne.

And then the door opens again, the clack of dainty heels dashing my hope. Is it Isabel? Has she come to comfort her betrothed like I failed to do?

"Farion came back to dinner looking disturbed. What happened?" Lyra's voice carries toward me on a gentle breeze.

Good. Better her than Isabel.

"It's all falling apart." Cassian's whisper is barely audible.

"Oh, Cassian."

There's a brush of fabric followed by silence. I risk a look. Lyra holds Cassian in her arms, the siblings comforting each other in the stillness of the night.

"I know it feels that way now, but it will work itself out." She rubs a hand over his back, and I wince, knowing the pain he's in. But instead of flinching, he leans into her touch, muscles relaxing, head falling onto her shoulder. Is Lyra a healer?

"They're dismissing Eden in the morning," Cassian murmurs.

Lyra's movements pause. "What? Why?"

"Farion thinks she's a bad influence on me."

"We'll find a way around this. After everything Father has done, he owes it to you to at least hear you out."

"Ever the optimist." Cassian pulls away. "Thank you, Lyra. Without you, I wouldn't still be here."

"Nonsense. My brother is one of the strongest people I know."

Cassian wraps an arm around her shoulder. "At least help me get through the rest of this wretched dinner."

"As if I'd leave you to suffer through the small talk all alone." Lyra scoffs as they head back inside, their voices muffled by the closing door.

I wait until the only sounds are cricket songs and rustling leaves, my mind still turning over snippets of conversation. Farion wants me gone, Cassian might be in love with me, and Lyra could be a healer. Thoughts swirl through me at a dizzying pace, and the walk through the palace drifts by in a mindless haze. By the time I reach my room, it's as if my door materialized in front of me, and I'm left with more questions than answers. Hopefully, no one thought twice about me wandering the halls in a stupor.

As soon as I cross the threshold into the safety of my room, weariness overtakes me, my body a leaden weight I can barely drag to the bed. I crumple onto the cool satin comforter. My limbs feel boneless, heavy, drained of every drop of adrenaline. I suck in a deep breath, the bodice of my gown pressing uncomfortably into my chest.

The paper. How could I forget?

Bolting upright, I pull the folded note from its hiding spot. A sudden nervousness prickles my palms as my fingers fumble with the little square of parchment. It's almost laughable now, to think I went through a daunting journey just for this. But after everything—the risk, the fear—I finally hold it in my hands.

It'll be her words. Her voice. One last piece of my mother. What will she say?

Gently, I unfold the parchment, still perplexed by its strange texture. It isn't like the delicate scraps my mother used for her poems; those were soft, like pressed petals worn fragile by time. This one feels different. Brittle at first, but with an odd, fibrous strength beneath the surface.

Unease circles my hope like prey, waiting for a chance to pounce. I don't let it. Who else would hide something inside the frame of a portrait, if not her?

I undo the final fold, breath caught in my throat. My pulse quickens, but not with joy. The ink, the shape of the words—it's all wrong.

My stomach turns as I tilt the page to catch the silver glow of my crystalline lamp, praying I'm mistaken.

But I'm not. The words are not my mother's.

And yet… the lettering is unmistakable.

Brows furrowed, I squint at the words, hardly believing my eyes. It looks as if it was lifted straight from the Royal Codex. My gaze snags on the torn edge at the top, jagged and raw.

The missing piece.

I draw the paper closer, my hands trembling. For a heartbeat, my vision blurs, the moment too heavy, too impossible.

The first sentence makes no sense.

I know this story by heart; the torn page in *The Origin of Fated Skills* ended with, *"Determined to disrupt."* What should follow is the Gardener's gift, a divine blessing meant to combat the Fallen's influence. This slip of paper says differently, the story going down a darker path. In this version, it's the Fallen who gives the gift.

And they aren't gifts. They're something else entirely.

…srupt the Gardener's connection to His flowers, the Fallen infected His flowers with pests—small, unassuming caterpillars.

In return for nurturing the creatures, the Fallen promised the flowers they'd become their own vine of life, but better—a butterfly able to reach divine heights. But as the flowers welcomed the caterpillars, they fed on the vines, gnawing away their very essence. Their vibrant colors faded as the pests ate away their spirit, completely severing their connection to the vine of life.

And from the decay emerged a butterfly. Though it had wings, it did not soar toward the divine but flew aimlessly, a shell of what it once was, forever separate from the Gardener's love.

A shudder crawls over me. The warmth of my room vanishes, replaced by a hollow, creeping cold. The world tilts. I re-read the page once, twice, as many times as my brain will process it, as if the words will twist into something different, something familiar.

But the story stays the same. The skills… they aren't blessings. They're parasites. Curses.

The air leaves my lungs in a rush as I curl in on myself, the paper trembling in my hands. Maybe it's a fake, or someone's twisted reimagining. It can't be true.

It *shouldn't* be true.

But deep in my soul, I feel it. A weight I've always carried but never named. I press my fingers to my temple, as if I could scrub the truth from my mind. I don't want this. I don't want to know.

But I can't unsee it now.

My gaze drops to my fatemark. The silver sands glimmer in the low light. It used to shine like a promise, a trophy of my hard work. Now, all I see is a countdown.

Not to glory.

Not to ascension.

To the death of my soul, each grain of sand a piece of myself lost.

And it's more than half gone.

My hand hovers in front of Eden's door. I picture her safe on the other side, refusing to believe our plan was anything but successful. With one last glance down the corridor, I knock.

Each second she doesn't answer the door is like an eternity. I slide my ring off my finger, then back on. Off. On.

Come on, Wildflower.

I'm inches away from rapping my knuckles against her door again when it finally opens. My lungs empty, a slow smile breaking through. "Twice in one night, Wildflower. I could do without the added worry."

She looks up at me, her red eyes stealing the smile from my face.

"What happened?" I pour over her appearance, searching for injuries, my hands itching to hold her. But I sense that same fragile look from the day she climbed the ladder, as if one touch will send her over the edge.

So I keep my hands to myself.

"I'm not hurt." Eden's voice is shaky. "Come in."

I step into her room. "Were you caught?"

She shakes her head.

"Talk to me, Wildflower."

Eden draws another shaky breath. Her normal energy is gone, skin pale. She looks like she encountered death itself.

"I found it." She points at her desk where a torn scrap of paper rests. "But it isn't what I thought."

Curiosity flickers through me, but it's not enough to tear my gaze from Eden. Something is wrong. "That's fine," I reassure. "I know you were excited to find something of your mother's, but I'm just glad you're safe. No harm done."

My words have little effect.

"Read it." Eden points to the paper again.

Warily, I walk to the desk and lift the page. I feel her watching, the comforter rustling as she settles onto the bed behind me. Unsure what I'm looking at, I scan through the page, mind still preoccupied with Eden's demeanor. It isn't until the last few sentences that comprehension dawns.

"What is this?" I lean against the desk to face her.

"The last page of *The Origin of Fated Skills*."

I reread the page. "No, it isn't. You're sure this isn't your mother's?"

A spark of determination flashes across her face. "Cassian, I'm sure. I know what her handwriting looks like. And—" Eden pauses, biting her lip. "It matches the Royal Codex."

I run a hand through my hair. "What do you mean, it matches? How could you know that?"

"I saw it tonight. In Farion's room."

Brow furrowed, I try to make sense of her words. She saw the Royal Codex in Farion's room? And now she thinks this page is somehow part of it. I touch the ragged edge where the paper was torn.

"While I agree the story is a bit…disturbing… It can't be part of the Codex," I say. "There's nothing to worry about."

Eden scoots forward. "It's ripped, I know. And no, I don't understand how that's possible when The Royal Codex is supposed to be indestructible." Her tone shifts, the trembling words replaced with an unexpected urgency. "But you have to listen to me, Cassian."

She really believes this is real. I look over the page again. If she thinks this is the true ending to the story, her earlier shock makes sense. But it's impossible. Our fated skills are gifts, not curses. Everyone knows that.

But Eden seems convinced. I'll hear her out. "I'm listening."

Her shoulders visibly relax. "I know I promised I'd be in and out, but the Royal Codex was right there, and I just had to look. So I did. And the bottom of the last page of that story," she points to the page in my hands, "was ripped out."

"Eden—"

She holds up a finger to silence me. "Yes, Farion holds the original Royal Codex, the unalterable word of Delayon, which can't be destroyed. It doesn't make sense. Just listen." Eden sits up straight. "I would be confused too, if I hadn't had an…encounter…with Delayon tonight when I was climbing the balcony."

"You did what?"

She gives me a stern look. I press my lips together.

"Farion's door was locked from the inside, and I had to find another way out. Anyway, as I was escaping, I called out to Delayon for help. And I felt Him, Cassian. It was like He was the wind, urging me onwards. Without Him, I would have fallen to my death. He helped me face my fears."

I try to keep my expression neutral, but her wide eyes say I'm failing miserably.

"I probably sound crazy right now, but it's true. And when I got back to my room and opened the note, I knew it was real." Eden places a hand to her heart. "I could feel it in my soul. I can't explain it, but you have to believe me. The fated skills are a curse. We've been lied to."

I lift the page. "Where did you find this?"

"No." She clenches a fist. "You don't get to dismiss this."

"I'm not dismissing it. I'm trying to understand." I soften my voice. "Was it behind Farion's portrait?"

Eden's eyebrows knit together. "Yes."

"Where your mother would hide things."

She closes her eyes. "I knew you wouldn't believe me."

"It's not about belief. It's about evidence. This—" I shake the slip of paper in my hand "—could be anything. Something your mother wrote, a forgery, a metaphor, or a strange, twisted reimagining of the story."

It's the only logical explanation. I just hope Eden will agree. Her reaction to this scrap of paper is starting to scare me.

"No, it's not her handwriting. It's not her words. It's not even the same paper she used!" She jolts to her feet. "I'm telling you, it *matches*, Cassian. The torn edge—this is the missing piece from the Royal Codex."

Farion was right, a voice whispers. The hairs on my neck stand on end. I glance behind me, but there is nothing but my shadow. *Her perspective is tainted*, it continues. *She doesn't understand.*

I shake the thoughts away. She's just overwhelmed. She'll see reason in the morning.

"You've been through a lot tonight, Eden. Let's revisit this in the morning."

"Give me the page." She holds out her hand.

My gaze flits between her open palm and determined stare. "No. You need time away from this. It won't do you any good to reread it all night. I promise I will be back first thing in the morning."

Eden's hand darts forward, fingers closing around the edge of the parchment. "I won't obsess over it all night, I promise. Let me keep it."

I hold fast. "No."

She gently tugs the paper toward her. "Please."

I jerk it back. "Let go."

"So should you!" Eden pulls harder.

The paper stretches between us, fragile as spider silk. It gives slightly, the fibers straining under the tension. One more pull and it'll tear.

Eden feels it too, horror contorting her features. "Stop— Cassian, *don't.*"

But it's the perfect way to prove it isn't real. I tug the paper hard.

For a second, neither of us breathes. The air between us crackles like lightning. The page trembles, suspended in the balance.

And then, in the moment between our heartbeats, something happens.

The parchment no longer strains. The fragile hairline tear stitches together, as if recoiling from the brink.

We both feel it. See it.

My eyes widen. "What…"

I slowly loosen my grip. She does the same. The page settles between us on the ground, whole. Untorn.

A heavy silence falls. I look from Eden to the page, and back again, trying to make sense of it. "Eden… if this is real…"

She meets my gaze. "Then everything we thought we knew is a lie."

A lie.

My mind is racing. Who else would know?

Farion is the most obvious answer; he always has the Royal Codex in his possession. The only other person who might know something, who stands to benefit from the power of the fated skills, is…

My father.

The king is a liar.

"The king is a liar," I say aloud. A laugh slips out.

Eden's eyebrows lift in a silent question. "We don't know that, Cassian. He could be just as deceived as we were."

"He knows."

She reaches for my hand. "Cassian—"

"He's the king, Eden. He knows everything that happens in Mentera."

"Why would he lie?"

"I don't know. Power?" I pull away from her and start pacing, my thoughts a tidal wave I can't outrun.

"At the cost of his soul?" she asks, tracking my frantic steps.

"You don't know my father."

Before she can speak again, I spot the page lying on the floor, forgotten in our shock. I snatch it up.

"Cassian, what are you doing?"

"Getting my freedom back."

And I'm gone, the page clenched tightly in my fist.

Eden calls after me, her footsteps following behind. I press on before I lose my nerve. This will solve everything. I finally have something to hold over my father's head. A lie this big would ruin him if exposed.

I'm the one in control now.

No one else.

Not Farion, who is threatening to have Eden dismissed.

Not the king, who's marrying me off.

Not even Eden, who simply wants what's best for me.

Her caution is warranted, but I refuse to let it deter me. She will understand when it's all over—when tomorrow morning, she's still the court artist and I'm no longer betrothed.

"Cassian, stop!" Her fierce whisper is closer than I expected.

I lengthen my strides. I could walk this path in my sleep, the labyrinth-like corridors burned into my brain. Eden has only been here for a month. If I keep this pace, maybe I can lose her. She doesn't need to be involved in this.

The halls blur as I move, boots pounding against the marble. My hand clutches the slip of parchment like a blade drawn for battle. I barely register the servants who press themselves against the walls to avoid my path.

"Cassian!" Eden's voice echoes behind me again, urgent, pleading. I don't slow.

I can't.

The doors to my father's chambers rise ahead, flanked by two guards. Eden's steps falter behind me. I spare a glance back. She looks torn—furious and afraid. But she doesn't call out again, moving out of sight. She knows better than to draw attention to herself.

Good. This part isn't for her.

I don't have a plan as I approach the guards. Not really. But I know this: power is a weapon, and I hold a lot of power in my hand.

The guards stand straighter, confused by my pace, my half-grin, and the wildness in my eyes.

"Prince Cassian—" one starts.

I wave him off, not slowing. "It's urgent."

They cross their weapons with a sharp clink to block the door.

"Prince Cassian," the other says, tone neutral but firm. "The king is not to be disturbed."

I step closer, the blades inches from my chest. "Move."

The first guard hesitates. "He retired for the night and—"

"I said *move.*"

They glance at each other, unsure. My pulse thrums in my ears, hot and loud. I keep my voice steady, dangerous. "Or would you like me to tell him you barred his own son from entry? Let's see how that goes over."

A long moment passes. One of them lowers his weapon. The other follows.

I push the door open without another word.

His room is dim. My father sits in an armchair near the hearth, half-turned, a crystal glass in hand. He doesn't flinch.

"Cassian," he says coolly. "To what do I owe the pleasure?"

"Oh, but the pleasure is mine," I say, strutting into the room with the page hidden behind my back. "I learned something rather interesting tonight."

He doesn't turn, just raises his glass and sips. "And it warrants barging into my chambers at this hour? Can't it wait until morning?"

"No, it can't." I keep my tone light, the way he taught me. "There's no time like the present, isn't that right, Father? Or, like you always say—don't waste an opportunity to take control. That's exactly what I'm doing."

That earns a small tilt of his head. "Finally taking control? Now you have me intrigued. What is it you must tell me, son?"

"It's not what *I* must tell you. It's what I want *you* to tell *me*." I pause. "There's a secret you've been keeping. Care to share?"

His gaze remains on the fire, expression unreadable. "Out with it, Cassian. I don't have time for your games."

"And I don't have time for your lies." I step forward, heart pounding. "I know about the fated skills."

He hums, amused. "I would hope so. Everyone does."

Anger flares up at his mocking tone. He never takes me seriously. "I know they're a curse, not a gift. And I have proof." I reveal the slip of paper from behind my back, the torn edge catching the firelight.

The fire pops.

"A curse?" he repeats, then chuckles, the sound low and condescending. He stands slowly, setting his glass aside. "And how does that tiny scrap of parchment prove anything at all?" His hand extends. "Let me see it."

I don't move. "You've already seen it, haven't you? That's why you're not surprised."

"Dear boy," he says with a sigh, "I have no idea what you think you've uncovered, but the hour grows late, and I am not in the mood for dramatics." A muscle in his jaw tics. The irritation is real. "I hold no secrets about the fated skills."

My chest tightens. "I don't believe you."

"You never do."

The doubt creeps in uninvited. What if this page is the first he's hearing of it? If I misread him, I lose every ounce of leverage I thought I had. And I know the punishment for false accusations. The welts on my back throb again at the thought.

"I'm not angry with you," he says, taking a measured step forward. "I'm simply tired. Let me see the page, son. Then we can both get some rest."

His voice is softer now, coaxing. That in itself sets off alarm bells. Still…this was the plan. To show him. To see if he reacts.

I take a tentative step forward and place the page in his outstretched hand.

He walks toward the fire, flames licking higher as he leans in, scanning the page's contents.

I watch him like a hawk.

Nothing.

Not a twitch. Not a crease in his brow. Not even curiosity.

Then, without a word, he tosses the page into the fire.

"No!" I lunge.

Father steps into my path. He grabs my shoulder, squeezing hard, the rough fabric of my doublet scraping against my back.

"Calm yourself, son. The fire will prove whether your claim is true, or if those are simply the ramblings of a madman."

I shouldn't be worried. I saw it practically stitch back together when Eden and I fought. And yet a part of me is still unsure.

He lets me go and we stare into the flames—waiting, watching. My palms sweat. Then the fire slowly parts, revealing the untouched page.

It really is a part of the Royal Codex. Eden was right.

Father whirls around. "Where did you get this?"

For one of the first times I can remember, there is fear in his eyes. Did he really not know?

"Where, Cassian." His voice is eerily calm.

Before I can step back, he places his hand on my shoulder again. Familiar pressure blooms beneath my eyes. I try to go blank, to clear my mind, but it's racing with all that's just happened.

A shout from the other side of the door pulls Father's focus.

"Cassian!"

It's Eden.

The king scowls, the force of his skill lifting like his hand from my shoulder.

"Cassian! What's happening?" Eden's voice is louder now, mingled with the deep protests of the guards as they forbid her entry.

Father brushes past me, his face contorted with fury.

My blood runs cold. I follow him. "Father, ignore her."

He throws open the doors. "What have we here? Miss Asher, you are a long way from the artisan wing."

"What have you done to Cassian?" Even in the face of the king, her voice is unwavering.

I step around him, eyes locking with hers. Relief flashes across her face, followed by fear as the king grabs her arm and levels the guards with a hostile stare.

"Insolent fools! Can you not guard a simple hallway?"

They lower their heads.

"Our apologies, My King," one of them says.

"Stop apologizing and do as you're told! Guard the end of the hall. If another unexpected late-night visitor bothers me…" He tugs on Eden's arm. "I will have both your heads."

Their armor clinks as they rush to the end of the hall, standing at attention. Father pulls Eden inside by her wrist, slamming the doors behind her.

Venom seeps into his tone. "I should have known you were behind this."

"Cassian, are you hurt?" She doesn't look at the king, focused only on me. "I heard you yell."

"I'm—"

"You will look at me, not him!" My father grabs her face. "I am your King. You are under *my* roof."

I step forward. "Let her go, Father. She has nothing to do with this."

His face is inches from hers. "Oh, but she has everything to do with this. Tell me, Miss Asher, where did you find that slip of paper? And how long have you been poisoning my son's mind?"

Eden's jaw is set, mouth unmoving. She tries to pull away, but the king tightens his grip.

"As expected. A witch never reveals her secrets. You, with your little brush and innocent eyes. You've been meddling. Whispering. Never fear, I will uncover the truth before the night is over."

His breathing deepens, muscles relaxing, and I realize he's channeling his fated skill.

"Father, don't!" I reach for Eden.

He turns, eyes black as they lock onto me. "If you interfere, dear boy, I will do much worse than intrude on her mind."

Eden's eyes widen, pleading with me for help. I want to, but I'm powerless to stop my father. She flinches as the weight of his skill presses into her thoughts.

"Stop!" I shout.

"Stay out of this, Cassian," he growls. "She's led you astray."

Eden pushes against the king's shoulder, but her attempt is weak, mind captive to his skill.

"You think I am a monster," Father says. "For what I do to Cassian."

She struggles against him again, jaw clenched tight. I wince, knowing her pain, the pounding in your head as his presence invades. They are like hooks, snagging your thoughts before they've fully formed, dragging them to the surface.

Father laughs. "Farion's room? Bold, my dear. Bold, indeed. And using my son to do it." He looks at me. "You are a weaker man than I thought."

I clench my fist at my side, nails digging into the soft flesh of my palm, grounding me. "It wasn't her idea, it was mine."

"Her mind says otherwise. Every word, every innocent-eyed look, sinking her claws deeper into you."

"He's lying," Eden grits out.

Is he? The room spins, the shadows suddenly alive with whispers of doubt. What if I *have* been played? What if getting into Farion's room was her goal from the start?

I close my eyes.

No. I refuse to be a coward any longer.

Even knowing the consequences, I retreat into myself, finding the comfort of detachment. The whispers fade. The doubts disappear. I feel nothing.

"Let. Her. Go." I place a hand on my father's shoulder, squeezing like he did to me moments ago.

His gaze flicks to mine. "You want to protect her? You don't even know what she is!"

His voice rises, a sign he's losing control.

Good. Direct your anger at me, not her.

Father snarls, releasing Eden. She crumples to the ground, holding her head.

His hand lifts to strike me.

assian catches the king's arm mid-air. In the deep golden glow of the room, his fatemark shimmers blood-orange, the sands moving.

He's using his skill.

"Cassian, don't!" I try to yell, but the sound comes out thin and useless. My head pounds as if it's been split in two.

Cassian's gaze never leaves the king's.

"Enough, Father. You always taught me to master my emotions. Shouldn't you do the same?"

King Leopold's jaw clenches. Muscles strain beneath his skin. For a moment, he wavers, his hand trembling in Cassian's grasp. But it's not enough. His anger blazes back to life, fiercer than before.

"You feel nothing!" Cassian's voice sharpens.

There's a shift in the air—the sudden, invisible press of something too heavy to name. Cassian's emotions are back, wild and alive behind his eyes.

But the sands still swirl.

He's using his skill on the king.

King Leopold fights against Cassian, shaking with fury. "You think you can control me?"

Cassian's face tightens with strain. "Isn't this what you wanted? Your son—cold, calculated, and in control? You should be proud, Father." His fingers dig into his father's wrist. "Detachment is power. And power is everything." His voice drops to a whisper. "So embrace it, Father. Let go of your anger."

I watch helplessly as Cassian uses the very weapon his father forged in him, turning it back on the man who made it. As Cassian's fated skill takes hold, the king's face contorts with resistance.

Cassian's grip tightens. The effort visibly drains them both. Sweat beads on Cassian's brow as he pushes his skill to the edge, forcing the king's emotions to ebb, to fade. The king gasps, his movements faltering, but still he resists.

"You feel nothing for her," Cassian continues. "She is like a speck of dust floating through the air." His voice breaks, only slightly, but I hear it. "She's beneath you, not worth your rage."

The king's resistance weakens. His shoulders sag. His fury falters.

Cassian presses on.

"That's it. Welcome the emptiness. The stillness. Welcome the power you taught me to crave."

His muscles grow slack. The king's body folds inward, knees buckling as he collapses to the floor. Cassian stumbles back, gasping as if he was on the brink of drowning.

"I did it," he whispers, staring at his trembling hands in disbelief.

I can't move. Can't breathe. This was never what he wanted—to become like his father.

But now I see it. The same steel in his spine. The same blind devotion to control. He used his gift to protect me, but it cost him something. Something I'm not sure he'll get back.

Don't become him, I want to say. *Please, Cassian. Don't lose yourself trying to survive him.*

But as his gaze shifts to King Leopold's motionless body, I fear it's too late.

"Father?" Cassian's voice cracks. He drops to his knees beside him, shaking his shoulder. "Father!"

The king's breathing is shallow. His mouth moves, but his whisper is barely audible over the roar of the fire. Cassian leans closer to hear him. My ears strain to block out the crackling flames.

"Finally becoming…" The king wheezes. "The man I wanted you to be."

His head lolls to the side, and I'm met with his dull, distant eyes.

Cassian's face grows pale.

"Father! Wake up!" Cassian shakes harder.

I stare in horror as the king remains unresponsive.

"Cassian…" My voice trembles as I crawl beside him, pressing my fingers to King Leopold's neck.

There is no pulse.

"He's gone."

Cassian stares at his father's lifeless body. "No… I didn't mean—I didn't mean to…"

I place a hand on his shoulder, but he shrugs it off, standing abruptly. He stares at his palms, his mouth slack.

"What did I do?"

"Cassian, you didn't know it would—"

"No!" he snaps, turning on me. "You don't understand. This wasn't supposed to happen. He wasn't supposed to die!"

I step back, shaken by the intensity in his voice. "You were trying to protect me. You couldn't have known what your skill would do—that he would fight back."

"I *should* have known!" His voice breaks, but he quickly composes himself.

He closes his eyes, his body rigid. When he looks at me again, his expression is hard.

"Cassian, don't do this. This isn't something you can escape from." I stand to face him, searching his ice-blue eyes for a sign of the real him. "Come back to me."

He stares at the ground. "No one must know what happened here. The king died of a heart attack. That is the story."

"Cassian, listen to me," I beg, my voice soft but urgent. "You can't hide this. People will ask questions, they'll want to know what happened—"

"They won't," he interrupts coldly, "because you won't say a word."

I freeze, his words sinking in. "What are you saying?"

He takes a step toward me, his face unreadable. "I need to control the narrative, Eden. And your silence is crucial."

"I—I would never tell anyone," I stammer. "But you can't just pretend—"

"I'm not pretending." His voice is icy.

Cassian turns, pacing between me and the hearth. I watch in silence, afraid to say the wrong thing.

His movements still. "You will be my betrothed," he says.

"What?" My heart skips a beat. Shock twists through me, sharp and sickening. "Cassian, no. You can't—"

"I can. And I will." His eyes lock onto mine, cold and resolute. "It's the only way. Farion wants you gone. You witnessed the king's death. If anyone finds out… This is the only way to protect you."

I shake my head, backing away. "You don't need to do this. I don't need your protection. I won't say anything about your father."

"You will." His voice is flat. "You're my Wildflower. Untameable. You'll tell the truth, even if it's only to your family, and it will destroy everything. I can't risk that."

Tears sting my eyes. "You don't have to force this. I would never hurt you."

His expression softens for a moment. The Cassian I know tries to break through. But then the coldness returns.

"I'm not asking, Eden. You will be my queen, and you will keep this secret. That is the only way."

I stare at him, my mind reeling. "And what about the truth of the fated skills? Are you asking me to hide that, too?"

Cassian turns to the fire, staring into the dancing flames. I follow his gaze—and freeze.

There, nestled in the embers, is the page from the Royal Codex.

"You didn't…" My voice is barely a whisper. "Did your father…?"

Cassian nods once, slow and numb. The fire's glow flickers in his eyes, but it's the only light left in him.

I don't think. I just move. Snatching the iron poker from beside the hearth, I reach into the flames. Sparks fly as I drag the page from the coals, a few glowing embers falling to the floor. I stomp them out, heart hammering.

The page remains untouched. Not a single burn.

"You can't deny it now," I say. "This is real. This is divine. We can't hide it, Cassian."

He doesn't look at me. "We will. For now. Until we have more proof."

"What more proof do you need?" My voice rises. "You'd rather let your people die like your father? Forever separated from Delayon?"

Cassian stares at his father's lifeless form lying just beyond the firelight.

"Sometimes," he whispers, "the truth has to wait… or no one will survive it."

My heart shatters for him, for the pain he carries, the crown already weighing on his soul. But that doesn't make it right. The truth can't remain buried.

"You're not the man I thought you were."

Something flickers across Cassian's face—regret, maybe, but it's gone in an instant. "The man you thought I was must die with my father."

I step closer, placing a hand on his cheek. His skin is cold. "No, Cassian. He doesn't. That man is strong. He'll be an incredible king—one who saves his people from an eternal death."

I place my other hand against his chest.

"Your emotions, your heart… they're not your weakness. They're your strength. Let them in. Let *me* in."

His eyes search mine, and I see him. The *real* him. But only for a moment.

"I can't." He pulls away. "Soon, I will be king, and you will obey me."

My breath catches, throat tight. I press a trembling hand to my chest, my heart heavy with sorrow. I stare down at the page—the one that changed everything. If I hadn't broken into Farion's room… if I hadn't found this slip of truth tucked behind my mother's painting… none of this would be happening.

Cassian wouldn't be shutting me out.

King Leopold wouldn't be dead.

And my world wouldn't be breaking apart at the seams.

But the kingdom would never be free from this lie.

Now Cassian wants me to keep that lie alive—to silence the truth I nearly died recovering. If I beg him not to make me queen, not to tie me to this deception, I lose my place beside the only person with the power to change things.

Cassian might be right. Maybe we need more proof, more people to dispel the lies we've lived for so long.

So I will stay.

For now.

He will listen when the grief softens, when the shadow of his father's death no longer clouds his judgment.

He needs me.

The kingdom needs me.

I sink to the ground from the weight of it all, my thoughts still racing.

I'm about to become queen, a future I never dreamed possible. I will have power and recognition—a crown to prove I'm worthy. But it all seems meaningless in the face of the truth. Never once did I think every choice I made, every brush with fate, was painting a future such as this.

If there's any hope for our kingdom, I must play the part.

And I'll wait for the moment when I can free us all. Even if it means locking myself in a gilded cage.

I lift my chin, my heart breaking. "As you wish, Your Majesty."

Turn the page for a sneak peek of Book 2:

A Breath of Hope

CHAPTER 1
Eden

*I*f looks could kill, I would be dead.

Farion is seething as he emerges from the throne room, an unfiltered rage trained on me as the door slams behind him. His eyes are black, like the cape draped over his shoulders—a bottomless, hollow darkness that chills me to the bone.

With Cassian's ongoing silence still echoing louder than the king's death, I didn't need Farion's anger joining the noise.

The guards on either side of the doors stand at attention.

"Farion," they greet in unison.

"Leave us," Farion says.

They obey without a moment's hesitation, leaving me alone with him as they move to the end of the hall.

Farion steps closer, eyes narrowed. "You unraveled everything like I knew you would. I should've dealt with you sooner. Before you made a mess of things."

I hold my ground, refusing to shrink under his glare. "Unraveled? All I wanted was to help Cassian."

Farion tilts his head. "And how exactly have you helped, Miss Asher? Other than exposing the crown prince's weakness for pretty women?"

I press my lips together, not taking his bait. I've never seen him like this. As the Ascended One, he always exudes power, control, and an almost detached kindness.

This Farion is different. Darker.

A Farion who could've easily killed my mother.

And then it shifts in a blink, a tight smile stretching his face as a servant walks past. He steps back.

"Watch yourself, Miss Asher. You may have wrapped Cassian around your finger, but his power is more than a commoner like you can handle. I trust the queen will agree in time."

The door opens again, and Cassian steps through. Immediately, the weight of Farion's presence lifts like a dark cloud dispersed by the sun. His gaze flits from me to Farion.

"I'm sure you have much to do, Farion," Cassian says. "And the queen would like to speak with Eden."

"Your Royal Highness," Farion bows his head. "I was hoping we could continue our discussion, just the two of us."

"What more is there to discuss?"

"Surely you realize there is much to prepare before you become king."

Cassian fidgets with one of his rings. His raven hair is an untamed tangle of wavy strands, and the dark circles under his eyes are more pronounced. He looks exhausted.

"Fine, Farion."

Farion grins, sparing one last glance for me, before striding down the hall, his cape swaying behind him. I try to catch

Cassian's eyes as he turns to follow Farion, but he avoids my gaze. My heart falls, stomach clenching with disappointment.

The last week has been hard, and Cassian has been more distant than ever, processing his grief on his own. But as he walks past me, the backs of his fingers brush mine, the slightest touch that lets me know he's still in there.

Somewhere.

He disappears down another hall with Farion, and the guards make their way back. My nerves return. The slight point of my arrow ring pushes into the pad of my thumb as I spin it in anxious circles around my finger. Queen Clarissa spoke with Farion and Cassian for some time.

What will she say to me?

Acknowledgments

First and foremost, I want to thank my Lord and Savior, Jesus Christ. It's because of your sacrifice on the cross that I have the hope and inspiration to tell these stories. Your Hand has been in my life since the very beginning, and I am humbled that you love me enough to rekindle my childhood passion for writing.

I never thought I'd have a published book, let alone two, and I couldn't have done it without the Lord's guidance. I've been writing since elementary school but never finished an entire novel until *Nowhere*. I truly feel it was my renewed faith and His gentle nudging that made what was once seemingly impossible, a reality in three short months. Now, I have a second novel finished, and the urge to write has made a permanent home in my mind. For that, I thank you, Lord. Thank you for this gift you've reawakened in me. I hope my stories will bring glory to your name and further your kingdom, even if it's only by touching one reader's life.

Next, I want to thank my amazing mom, who has been my best friend, biggest cheerleader, and sounding board all my life. Thank you for talking through book ideas for hours, lending me your creative mind and encouraging spirit to reignite the spark when I'm lost in the slog of writing. Thank you for reading every word, sometimes mere hours after I've written it, and telling me to "write faster" because you didn't want it to end. Thank you for your unfiltered opinion, even when I don't want to hear it (you know I'm not the best with criticism). And thank you for always believing in me.

Thank you to my loving husband, who reads my books, romance and all, even when it's "not his thing." Your keen eye for detail has been an asset during the editing process. Thank you for promoting my books to your friends and random people on the internet (even though it got you banned on a Reddit page.) It means a lot that you are proud of my accomplishments. And most of all, thank you for reminding me why I do this—not because I have something to prove or followers to gain, but because I enjoy creating. You keep me grounded, my anchor amidst these new waters I'm navigating.

Thank you to my dad, who believes in my talent even without having finished my first novel (you better get to reading). Thank you for your wise advice and unwavering hope that my books will reach more readers.

Thank you to my little brother for letting me steal mom away for brainstorming, for your blunt advice, and your support from the sidelines. Maybe one day your fear of second-hand embarrassment will fade enough that you'll take a stab at reading your sister's writing.

Thank you to my two lovely grandmas who make the most wonderful beta readers. Your enthusiasm for my writing keeps me going, and your (mostly) unbiased feedback helps make my novels shine.

Thank you to my entire family for supporting my writing. It means the world to me that you take the time to read my words, attend my events, and share my work with others. I am beyond blessed to have such a loving group of people surrounding me.

Thank you to my church, Redeeming Grace, for providing the nutrient soil I needed to plant myself and start growing my calling. I truly feel the Holy Spirit at work in our midst and am incredibly grateful to be part of this family of believers. Your support of my writing means a lot.

And lastly, I want to thank *you*, the person reading these words right now. Thank you for taking a chance on this story—on me. I hope in some way my words resonated with you. It's crazy to think my writing is out in the world, and someone out there, someone like you, chose to spend their precious time and money to explore one of my imagined worlds.

I hope you'll stick around for the next one.

CAMRYN VAN LINGEN is an artist and avid reader who lives in the Midwest with her husband and two cats. Though she started writing in elementary school, it wasn't until her first year of teaching that she published her first novel. She strives to craft character-driven stories with a deeper meaning (and a good  plot twist), weaving elements of her faith into each one.

Camryn has a degree in Art Education and currently teaches high school Media Production and Cybersecurity. If she's not teaching or cuddling her cats, you'll likely find her dreaming up her next book.

DON'T MISS A MOMENT.
FOLLOW FOR UPDATES & NEW RELEASES.

camrynvanlingenbooks.wixsite.com/cvlbooks